Praise for *Charming the Snake*

Charming the Snake will charm you from the beginning. Davidson, Anthony and Schroeder have written outstanding tales of love. The mix of humor, action, adventure and very intense sexual attraction has earned this book a place on my keeper shelf.

—Tewanda, *Fallen Angel Reviews*

MaryJanice Davidson's *Savage Scavenge*

...The reader can't help but fall in love with her characters. Once more I found myself smiling all along as I was reading Gladys and Jasper's antics ...*Savage Scavenge* is a highly amusing, lighthearted short read, the perfect appetizer to start the anthology.

—Mireya Orsini, *Just Erotic Romance Reviews*

Melissa Schroeder's *Seducing the Saint*

Ms. Schroeder is known for writing sensually enticing stories and this is another one. Bringing together the sensual nature of her characters and a story line that has a hint of danger to it, *Seducing The Saint* is a HOT read and another winner for sure.

—Sheryl, *Coffee Time Romance*

Camille Anthony's *Carte Blanche*

Carte Blanche is the perfect blend of mystery, sexual chemistry and humor. The author has created two very intense characters in Chastity and Dare. I will definitely be looking for Ms. Anthony's next book

—Tewanda, *Fallen Angel Reviews*

Looseld

ISBN 1-59632-099-0
CHARMING THE SNAKE
Copyright © 2005 by Loose Id, LLC
Cover Art by April Martinez
Edited by: Raven McKnight, Linda Kusiolek, and Maryam Salim

Printed in the U.S.A. by
Lightning Source, Inc.
1246 Heil Quaker Blvd
La Vergne TN 37086
www.lightningsource.com

Contents

SAVAGE SCAVENGE

MaryJanice Davidson

Dedication

For the readers who wanted to know more about Mutes.

This story takes place three months after the events in Beggarman, Thief.

Prologue

Summer 2072
Minneapolis, Minnesota
A-Block
Midnight

Jamie Day, blushing bride-to-be, stretched, scratched, and yawned.

"Grace, thy name is Jamie," her fiancé observed.

"Off my case, metal man. It's not my fault you've worn me out again."

"Well, it certainly isn't mine," Mitchell said wryly. He pulled her close for a sweaty snuggle and stroked her hair. "One of my PR people was up here again today," he reminded her.

"So?"

"So, I think it's time I announced my intention to make an honest woman of you."

"Why? Why can't we just get married downstairs—or in here, even? And not make a big deal out of it? Be honest—like a judge wouldn't come up here if you asked? If Mr. Mitchell Big Dick Zillionaire asked for a favor?"

"Leave my dick out of it."

"I'm just saying, why make a big thing of it? Why tell anybody, never mind your PR people?"

"Because I want the world to know you're mine," he said simply.

"Dammit! See, there you go. You say something like that and I just melt. How can I argue with that?" she griped. "Easy: I can't."

"Excellent."

"Oh, excellent, shut up with your excellent. I'm only letting you win this one because you said such a nice thing."

"Darling, I always win them; sometimes it takes a bit longer, that's all. And Jamie, I have to ask…isn't there anyone you wish to tell? To share our day with?"

"No."

"Because you could invite whomever you wish. The ballroom accommodates five thousand, but if you need more, we can get married uptown. We—"

"There's no one."

"Ah… I know you were an orphan, but surely you have some friends?"

"No."

"That's ridiculous. Anyone as charming and, uh, gifted as you must have loads of friends."

"You're the only one who thinks I'm charming. And thieves aren't well-liked in C-Block. It's hard enough getting stuff without worrying about somebody snatching it out from under you. We all pretty much kept to ourselves."

"That's horrible."

"It was a living, is all. Growing up, I had either allies or enemies. It wasn't really a friend-type environment."

"Oh."

"It's no big deal."

"I disagree."

"Maybe there's one woman I could ask," she continued thoughtfully, "but she wouldn't come."

"Really? Who is she?"

"Never mind. Like I said, she wouldn't come anyway. She's really busy all the time, kind of digs into her work."

"Is she gifted like you?"

"It's okay, Mitch, you can say it: mute. No, she's not. But she's one of those people on the fringe…if a mute got hurt, you could go to her and she'd fix you up, and she wouldn't tell the government about you. There's a whole bunch of underground doctors and clinics. She's the best one. But I wouldn't say she's a friend, exactly. Like I said, more an ally than a pal."

"I'd like to meet her."

"Never happen. She never leaves B-Block."

"West St. Paul?"

"Right. We come to her to get fixed; it's not the other way around."

"It makes me feel bad," he admitted, "that you have no one to attend our wedding."

"Well," she pointed out, "now I'm one of those annoying women whose entire life revolves around her boyfriend."

"Husband," he reminded her, with a light kiss.

"Right, right."

Chapter One

Minneapolis, Minnesota
B-Block
8:35 a.m.

Dr. Gladys Loder glanced up from her cornflakes when she heard Jamie's name, and waved a hand in front of the feed. A picture popped up, accompanying the news story.

"...announced her engagement to billionaire developer Mitchell Hunter, recently known for donating the Moon Rock to the Minneapolis Science Institute. Ms. Day is from South St. Paul."

"South St. Paul!" Gladys snorted, nearly sneezing into her cereal. "Call it what it is, you feel-good morons."

"The couple has plans for a European honeymoon."

Gladys raised her eyebrows until she thought they'd fall off her head. European honeymoon? Jamie Day? That blue-haired, sticky-fingered, sharp-tongued mute? The girl was an absolute magnet for trouble; Gladys had lost track of the number of times she'd set an arm or leg for the charming crook.

And now she was marrying Mitchell Hunter? The country's most eligible bachelor? How had *that* happened? The last Gladys knew Jamie was still lifting pretties for Brennan. Now she had gone straight (ha!) and was getting married to no less than Mitchell Hunter. The man's breeding was impeccable; he could trace his family back to Ellis Island. Jamie, of course, couldn't trace her family back even one generation.

Did he know?

Would she tell him?

Gladys scraped the last of the skim milk out of her cereal bowl. It wasn't her business, either way. Jamie was a good kid; she deserved every happiness. If Mr. Hunter knew his bride-to-be had special gifts, it wasn't her problem, or her business. And if he didn't, that wasn't her problem, either.

She wondered if they would try to have a baby.

Chapter Two

Twelve hours later, pleasantly exhausted from the clinic, Gladys went out to the small patio and picked three grapefruits from the dwarf tree she had been coddling. Unlike the fruit she saw on TV or in the store, the skin on these fruits was an ugly greenish-brown; from the pollution, she knew. They didn't look pretty, but they tasted great and were better for her...was there a message in that? The fruit in the stores was bleached and prettied up, and that's what everybody wanted.

Hmm.

She studied the tree and made a mental note to buy more fertilizer, pretending that lugging it to the eighth floor wouldn't be a giganto pain in the cheeks. The things she did for the stupid tree!

Not that such things needed *that* much work these days, not once the botanists got done with them. Steady watering, some fertilizer, watch the roots, take it inside if it was going to get below freezing. It was hard to believe the Minnesota winters used to be so cold, tropical fruits wouldn't grow.

She glanced out and saw the distant silver gleam of the river. Four years ago, she'd rented the two-bedroom, one-and-a-half-bath apartment because it was convenient to work; the view (the very very very very faint view) of the Mississippi River was a bonus. A four-hundred-dollar-a-month bonus. Now Gladys was sorry she hadn't taken the cheaper apartment on the third floor; she almost never noticed the view, and never appreciated it.

She went back inside, juiced the fruit, and pulled the latest pill-pak out of her purse. She sat down at her small kitchen table and frowned at the tiny pearl-colored tablets. This would be the first day of the sixth week she was taking them.

Difficult to believe they were so hard to get; for her, it had been quite simple. A colleague had written the scrip without a blink; she'd had it filled at the local Valu-Mart, as well as picked up a bottle of Coca-Pepsi.

Was she really going to do this thing? It wasn't like a library book; you couldn't take it back, and the fees weren't small, either.

Well, she thought, popping a pill out of its protective packet and swallowing it with a sip of juice, *it's not like I've got candidates knocking down my door, anyway.*

Then her patio door split down the middle.

Chapter Three

Although Gladys had worked emergency wards for half a decade and was used to any manner of startling happenings, the suddenness of the man's entry shocked her into immobility. Her immediate thought was that there had been an accident. Other than the one that wrecked her glass door, rather.

"Gods, are you all right?" She had dropped her juice, but the plastic cup held. The same could not be said of the door.

He was shaking glass out of his dark red hair, so dark it was almost purple. "What?"

When he looked at her, she saw his eyes were a lighter shade of red, the color of cherry cough drops. She couldn't believe he walked around like that...wasn't he afraid of being picked up? Wasn't he afraid of scaring people?

He said it again, louder: "What?"

Oh, dear. A mute. And, as in many cases, a not terribly bright one, either. She stepped closer and raised her voice. "Are. You. All. Right?"

"I will be as soon as you stop yelling," he said cheerfully. Glass crunched beneath his boots as he came further into the room. "Yucka, my ears are still ringing!"

She blinked. She was having trouble following current events, and was embarrassed she was having trouble. *Get hold of yourself, Gladys. Right now!* "Are you hurt?"

"Besides the obviously not-glad-to-see-me look on your face? Nuh-uh. Well, I'm a little hurt, but it's nothing I can't recover from. Still, would 'good morning' kill you?"

"It's evening," she pointed out through numb lips. His voice...it was difficult to describe...like verbal velvet. Rich and deep, a radio star voice. It perfectly matched his blunt good looks—the broad face, the unusual hair and eyes, the wide shoulders, the long legs. He towered over her, and she was a bit tall for a woman, a hair away from six feet. "Not morning."

"The rules of good manners still apply." He bowed from the waist as if he were thanking an audience after conducting an orchestra, and shook his head like a dog. More glass flew. He looked up at her, and the corners of his mouth twitched. "I need you, Dr. Loder."

She tried again to collect her scattered wits. *Oh, those eyes...those shoulders!* "Of course. Where is the accident? Are many people hurt?"

"Uh..."

"Are! Many! People! Hurt!"

"Dr. Loder, honest to megatroid, if you don't stop screaming, I'm probably going to barf all over you."

"Sorry. It's just that I'm not sure you're following what's going on."

"I'm not sure *you* are, honey. Come on, let's go."

"I'll get my bag," she said, and darted to the hall closet. Thank gods she had restocked just that morning! "It's all fully supplied and ready to go." Since most mood-altering drugs had been legalized by Shea's Act of 2021, not only had crime rates dropped like rocks, but nobody had to worry about junkie break-ins. Thus, she could say something like "it's all fully supplied and ready to go" to hold up her end of the conversation, and not worry about being robbed.

"What?"

"Never mind. Just take me where I'm needed."

"Yowza," he muttered, giving her a sudden appraising look, his eyes glowing like coals.

"What?"

"Never mind."

Chapter Four

So far, he wasn't impressed with the great Dr. Loder, the Angel of C-Block.

But then, he was in a bitchy mood. He probably wouldn't have been impressed if he'd met the president. He was in this thing to win, and if meeting the Angel hadn't been everything he'd hoped (she seemed a little slow on the uptake, for starters), then that's how it was, too bad, so sad, pass the gravy.

"Nice elevator," he said as they stepped inside. "I can't believe they turned 'Livin' On A Prayer' into Muzak."

She pressed *B*, then turned and looked at him with sober, dark eyes. Brown hair, brown eyes, too skinny, too tall. Your typical twentieth-century *Homo sapiens.* He felt a little sorry for her...it must suck not to evolve. "What?" she asked.

"Never mind."

"Didn't you see the elevator on your way..." She trailed off, and he waited for her to put it together. "No, of course not; you didn't come in the conventional way. How did you get up to my floor?"

"Oh, ways and ways," he replied cheerfully.

"I'd like to know. Can you fly? Walk up walls? Teleport? Can you disrupt the air around you—is that what happened to my deck door? Can you—"

"What rude questions from the great Dr. Loder," he said with mock amazement. Actually, not so mock. By contemporary standards, they *were* rude questions. The twentieth-century equivalent of asking, "So, are you planning to ever lose all that weight?"

"I'm sorry," she said at once, and a little color came into her cheeks. She was a great-looking woman, no question—when she wasn't blushing like a virgin her skin was the color of whole milk, not a freckle or a mole anywhere (that he could see). Too thin, yeah, but she probably couldn't help her metabolism. If she spent all that time in C-Block, ministering, she probably didn't have time for many six-course meals. "I didn't mean to butt into your life."

"That's all right," he said as the doors opened. He followed her out into the garage. "I butted into yours."

"Yes, but it's my job. It's what I'm here for."

"Yep, Humanitarian of the Year, that's you."

She gave him a sharp look, and her dark brows crinkled together. "If you have something to say, by all means..."

"What? You're swell. We of the C-Block are so grateful." He said it in a tone so honeyed, he almost made himself sick.

"There's no winning with you people, is there?"

He nearly tripped. "'You people'?"

"You heard me," she snapped. Now there was a *lot* of color in her face. Damn, she was a cutie when she was torqued off. "I'm down there pretty much every day, helping run the free clinic, and you all know I won't turn you in, but when I try to get an apartment in C-Block, it mysteriously doesn't happen. I bust my ass helping *you people,* and what thanks do I get?"

"So you do it for thanks?"

"No." She clicked a button on her keychain and her car, a navy-colored, boxy electric model, beeped at her. Then she turned to him and practically snarled, "I do it for some *Goddamned respect.* I'm good enough to come down and help at eleven o'clock at night, but I can't live down there? *You people* put the fences up, not me. *You people* don't mind taking up all my time, but I'm not good enough to live with you. So don't show up at eleven at night, break my door, expect me to drop everything and come with you, then make snide remarks about my lifestyle, okay, Cherry?"

At last, something he maybe had the moral high ground on! "Don't call me Cherry."

"Well, you haven't told me your name, fuckduck, so what choice do I have?"

"Fuckduck?" he cried, delighted.

She had started to swing herself into the front seat, then stopped and put a hand over her eyes. "I can't believe I called you that. I'm so sorry."

"No, no, it was great! Jeez, the whole thing was great. I didn't know that you tried to live—I mean, I didn't know any of that stuff. I guess you're right, some of us stick to ourselves maybe a little too much; but between staying off the government's radar and trying not to scare ordinary folks, and make a living, it's—it can be hard sometimes."

"Yes," she said quietly. "I can't imagine. Even though I've seen it, it's still beyond my comprehension. Because at the end of the day, I get to go home to B-Block, don't I?'

"Well, yeah." The way it came out, it was almost an apology. Well, he *was* sorry for her.

One thing for sure, he was looking at Dr. Loder in a whole new light.

He stuck his hand out, and they shook across her car roof. "Jasper Savage. But my friends call me Jaz."

"I'm Gladys—"

"Yeah, I know." He let go of her hand, which was cool and small, incongruous with the rest of her lanky frame. "We're just too trendy, aren't we? I had, like, four Gladyses in my class—"

"And there were two in mine, and you're probably the thirtieth Jasper I've met in the last year."

"Well, someone's got to set the style trends for you people."

"Now you're just being nasty," she said, and ducked inside her car.

Chapter Five

Jaz looked at his watch, did something to it, then said, "Okay, we've got to make one more stop, and then we'll go back to my place."

"What's the stop? How many people are hurt?"

"It's just this quick thing," he said. "Pull up there...sit tight, I'll be right back."

He darted into the Super-Wal-Value, and even through the scores of people, she easily kept sight of the arresting dark head and those broad shoulders moving through the crowd. Several people turned to look, but nobody stopped him.

They must assume it's hair color, something he has professionally done, she thought. *And colored contacts.* She remembered the first time she'd met Jamie and realized the blue hair was natural.

The first, irrational thought had been, *Mute! Get away from it! What if it's dangerous?* She'd managed to stay and finish the exam, and was shocked to find Jamie was smart. Smart and funny and fearless—not at all what she had been expecting.

Gladys had been taught since she was old enough to watch a screen that mutants were few and far between; they were cataclysmically retarded (read: too dumb to hurt us, or uprise, so don't worry, nobody worry); they weren't dangerous; and even if they were (which they weren't), the government kept tabs on them.

When she was in medical school, she figured out each lie, one by one. And she'd come to decide that mutes were like rattlesnakes. She'd spent enough time in the woods to know: *Yes, just like a timber rattler...lethal, but far more scared of us than we are of them. Let them stay to themselves, and they will. Mess with them, and you'll get bitten.*

She stared at the doorways to the store. What could he be doing in there? What was more important than getting to the sick, the hurt? Perhaps he thought he needed medical supplies to augment her bag? Noooo...he didn't seem dumb, and that would truly be a boneheaded move.

What was he *doing?*

After a few more minutes of fretting and glaring at her watch, there he was again, shouldering his way through the crowd, the bright blue "I just saved eight percent, thanks to GC #1298!" bag clutched in one of his hands.

"Great!" he said, practically jumping into the car. "Now we can go."

She instantly pulled away from the curb. "It's about time, I must say! What was so important that we had to stop? People's lives could be at risk, you know."

"Hey, I can't show up without these babies, baby. Take a left at the light, and take a right at the one after."

"What is it?"

The bag rustled as he showed her what he had bought. She stared at them and nearly ran the red light.

"Maybe I should drive, Dr. Distracted."

"But those are...they can't be."

"Sure they are." He squeezed one, and the plastic crinkled.

"We stopped so you could get those?"

"Sure. Like I said, we need them. Can't show up without them."

"Is it possible you're going to use them for an intent for which they are not designed?"

"What?"

"I meant—"

"What's so hard to understand, Dr. Dim?" He inhaled the aroma of cheap plastic. "They're water wings."

Chapter Six

He burst into his apartment with the two bags and Dr. Loder. The place was full of people, but there were probably only a dozen or so inside...his apartment was ludicrously small. A typical bachelor pad...messy, tiny, smelly, and in desperate need of a woman's touch.

A woman's touch? That was the first time in twenty-four years he'd had that thought. What was the matter with him? A woman's touch. Jeez!

A woman's touch?

"So?" his friend Jody asked. She was a small brunette—fake brunette, of course—wearing (barely) a strategically ripped tube top and a skirt made out of lastic. "How'd you do?"

"I *won*, babies! Check this: I got water wings, a quarter from 2005, a classified ad from someone who *doesn't* want a picture, a can of vegetables starting with the letter C, a Crayola crayon in Burnt Umber, and..." He grabbed Gladys's elbow and pulled her forward. "...Dr. Loder!"

"Holy shit, he did it," Tim muttered around his beer. "He got her. Them."

Jody checked her watch. "I think...I think that's a new record."

"It's Miller Time!" someone else shouted, and a cheer went up.

"Wait," Dr. Loder said.

"What can I say?" he said modestly, accepting backslaps and, in Jody's case, a wriggling hug. "You want the best, you got the best. And I think we can all agree that right now, at this moment, I am the best!"

"Just a minute," Dr. Loder said.

"I can't believe you got all that shit in under two hours," Jody said. She stuck out her hand, and Dr. Loder shook it automatically. "Hi, Doc. You probably don't remember me, but—"

"I remember you, Miss Lange. It looks like your flu cleared up nicely."

"Yeah, yeah, it did. The meds helped, though. Thanks for coming out so late. Uh...are you all right?"

"Fine," Dr. Loder grated, sounding like she was twenty years older, and a different sex, to boot. "Mr. Savage, may I see you outside?"

"Whoa," he said, "honey, Mr. Savage is my father. You— hey!"

She had a surprisingly strong grip, and in about two seconds she had hauled him into the hallway and slammed his front door shut on the amazed faces of his pals.

She growled, "What the hell is this?"

"Hey, I was just about to ask you the same thing!"

"Explain yourself. Right. Now!"

"Well, it's an apartment building in C-Block...I'm surprised you don't recognize it." He was joking to cover the sudden case of nerves—she looked *really* torqued off.

"You dragged me out of my home for this—this—"

"Scavenger hunt," he supplied helpfully.

"You told me there were people who needed me! That there was—was an accident or—or—"

"No, no, no." He wagged a finger in her face, then jerked it back when it looked like she might bite it off. *"You* said those things. I just didn't argue with you."

"I was an item on a scavenger hunt?" She sounded like she didn't know whether to be mystified, amused, or pissed. "Me and—and water wings?"

"Hey, we won! We're the Scavenge Champs of C-Block. Rejoice!"

"I have to get home," she muttered, and turned to go.

He leapt forward and caught her elbow again. "Wait, wait. Come on, don't be mad. Okay, I was a jerk; I tricked you. But look at what high regard you're held in—you were the last thing on the list, and you know they do those things in order of difficulty."

"I was harder to get," she said, totally emotionlessly, "than a crayon?"

"Way, way harder. They don't make Burnt Umber anymore, you know. It went the way of Redskin Red."

"Did it."

"I don't think you're appreciating the difficulty I had."

"Possibly because I don't care."

He doggedly continued. He didn't want her to leave mad. Hell, he didn't want her to leave at all.

Didn't want her to leave at all?

What was the *matter* with him tonight?

"First I had to figure out where you lived. Okay, Jamie told me that—she got her rich new boyfriend to track you down—"

"You know Jamie? Jamie Day?"

"Yeah, we grew up together. Girl's got a big problem—she'd steal the Empire State Building if she could get away with it—but she's basically okay. Anyway, Jamie told me where to find you. I didn't know what kind of security you'd have and, frankly, I love love *love* the dramatic entrance, so I used my power to get in." Instantly he saw a way to make it up to her. "You know, my power? That thing you were wondering about?"

"I don't care anymore," she said, which was a total lie.

"I can make forcefields of any kind or shape or density. So I just sort of made a field around me and walked up the side of your building, and then I used another one to break your door. I figured if it was all dramatic and quick, you wouldn't have time to argue."

"I see," she said neutrally.

He eyed the old-fashioned fire extinguisher hanging a foot to her left; he was pretty sure he could get a forcefield up in time, but you never knew...

"Look, come in and have a beer, okay?"

"Just because you confided your power to me does not make me less angry with you."

"So that means..." He thought for a second. "You *are* still angry. A better reason to come in for a beer! If you leave now, all the things they say about you will be true."

"What things?" she asked indignantly.

"Stuck-up, too good for mutes, only cares about you if you're sick...you know. Things."

"I don't care what anybody thinks." She folded her arms across her chest and looked, for a moment, as if she did care. A lot. "You tricked me, and you used me, and now you want me to have a drink?"

"Come on," he coaxed. "I'll owe you one."

Suddenly, she smiled. "That's right," she said. "You will."

Chapter Seven

"I can't believe we're doing this! Actually, I can't believe *you're* doing this."

"Shut up," she mumbled with her mouth full.

He propped himself up on his elbows to watch. "Seriously, this is *not* how I pictured the evening ending. Nope. I figured—ah!—you'd have a beer to prove you didn't care—when we all know—oooh!—you do care, and then you'd insist on a ride home and—and—and s-sulk all the way, and that would be that. Ouch! Watch the teeth."

"Sorry." She sat back on her heels and watched him. He didn't mind because she was, if possible, nakeder than he was. Nude in the semi-gloom of his room, she was a discovery of near classic proportions. Her small hands were resting on her thighs, which were long and muscular, like a champion thoroughbred's. Her head was tipped back so she could study him, gasping on the bed. Her dark hair had been unpinned during one part of the evening's festivities and flowed over her shoulders in a dark cloud. Her dark eyes were intent on his.

And she had the devil's mouth. Because he was *not* normally this easy. Well, mostly not this easy. Okay, he was easy, but he drew the line with norms. In fact, she would be his first—

"In my clinical opinion, you're ready."

"In my clinical opinion, you studied more than anatomy at medical school."

"I put myself through by servicing all the other doctors," she deadpanned.

"Get out of town!"

"Soon," she promised. She slipped gracefully to her feet, straddled him, spread her knees on either side of his hips, and then she was impaling herself on him, sliding down with delicious friction.

"Oh, my Gaaaaawwwddd" was the most he could contribute to the conversation. She was all hot silk and, when she swung forward, he could smell her hair, a clean, dark smell, like jungle orchids. "Holy Mother!"

"Yes."

"Jesus H. Christ!"

"Yes." Her hips had quickened. He was rising to meet her, and suddenly had That Feeling. It was mortifying, but, like the IRS of old, it would have its way.

"I'm really sorry," he groaned, "but I'm going to come now."

He could see her teeth in the dark as she smiled at him. For some reason, that gave him a chill. He didn't like that smile. At all.

"That's all right," she said. "I've just about got what I needed."

"No way are you even close to coming," he began, and then she leaned back and tickled his balls, and that was it; he was done.

Chapter Eight

"Well," she said brightly, beginning to put her clothes back in order. "That was…"

"Embarrassingly brief. Ludicrously quick. Speedy. Fast. Rapid."

"Now stop that," she reproved him, slipping into her underpants.

"Prompt?"

She laughed; man, what a great laugh. Low and deep, like a secret.

"It was wonderful," she was saying, and *that* was pretty nice of her. "I haven't done it in years."

"Never with a mute, either, I bet," he said smugly, and stretched. He caught a whiff of the pillowcase and jerked his head back. Errgghh. Time to create a forcefield that does laundry.

"Don't flatter yourself," she said shortly, stepping into her pants and zipping them.

"What? Seriously? Oh, come on. You've never gotten down and dirty with one of us. You? No way. You fix us; you don't fuck us. And I say that in the nicest way possible," he added when her eyes went narrow and squinty.

"It's really none of your business, first; and second, your bigotry is beyond belief. Get it through your head: it makes no difference to me if you have blue hair or can create forcefields or have blond hair and can type a hundred words a minute. You've got eyes the color of a stop sign—ooooooh, I'm impressed; I'd better never even think of having sex with one such as you. So godlike, so annoying."

"Anything sounds bad when you say it like that," he snapped, feeling the heat climb to his cheeks. Was he a snob? Well, yeah. About some things. Some lines you just don't cross, and that's how things were.

"When you live alone, and you meet someone nice, you take what you can get. That's all."

"The secret of life," he said mockingly.

"If you like." She pulled her shirt over her head.

"So, you're a slut!" he said, with an exaggerated *ah-ha* in his voice so she'd know he was teasing.

She did (whew!); when the shirt was down where it belonged, she smiled at him again. A much nicer smile this time. "I guess so. This will be the second time in twenty-two months I've had sex."

"Oh, my God!" He nearly rolled off the bed. An old line from a twentieth-century movie came to him. "How do you *live?*"

"Men," she snorted, and began searching through the laundry heaps for her bag.

"Maybe I could go twenty-two days. Maybe."

"You couldn't go twenty-two hours and you know it."

"Well, okay, you got me. Listen, let me find my pants, and I'll drive you home."

"Don't forget your underpants this time."

"Never wear 'em," he said cheerfully.

"Yes. I noticed." She sniffed disapprovingly, dug her bag out of a pile by the door, and said, "I can drive myself home. You'll recall I drove us here."

"Aw, come on. I'll go with. It's the least I can do after dragging you out of your place in the dead of night on false pretenses."

"I notice you haven't offered to let me stay the night."

That caught him; stopped him cold. "Uh...I guess I figured you didn't want to...the place is kind of a mess...and I thought...I mean, I thought you would think...and you got dressed in a hurry, so I figured..."

"Never mind," she said quietly. "I'll be waiting in the car."

Shit, he thought as the door closed quietly behind her. What was the matter with him? The lady comes with him without questions, is actually a pretty good sport about the whole thing, *fucks* him, is totally fine about not getting her fair share of the good stuff, and he still doesn't want her to linger.

He gasped and thought, *I am a snob!*

It was a sobering thought. When he pictured a snob, he thought of an A-Block jerk like that Mitchell Hunter guy, rich and oblivious. Not a regular joe like himself, a guy just trying to get through life.

He hunted desperately for underpants for five minutes, knowing he didn't have any, but trying to find some way to please her.

Maybe when they had sex next time, he could—

Whoa. This was a one-time thing; he knew it; she knew it. So what was the matter with him, already trying to get her into bed again? She'd go back to her life and he'd go back to his and, by God, that's the way things were supposed to be.

Right?

Chapter Nine

"I'm really sorry," he said again, but Gladys cut him off with a wave of her hand.

"For the fifth time, don't worry about it. I could have asked to stay, and I didn't. It isn't all on you."

"You know, I've never done it with a norm before."

"Yes, I gathered."

"It was great! I mean, you were great."

"Thank you." *Great,* he says. Yes, great. Just really great. She bit her lip and looked out the passenger-side window—Jasper had insisted on driving her car—and tried not to snap at him.

Great, was it? That was putting it mildly. The feel of him, slick and hard, filling her up; the look on his face, his hands stroking the small of her back, his groans and loss of control…wildly flattering, wildly shattering.

She would love to go again, now that he would be able to last a bit longer, would love to take him to bed on her warm flannel sheets for about the next six hours, then make bread pudding for breakfast and watch one of her *Wheel of Fortune* discs.

Clearly, not in the cards. It was almost a relief he'd turned out to be such a swine. It made tricking him so much easier.

"...good thing, too, huh?"

"What?"

"I said, good thing this wasn't a hundred years ago—I mean, we just went *wham bam*. In the olden days, you could be knocked up."

Here was a chance for revenge, gold-plated; she went for it like a hound went for a rabbit. "I still could be."

He laughed.

"No, really. I've been on the Pill for the last few weeks, and I'm ovulating right now."

"You've been *what* and you're *what?*"

"Oh, I think you heard me." She folded her arms across her chest and tried not to wince as he ran the red light. It was clear, since he was staring at her, he didn't even *see* the red light.

"Maybe I should drive."

"You're on the Pill? You got the exam and permission and all that?"

"Yes."

"But...but I'm still on city water." Shaken, he seemed to be trying to give himself good news. "It only works if both of us are taking it, right?"

"That's what they tell us, isn't it? But anyone with a little education can figure out the lie. Jaz, it's much, much easier to repress ovulation in a woman than repress sperm production in a man. The water being necessary for both is just an urban legend; the Pill being necessary for both for a baby is a lie."

"What—what are you—I don't get it."

"The contraceptive in the water prevents women from ovulating...which is something their bodies do naturally anyway, when they're pregnant. The Pill counteracts the stuff in the water, so they—I—ovulate, I have an egg ready to fertilize, and if I pick the right candidate at the right time, I could get pregnant."

"But you—" Another red light flashed by; luckily, no one was on the streets at this hour. "You didn't tell me!"

"No," she agreed. "In fact, you might say I tricked you."

"So you might have a baby? *My* baby?"

"Might."

"That's disgusting!"

She raised an eyebrow. "Disgusting?"

He stood on the brakes and the car came to a smoking, sudden stop. He turned to look at her, and his eyes were like coals burst to flame, a demon's eyes, and for a second, she was scared of easygoing Jaz. "Why didn't you say anything before?"

"Because you're a pig and a snob, and I don't want you—I want your genetics."

"But I don't want a baby with a norm!"

"This is what being a snob is."

"My baby—it might not even be evolved. It might be like you!"

"Also what being a snob is."

"Goddammit!" he roared, pounding his fists on the steering wheel. The back window shattered, but she didn't flinch—barely. "You bitch, you cheat!"

"Cheer up," she said flatly. "Maybe the baby will be a mute."

"Raised by you in B-Block? Raised to look down on us and think up ways to lock us up? No fucking thank you. You bitch." His eyes narrowed, slits of fire. "I hate you."

"You don't even know me. And that's the problem. Take a left at the stop light; don't run this one."

"Forget it. Get out!"

"But it's my car."

"Tough noogies. Out!"

She shrugged and moved her hand toward the door handle, but he grabbed her by the shoulder and said, "Don't do that!"

"What?"

He started the car and darted down the next few blocks. "This is a shitty neighborhood; I'm not dropping you off in a shitty...here!" He hit the breaks again. Gladys wondered if the airbags would deploy. "Get out here."

"All right."

"No, wait!" Another few blocks, then, "Here! No, wait!"

After a minute, she pointed. "That's my building."

"Fine, now get out!"

At last, he let her. She stood by the window and said, "It's been a fun evening."

He shook a fist at her. "You've *ruined* scavenger hunts for me." Then he was roaring away from her—well, as loudly as the efficient electric engine would allow.

She stood in the street and laughed and laughed, and after a moment, her laughter turned to sobs, but it felt the same, inside.

Chapter Ten

"Can you believe it? Can you *fucking* believe it?"

"Well, I can believe any guy would fall into bed with any woman, because you're all just pitiful when it comes to sex. But it's weird to think that Dr. Loder would be interested in one of us." His friend Jody took another sip of the beer, which had been flat for hours, and grimaced. "No accounting for taste, I guess, and who brought the beer this time? Yerrgh."

"That's what I said!"

"You said yerrgh?"

"No, I thought it was weird she was interested in a mute. But she's all 'everyone's equal, it doesn't matter, the important thing is a healthy baby' and...I kind of missed the rest; I was plenty pissed."

"Still, that's something." Jody smoothed her brunette wig. Jaz knew that she was completely hairless, that her hair, eyebrows, and even eyelashes were fake. They'd jumped into the sack together a few times, more out of loneliness than desire, but this was better. Friends was better. "Out of all the people she could have picked, she picked you."

"I was just a convenient cock, a drippy dick, a—"

"I get where you're going with this," Jody said dryly. "Look, Jaz, it's not her fault she doesn't get it. She can't, okay? She's not the one worried about the government or Brennan and his goons—"

"Brennan's dead."

"Get out!" she gasped.

"Swear. Jamie Day told me."

Jody dismissed Jamie with a wave of her hand. "She lies like rugs."

"Not to me. Anyway, Brennan's dead. And I see your point. Gladys doesn't get it. Her 'we're all equal' shit just doesn't cut it, because we aren't."

"Because you can do things she can't. Because you're genetically superior to her."

"Well…"

"Wow, you *are* a snob!"

"I'm a realist."

"Because most people would think she's lowering herself to have a baby with you. When you think you're lowering yourself to have a baby with her."

Jaz said nothing.

"Wow, no wonder she was mad!"

"Hey, hey, this is about me being the victim, if you don't mind."

"Poor thing. You got laid, won the contest, and maybe you'll have a baby with the smartest, most compassionate woman any of us have ever met. What a living hell your life must be."

"But she tricked me," he whined.

"And she came to the party how, exactly? Did you send her an invitation?"

Silence.

"Look, there might not be a baby, number one. It's not a guarantee. Even married couples with permission from the state and all the meds they need, even they sometimes try for months and months. So you might be totally off the hook."

"No baby?" He was shocked. Then shocked he was shocked. "But she really wants one."

Jody threw up her hands; beer spilled everywhere. "Jesus, Jaz, make up your tiny little mind, willya? Are you mad at her, do you like her, want to help her, want to kill her, want to fuck her, what? What?"

"Well, what if she isn't pregnant?"

"Then next month she'll find someone else. Someone who won't be such an asshole about it." Jody took another sip of flat beer. "I mean, she could hardly do worse..."

"My ass!"

"Just once," she sighed, adjusting her black tank top, "I'd like to have a conversation with you that doesn't involve your ass or my tits."

"Never mind your tits. If she wants to have a baby so bad, fine, but she should talk to me about it."

"Why? I'm sure your horror and disgust came through loud and clear to her. You'll be lucky if she ever talks to you again."

"But *she* tricked *me*. She was the sneaky one!"

"Yep. It was real easy for her, too, I noticed. She's not one to let an opportunity slip by, that's for sure." Jody made the comment with total admiration. "I mean, she was here, pissed, then you guys were in your bedroom, probably not so pissed..."

"Right, see how sneaky and evil she is?"

"See how she does the best she can, just like any of us?"

"What, you're on her side? Jody, she's a norm! She's the kind of people who want to lock all of us up!"

"Dr. Loder would stick a gun in her ear before she'd try to have any of us locked up, and you know that. She gave you a gift, you mute motherfucker. She basically said, 'I'm not getting any younger; I want a baby; I want *your* baby.' And you threw it in her face."

"I didn't exactly throw..." he mumbled.

"Oh, don't even start with that sad shit."

"She *is* kind of cute. If you like them tall and bony with eyes the color of good chocolate."

"And brilliant, and devoted to the community, and with determination in spades. God, I hate that type. I guess you'd prefer some scumshank from the neighborhood."

"Jody!" He was honestly shocked. If a non-mute had used the word, he would have punched them in the face. Repeatedly.

"Hey, if the girls around here were so great, you'd have settled down ages ago. But they drive you crazy. I'm the only one you ever liked, and we were more fuckbuddies than, you know, in a relationship. At least—at least with Dr. Loder, you could have a baby."

"But...I never wanted one."

"Yeah, but you could. None of us on our own would pass the screening tests. But if what you told me is true, you don't have to pass anything. You just have to keep having sex with Dr. Loder."

"Okay, okay. Will you take me to her?"

"What, now? I'm supposed to play Naked Twister downstairs with the guys."

He grabbed her hand. "Later."

"If I pop us over there, and pop me back, I'll be way too tired to—"

"I'll owe you, okay?"

"Fucking right you will, buddy-punk," she muttered, and squeezed his hand, and the apartment disappeared in a white roar inside his skull.

Chapter Eleven

Gladys had just gotten ready for bed when there was an extraordinarily loud *pop!* from her living room. It was a sound unlike any she had ever heard.

Gods, what is it now?

She hurried out of the bathroom, down the short hall, and found Jaz and that cute brunette from the party—Jody, that was it—staggering around her living room like two drunks on a bender.

"Your power sucks," he groaned.

"Got us here, didn't it?" Jody moaned, and let go of him so she could collapse on the couch.

"What's wrong? Are you two sick?"

"He'll be throwing up for about five minutes," Jody said. "But remember, he asked me to do it. I was happy to play Naked Twister." She staggered to her feet and popped out of sight. Literally popped; Gladys realized the sound was the noise of air rushing in to fill the space she'd just occupied.

"I'm just taking the bus next time, I swear to—urp!"

Quick as thought, she hauled Jaz to his feet and hustled him down the hallway—she'd just had the carpeting done and had no desire to do it again. He made it to the bathroom, barely.

"So anyway...I thought...after I talked to Jody...don't worry, she's very...discreet..." All said between heaves. Gladys had never seen someone try to puke and have a conversation at the same time. It was grisly, yet fascinating. Like an audit. "Anyway, I thought...I thought we could...talk. About the..."

"Jaz, it can wait until you're feeling better." She ran cool water over a washcloth and handed it to him.

"I just...want you to know...that I don't let Jody...zap me...for anybody...'cuz it's horrible...it's like being stuck...in a blender...with a hyena..."

"It's all right," she soothed. "I'll give you a ride back."

He shuddered, hunched over the toilet bowl. "I'm not leaving this bathroom, ever."

* * *

"Feeling better?"

He was sprawled on her couch. She'd pulled his boots off and tossed them in the hall closet.

He cracked a red eye open. "Much. I'm amazed I didn't die in there."

"*Is* there an emergency?"

"Yeah. I was a dick, and I wanted to tell you that as soon as possible." He shuddered. "Not the best plan, come to think of it."

"Jody's a teleporter."

"Yeah, she can go wherever she's been, or wherever the person she's touching has been."

"I imagine moving through space like that, at speeds like that—it looks to me like it wreaks havoc on the system."

"And the stomach. Jody can stand it better than anybody, but nobody likes to do it."

Gladys sat down beside him on the couch and patted his damp hand. "How sweet. All that vomiting, just for me."

"I was a dick."

"Yes, you were."

"I shouldn't have reacted like that."

"No, you shouldn't."

"And you shouldn't have tricked me."

Gladys thoughtfully bit her lower lip. "Well…"

"Gladys!" he groaned. "Give me a little something. Anything."

"Well, I really do want a baby. And I didn't think I'd ever see you again. In fact, after you stole my car, I was sure of it."

"I would have given it back. Eventually." Then he added, "You could have called the cops."

"I didn't want to have to pick out my baby's father from a line-up," she admitted. "It could have been awkward."

"To say the least! 'Yes, Officer, the one on the right is the one who knocked me up and stole my car. I don't mind about the first, but I'd like to get the car back.' Ack!"

Gladys smiled a little. "I admit I was surprised you were so angry. And sad you were so angry."

"Look, it's going to take some getting used to, okay? I mean, twelve hours ago, I only knew you by reputation. I never thought of you as a person like me, someone who, I dunno, hates—"

"Broccoli," she supplied helpfully.

"And loves—"

"Daisies."

"Right. Daisies, huh? Weirdo. And I'm not saying we have to, you know, get married or anything—"

"Not until we're sure you've stopped vomiting, at least."

"—but if it turns out you're not pregnant, I don't want you running around looking for some other guy to seduce. *I* want to help you, okay? Not some dildo-brain from A-Block or whoever you were going to pick."

"You're the only dildo-brain I want," she said.

"Oh, shut up. And help me go lie down. I'm dyin', here."

She helped him up and he hobbled toward her bedroom. "You know," she said, "you really could have taken the bus."

"Tell me."

But I'm so glad you didn't. She was grinning ear-to-ear; it felt like Christmas and her birthday rolled into one. Sure, they had about a thousand hurdles to clear, but him being here with her was a grand start.

He flopped down on her bed, then rolled over to look at her. "What's the plan if you're not pregnant?"

"You know what they say." She smiled at him, and his eyes actually lightened as she watched, got brighter as he smiled back. "Practice makes perfect."

MaryJanice Davidson

MaryJanice Davidson is the award-winning author of several books, most recently *Undead and Unemployed* from Berkley, and *The Royal Treatment* from Brava. She currently writes for Loose Id, Kensington, and Berkley. She lives in Minneapolis with her husband and two children, and is currently working on her next book(s). She loves getting e-mails from readers at maryjanice@comcast.net and you can visit her Web site (and read lots of sample chapters!) at http://www.usinternet.com/users/alongi/.

SEDUCING THE SAINT

Melissa Schroeder

Dedication

To the Quad:

To Allie, for always being there when I needed to whine and gripe;

To Doreen, for her thoughtful words of encouragement;

To MT, for her outstanding editing and gentle reassurances that I can actually write;

and

To Treva because, well, you understand most of my jokes, and if you don't, you play along and pretend I'm normal.

Thank you for taking the chance on a newbie writer who submitted her first futuristic, assigning me to Linda Kusiolek, and giving me the opportunity to grow.

I will always be in your debt.

Ladies, you're a class act.

Chapter One

It figured she'd find him here. Liberty Wainwright studied some of the worst scum of the universe through the haze of reefer smoke. Just her luck that Brady St. James would spend his time working out of a bar where saying the wrong thing could get your throat slit. She glanced around the room looking for him. At six-foot-four, he was usually easy to find. And knowing him as well as she did, she knew there would be a crowd of admirers surrounding him. Brady loved an audience.

A burst of laughter from the back of the room caught her attention. Instinct told her she'd found him. Carefully, she walked through the room, avoiding eye contact but keeping a close eye on hands, tentacles, and other appendages. Throughout the area people drank, played kinos, and danced. The all-horn band's techno beat had several people out on the floor, but most of them were too wasted to dance. They were here to forget, because most of them lived lives to be forgotten. So they would drink, they would smoke, and they would forget the other life forms they'd killed. Or would kill. Even tonight, she thought as she kept an eye on a group of Awsarians. Short, round, and purple, the race was known for their love of killing for pleasure. Or for a price.

She ignored the chill running down her spine and willed herself not to sweat. Libby knew just how to handle herself in situations such as these. She came well-equipped with a laser on her hip, handgun in her boot, and more than a few knives. Sterling Wainwright hadn't raised a fool.

As she neared the group, she noticed females outnumbered the males. Inwardly she snorted. It figured that some of them would probably see her as a rival. She reached the outer edge of his admirers. From the looks of some of them, they had to be mercenaries. Tall, dressed in dark colors, they were heavily armed and had a lean, hungry, cold look in their eyes.

Brady's deep baritone flitted over the crowd, and she sighed. He was telling the story of the mines on Alcazere. She shook her head. The man needed new material. And he always got the story wrong. Libby was the one who came up with the idea of rappelling into the mines at night. Brady fought the idea, since he has a little problem with dark places. Her father, for once, had listened to her.

She eyed the crowd again, walking around the outer rim. Shoving her way to the front wouldn't work. Besides, even if she could, she didn't want to chance touching some of them. Who knew what weapons they hid, or what toxins some of them could spurt? There was only one way to get Brady's attention, and that was to steal the audience.

"I think you have that wrong, Brady. You didn't want to do the jump, remember?"

All conversation stopped around the table, and a chorus of curious eyes swung her way. The group parted in front of her, and she felt a wave of satisfaction, however snarky, that she had stolen a bit of his thunder. She ignored the fact that her pulse had jumped and her mouth had suddenly gone dry. Long ago, it would have heralded another stuttering fit, but she'd gotten over her infatuation with the idiot.

"Well, well, well. If it isn't little Liberty Wainwright." She couldn't see him as she waited for a tall, yellow-skinned Semian male to step out of her way. The irritated look the alien shot her with his blue-green eyes told her Brady had won another admirer.

When she finally made it to the table, she cursed herself for the shiver running down her spine. He looked the same. His ebony hair, a tad too long and needing a trim, did have a bit of gray threaded through it. A few more laugh lines had appeared around his cobalt eyes. His nose had been broken, again. It just made him even more attractive. He was surrounded by females, of course. Brady always liked women of every shape, size, and species. Including, she was sure, the human bimbo sitting on his lap.

"I see you're still holding court in bars, Brady. And that's *Dr. Wainwright* to you, dickhead."

His lips turned up in a mocking smile. She curled her fingers into the palm of her hand. Smacking him would probably land her in hot water. It always had before. His gaze traveled down her body, taking in her wrinkled shirt and pants, her dusty boots. Slowly, he brought his attention back to her face.

"I thought the last time you saw me, you said you wanted nothing to do with me."

Yeah, she had said that, as she was heading out the door. She meant it at the time. "This has nothing to do with you...or me. It has to do with Sterling."

His eyes narrowed and he frowned. "I haven't seen him in months."

"You or anyone else."

"Did you two have another fight?"

"Sterling and I...we had a disagreement about a year ago."

His eyebrow rose and that damn smile returned. "What was it over this time? You thought he was taking too many risks, and he thought you had your panties in a wad about life?"

She swallowed the retort she really wanted to make. Something that would be anatomically impossible for him to do. It galled her that she needed his help, but she did. And to rescue her father, she would do anything. "No. It had to do with my divorce."

His smile faded and he actually pushed aside the blonde. The woman shot him an angry look and slid out of the booth.

"You're married?" This time irritation threaded his voice.

"Was. Sterling wanted me to work it out; I didn't. Hence, we stopped talking."

He pursed his lips. She knew he was seriously considering it from that gesture. A cautious sense of hope unfurled within her. His next words stopped any idea of help from him.

"What's in it for me?"

She sighed. She should have known. Bitterness that she'd thought she left in the past balled in her stomach. The man was always out for number one. The so-called Saint did everything for his own notoriety, not because giving his finds to museums and historical societies was the right thing to do. Knowing she was close to begging—and Liberty Wainwright did not beg— she curled her lips in disgust.

"Tell you what, Brady. I'm staying over at Delorosa's Inn. You want to hear about it, show up. If not, kiss my ass. I'll go it alone."

With that, she turned on her heel and strode out of the bar. She pushed open the door and stepped outside. The cool night air washed over her, but it didn't help her temper. Fighting the tears that threatened to spill over, she drew in a deep breath. Fatigue. That was all it was. It had been a long ten days since she'd started searching for Brady, and now it seemed she'd wasted precious time.

Damn him for being a fucking mercenary.

* * *

"Hey, Saint. What was up with your lady?" Masters asked as he slid into the booth.

"Not my woman." Not anymore. One time...

"Your loss."

He shot his friend a deadly look. "We had a thing when we were younger."

"Ahh. Is she really Wainwright's daughter?" Brady nodded. "Hard to believe that old pain in the ass with a sweet thang like that for a daughter."

Brady snorted. "Sweet isn't what she is."

Masters smacked his lips. Brady used every ounce of control not to punch him. "I bet she's a bit on the tasty side. I always liked a gal with a little spice."

He scowled at his friend. They'd never competed for women. Both of them always had plenty to choose from. Robbie Masters was an inch or two shorter, but the ladies had a thing for that blond hair and those green eyes. Brady really didn't care if he'd lost out any other time. But Libby was a different matter. No one was supposed to even fantasize about her.

His mind drifted back to Master's comments about Libby. *Spice.* She definitely had that. Six years had passed, and damned if he didn't have the same reaction the moment he heard that smart-ass comment—instant hard-on. She'd been an itch under his skin for years, growing up right before his eyes. Two years younger and as horny for outerterrestrial archeology as he was. Not many women with mile-long legs understood a dig. She'd aged well in the last six years. She'd let her dark red hair grow. He wanted to know how long it really was, but she'd had it piled on top of her head. And the way those honey-brown eyes snapped fire. Hmmm... Brady understood Masters's attraction.

"She's out of your league, Masters. And, for once, the woman knows it."

"What she say about her father?"

Brady watched him suck down his drink before answering. He was still trying to sort it out in his brain.

"Something about him being missing. Nothing new."

"Yeah. That old man is constantly disappearing. When was the last time you talked to him?"

"Six months ago. He wanted me to look for some dumbass legend."

Suddenly, Masters wasn't so laid back. "Legend?"

Brady cut him a derisive look. "The legend of the Snake King."

"Oh. Well, that *is* a dumbass legend. How many people have disappeared looking for that?"

"At least one more." Knowing he didn't have a choice, Brady threw a few coins on the table and stood to leave.

"Where you going, Saint?"

"To see an old friend."

He just hoped he didn't get his balls cut off in the process.

Chapter Two

Liberty stuffed the last of her gear into the bag and took another survey of the room. Everything was ready. She could skip out in the morning before the suns rose. Sooner, if need be. Confronting Brady in the bar might have earned her a few enemies. Male and female.

After stripping out of her clothes, she used a rag and some warm tap water to clean off. Delorosa's wasn't the best accommodations, but then, it was better than most on Relecita. The room was sparse but halfway clean. The foam mattress bed was simple, without a headboard or footboard. The only other furniture in the room was a faux wooden table with a matching chair. Both of them had seen better days.

As she pulled on a clean pair of pants—she wanted to make sure she was ready to move if needed—Liberty thought about her encounter with Brady, and frowned. She'd thought for sure he would have heard from Sterling by now. Buttoning her shirt, she thought about the last time she'd talked to her father and the bitter words they'd shared.

She sighed and pushed off the guilt. They had been at each other since she hit fourteen and wanted to become an archeologist like him. But not like him. Liberty believed in ethics, not fortune-hunting. She believed in study, not adventure.

Knowing that she wasn't likely to get much real sleep, she decided to hit the bed early to get as much rest as possible. Before she could slide under the covers, a knock sounded at the door. She grabbed her stungun and walked slowly to the door, trying not to make a sound. Her heart stuttered and her breathing hitched when she stepped on a squeaky floorboard. She froze, waiting for another knock. What she heard was an aggravated sigh.

"Libby, open the damn door. I'm too tired to play games tonight."

Relief rushed through her when she heard Brady's voice. She knew she should feel irritated, but there was no reason. If he was here, he was planning to help.

She reached the door and held it open just wide enough to look at him.

"Whatcha want, Brady?" Liberty tried her best not to sound relieved, but it was hard. She knew she could go it alone and find her father, but it would be much easier with Brady by her side.

"What I want..." His gaze traveled down her body and then back up. "Isn't on the menu. Unless you changed your mind."

Heat tingled down her spin. Her nipples hardened. "No, I haven't."

He shook his head. "Damn shame, Libby. We used to have some pretty good times."

She snorted and then opened the door wider. "Hmm, I think we remember our time together differently. But that's neither here nor there. Come on in."

He brushed past her. She drew in a deep breath. His scent lingered in the air. Male, with a hint of soap.

She closed the door and watched him as he walked around the room.

"So you haven't heard from Sterling in a year; I haven't heard from him in six months." He glanced at her pack. "Going somewhere?"

"Brady, I was raised by Sterling. Do you think I would sleep without my gear ready to go at a moment's notice?"

His lips quirked. "No. You should've been a boy scout."

She rolled her eyes and settled in a rickety chair. "To get back to the matter at hand, no, I haven't seen him since our argument. You know how he is."

Brady nodded. "Care to tell me who Mr. Doctor Wainwright was?"

His tone was condescending, and for once she was happy she could put him in his place. "Anthony Freemont."

The smile faded from his face. "Anthony Freemont of Freemont Inc.? The company that finances most of these bloody fact-finding missions?"

She could tell he was angry, because his Irish accent had slipped into his speech. Brady tried his best to keep people guessing about his background. He took perverse joy in letting people think he was American. Idiot. The only time he lost control of his accent was when he was angry, irritated, or really turned on.

Not a good thing to be thinking about, Libby.

"Yes. Hence our problems, along with a few other areas."

His gaze caught hers and she couldn't look away. "What other areas?"

"Just some problems we had."

"You knew who the bastard was when you married him."

"Yes, I did. But he wasn't working for the family business five years ago. When he was drawn back in by his father, he...changed." She swallowed the resentment. Bitter anger would do her no good.

"So, what was Sterling doing when you talked to him last?"

"Ever heard of the legend of the Snake King?" Brady thought Libby was about to faint, since all the color left her face in one fast rush. He stepped forward, ready to catch her if she should fall out of the chair.

"The Snake King?" Her voice was a whisper, and she closed her eyes. "Jesus. I can't believe he actually bought into that crap."

"I agree." She opened her eyes and stared at him. "Hey, I'm not a dumbass."

She snorted. "No comment."

Irritated with her. Irritated with himself. Dammit, the woman had him in knots and he had been in her company less than five minutes. Just hearing her snort sent a wave of heat through him. "I turned him down. I was teaching in New York at the time."

"What did he say? Did he say anything about his plans, where he might go?"

"I'd hoped that I talked him out of it. Even if the damn thing was true, too many men have died trying to find it."

She sighed and her shoulders slumped. He had to fight down the urge to go to her and pull her close. Because that would lead to feeling her curves pressed up against him. And that would lead to kissing, and that would lead to...

"Well, I have no idea where to start. I found out he hired Dracon to fly him to Gelwan, but that was the last thing I can find."

"Dracon? I thought they were at odds."

She smiled, sadly. "You know those two. Sterling and he have been arguing for the last twenty years. At least someone levelheaded was with him. Dracon, from all reports, wasn't happy about going, but when Sterling threatened to go it alone, he caved. I had no idea the Snake King was what they were after."

"You know all about it, then?"

"The legend of an emerald from the Quantanz sector so brilliant that several wars were fought over it. Not for the price, but for the magical powers it is said to posses."

"To rule without fear of being conquered." He sighed and placed his hands on his hips. "So, why was Sterling upset with your divorce? He isn't puritanical, is he?"

Her lips twisted into a cynical smile. "It had nothing to do with me, per se. You know him. Why would he not want me to divorce my husband?" When he shook his head, she continued. "Why, to benefit him, of course. Freemont Inc. was supposed to fund his latest adventure."

"Ah." His voice was calm, but the anger boiling in his gut wasn't. Damn Sterling for treating his daughter like a commodity. Again. Brady flexed his hands and tried his best not to pick up something and break it. The way the man had raised her had been one of the problems that had broken them up. The other part had to do with Libby not being able to accept things one day at a time. Always had to have a fucking plan for everything, and it drove him crazy.

"So there is nothing really in it for you, as you can see." She rolled her shoulders, which thrust her breasts against the soft fabric of her shirt. Momentarily his thoughts, and most of his blood, drained from his head. Libby looked to have finally grown into her almost-six-foot height. In more than one way. He licked his lips.

"Excuse me."

He barely noted her voice as he watched her puckered nipples pressed against her shirt. He knew just the way they felt when he brushed the back of his hand against them.

"Brady."

He glanced up at her face and felt a flush of embarrassment creeping up his neck. Damn, caught. He cleared his throat.

"Sorry. So nothing, no money involved?"

She tsked. "You should know better than that. If someone financed the trip, they'll get a percentage of what he finds. Which I am sure is nothing. And you know he spent all the money on the trip. Sterling Wainwright always travels in style."

Brady heard the love and concern beneath her scorn. He'd known the Wainwrights since he'd been fortunate enough to stow away on Sterling's hired ship. He'd been fifteen and green. Damn, he'd been lucky he'd picked the ship he did. When Libby found him hiding in the overhead compartment, he'd thought he would be sent back. Sterling took one look at him and saw a comrade. Libby acted as if he'd committed a crime. He took her place. But even with their estrangement, Brady knew she loved her father and worried about him. Truthfully, it usually didn't take her this long to go looking for Sterling.

"Must have been one helluva fight."

She sighed. "It was, and there were some things both of us said that may not ever go away, but…well, I have to find him. He has a habit of finding trouble. And since neither one of us knows where he is…"

"Who knows where the hell he is?" He sighed and then a smile tugged at his lips. "Hey, you remember that job on Yentalan, where those Saber Tooths came after us?"

Her eyes widened and her lips parted as if in surprise. She swallowed, visibly. "Of course I remember that." Her voice had turned a shade colder, and she wouldn't meet his gaze. "We better get going. I take it you have your own ship?"

"Yeah. I figured you might know where to start."

She stood and started to gather up her things. "Yes, I tracked him to Bulivenia. It wasn't fun. The last I heard after that was they were headed to Dranirick."

"Good God." Dranirick was barely surveyed. Several species inhabited the overgrown rain forest. One was a group of humans who thrived on strange sexual practices.

"Yeah, that's why I came to find you. I couldn't trust anyone else."

He grunted and grabbed her arm as she tried to walk past him. "What the hell is the matter?"

Every muscle in her arm grew rigid, and that same damn broom handle stiffened her spine. "Forget it."

"Listen, sweetheart, we're going to be in each other's pockets for a few days, if not a few weeks. We should make the most of it."

She glanced up at him. Instead of the cold look he expected, there was something else, something that struck him as hurt, portrayed there. "I think we'll both survive. We did last time."

"Libby—"

She wrenched her arm away. "Listen, *Saint*, I have no problem with it. It was just the mention of Yentalan. That's all."

"What? So I was reliving some of our old times together."

"Nothing. Listen, I'm going to use the bathroom, and then we can get out of here before any other admirers come after me."

Before he could say another word, she left him, locking the bathroom door with a definite click. What the hell did he do now? If it wasn't one thing with Libby, it was another. The woman was harder to please than anyone he'd known. All he'd done was mention Yentalan.

Then it hit him like a right hook to the chin. He shut his eyes as he realized what he'd said. What he'd brought up. Damn his fucking mouth. Sterling always said it was the thing that would get him in trouble. Brady shook his head and opened his eyes, thinking of what an ass he'd made of himself.

They'd been after some Yentalianese artifact that Sterling was sure would make them rich beyond their dreams. Brady was twenty-one to Libby's nineteen, and the two of them had bickered the whole trip. Her damn ethics were always getting in the way.

As the past came roaring back to him, he walked to the window and stared blindly out, allowing the memories to wash over him. They'd found that damn treasure. It hadn't been worth as much as Sterling had suspected, but they'd still celebrated. Too much. Sterling had gone off to bargain. Brady and Libby decided to split a bottle of wine. Dressed in camos, dirty from the firefight they'd been through, they'd found a deserted cave and collapsed.

"You know that one of these days both of you are going to get caught doing something illegal, and you'll both end up in jail."

The flickering light from the campfire washed over her, casting a golden glow to her skin. Brady knew at the moment he'd never seen anything as beautiful as Liberty Wainwright. All that red hair, those slanted golden-brown eyes...even the freckles that danced across the bridge of her nose turned his mind to mush. They had since she was fifteen.

"And you'll bail us out, as usual." His words were slurred, and even he heard his Irish slipping into his speech. He reached out and brushed the back of his fingers along her jaw. She shivered. "You know, lass, that every time we do something on the border of illegal, you come to the rescue."

She took a swig of wine and looked away. "Maybe one of these days I won't."

"Is that some kind of threat? Come on, sweetheart, you know better than to threaten us. Your da and I both know you aren't going to leave. You've been threatening it for three years."

"Just don't count on it."

"We can always count on you."

"I was accepted into training at the Freemont Center. They have ethics. I want to learn about real archeology. Not fortune hunting."

Panic clawed at his throat. He took a deep breath and reminded himself that she'd threatened this before. She'd never followed through.

"Lying again, are you, Libby? You know you won't leave your da."

"Really, why?"

"He needs you."

She laughed without humor. "Do you think he'd actually notice if I disappeared, Brady? I sometimes think it would be better if I left."

Her voice was so sad, so filled with need. He swallowed the lump in his throat, knowing what she was feeling. He'd been there with his own family too many times to count, but in this case, she had no one else. Damn her father for being a shit. He heard a suspicious sniff and leaned forward, bridging the gap between them. Cupping her chin, he tilted her face up. Just touching her soft skin sent a shock of heat roaring through him. She'd been under his skin, driving him crazy.

Unshed tears shimmered in her eyes, and the sight almost broke his heart. "Ah, lass. Don't let Sterling get to you."

She tried to pull away, but he held her chin firmly. Before he could think twice about it, he leaned down and brushed his mouth over hers. He held her gaze as his tongue darted out and traced the seam of her lips. Her eyes drifted closed and she opened her mouth. Any blood left in his brain traveled south. He closed his eyes and took possession of her mouth. Her arms slid around his neck and his dropped to her lower back. In one move, he pulled her forward and covered her body with his.

The heat between them went from spark to inferno within seconds. All the years they'd been holding back, broke free.

They tore at each other's clothes between kisses. When he'd finally stripped her to her waist, he slowed down. The cool air washed over them; her nipples puckered.

"Brady?"

He'd have been a fool not to hear the fear in her voice. "Shhh, lass."

He bent his head and took the turgid tip into his mouth. Instantly, her fingers speared through his hair as she pressed him closer. Her moan echoed in the cave, but he didn't notice anything but the feel of her flesh against his, the taste of her skin, and the feel of her heat against his groin. He pressed his cock against her pussy. Even through the layers of clothing, he could feel her damp core.

"Brady." He didn't say anything, just moved to her other breast, pausing to lick the skin between them. "Brady."

It finally hit him she was pulling on his hair. He looked up and smiled at her. Ever neat and in control, Liberty Wainwright was a mess. Her short hair stood on end. He could already see the razor burn on her neck left from his beard. Passion clouded her eyes.

"What?" His voice was soft, coaxing.

"I've never..."

Even in the dark cave, he could see her flush.

"Ahh, Libby." His mind couldn't function, not without one drop of blood in it. He'd never slept with a virgin. It had never mattered to him before. Now it frightened the hell out him. It was also damned arousing. "You trust me, don't you?"

She nodded, and he swooped in for a kiss. By the time he raised his head, both of them were breathless. "I promise it will be fine."

A husky laugh bubbled out of her. "I know that, Brady. I just wanted you to know."

She was offering something to him that she'd never given to another. Something trembled around his heart, but he pushed it aside. "Well, first off..."

He slid down her body, kissing her stomach and undoing her pants. He pulled them away—

"Brady?"

Her voice jolted him out of the bittersweet memory. He tried to ignore her and move back into his memories, but she'd broken the spell. Wiping his forehead, he looked at her and inwardly sighed. It was damn bad luck to want a woman as much as he wanted Libby. His body vibrated with unrelieved passion as if they had been making love just moments earlier.

"Are you ready?" His voice was rough, but he couldn't help it. Whispers of his earlier thoughts still washed through him. She still got to him.

"Sure."

He followed her to the door, trying to ignore the throbbing in his cock and the sweet sway of her ass. Drawing in a deep breath, he reminded himself why they split up six years ago.

But damned if he could remember one reason that outweighed his feelings for her. He just hoped they found Sterling, quickly.

A knock sounded at the door, and both of them froze.

"You expecting company?"

She looked back over her shoulder at him. "Whadya think?"

He braced himself against the wall next to the door. She watched him, and when he nodded, she followed right along.

"Who is it?"

"Robbie Masters. I heard you were looking for help."

Chapter Three

Liberty watched Brady raise his finger to his lips. The muscle in his jaw twitched as he ground his teeth together. From the narrowed-eyed look he sent her, he wasn't happy with the situation.

Masters was a slimy gunrunner, and all-around gopher when needed. There'd always been rumors about one deal or another he'd been involved in, but he seemed to come through it clean. She needed to buy a little time.

"Who did you say you were again?" She tried her best to sound like the scared little woman. Macho jackasses always fell for it. Glancing at Brady, she noticed his lips twitched. He knew exactly what she was pulling.

"Robbie Masters. I'm a friend of the Saint's."

She arched her eyebrows. Brady bit his lip, probably because he was ready to laugh out loud.

"You don't say?"

"Yes. He told me you might be interested in hiring someone to help find your father."

The laughter faded from Brady's eyes and a different light altogether flashed in them. Ohh, boy, she'd seen that look before. Suspicious and predatory.

He moved in behind her, pressing against her back. Instantly, every thought in her brain faded as heat singed along her nerve endings. The scent of him filled her senses. His breath brushed her earlobe, and she suppressed a shiver.

"Open the door, slowly. Get him in the room." Whisper-soft, his command should have irritated the hell out of her. She liked to be the one giving orders when working. It was something that had always been a problem between the two of them. But she couldn't get past the fact that his breath was against her skin or that her nipples had hardened the moment he stepped behind her.

Liberty turned her head and looked up at him. The moment his gaze caught hers, the breath she was taking tangled in her throat. The intensity in his blue eyes sparked a fire in her stomach. A wave of sensual longing wound through her. She could feel his heartbeat against her back accelerate the moment they made eye contact. Damp heat slid from her belly to between her legs. Shifting her weight, Liberty brushed against his erection, and both of them stopped breathing. Brady closed his eyes, visibly swallowed, and drew in a deep breath.

Her whole body throbbed. She didn't understand it at all. Less than a day in his presence, and she was panting after him. She'd never been able to respond to her husband the way she had to Brady. An innocent touch and she was ready to jump him like some cat in heat.

He opened his eyes, and she noticed the banked fire simmering; the look he shot her told her he wouldn't let this go. Nodding his head to the door, he stepped back. Cold air replaced his heat, and she shivered as she opened the door.

She didn't know what to expect, but it wasn't the tall, handsome man standing across the threshold. Short blond hair and sparkling green eyes stood out against lightly tanned skin. Long and angular, his face sported a more-than-once-broken nose and full, smiling lips. He wore camos, just like every other human in the business.

"Ms. Wainwright?"

She smiled. "Mr. Masters, I have a feeling you already know who I am."

His own smile broadened. For a moment, she was held mesmerized by the boyish good humor on his face. She knew now that the other rumors, those of his many conquests, were probably true.

"Why don't you come in?" She gestured with one hand while keeping the other on the door. Masters nodded and walked into the room. The moment Masters crossed the threshold, Brady came forward, stungun raised. In one fluid movement, he grabbed Masters by the arm, twisted it behind him, and shoved him against the wall.

"Shut the fucking door."

She bristled at the harsh tone, but did his bidding.

"What the hell is wrong with you, Saint?" Masters words came out muffled since Brady held his head against the wall.

"What the hell is wrong with me? Jesus, Masters, what the hell is wrong with *you?* What the fuck do you think you're doing here, anyway? Retrieval is not your forte."

When Masters didn't comment, Brady squeezed his neck harder. Brady's anger was making her uncomfortable. She'd never seen him in such a rage.

"Brady. He can't talk. You're holding on to him too tightly."

He glanced at her as if he'd forgotten she was there. She recognized the moment he realized what he was doing. Shaking his head, he let up the pressure. The breath Masters drew in was audible.

"Now, hand Libby all your weapons."

Masters, apparently terrified of the murderous look on Brady's face, quickly handed over a stungun and a couple knives.

She walked over to the bed and dropped them by her bag.

"That's good. I'm going to let up, and you are going to park your mangy ass in that chair."

Masters nodded jerkily and followed Brady's directions.

"Now, what do you want with Libby?" Masters opened his mouth, but Brady interrupted him. "And don't give me that crap about wanting to help her find her father. I know you better. There has to be something else in it for you. Money."

Masters rubbed his neck then smiled. "Not always money. I have other wants."

She heard the challenge in his voice, but didn't understand anything. Whatever it was, Brady's fist shot out before she could stop him. Masters flew backward, chair and all. Both crashed against the wall. So much for keeping it quiet.

"Brady, stop it this instant." He'd stepped forward and was towering over Masters like a raving lunatic. "All this noise is going to draw attention."

His face was flushed with anger, but he nodded and stepped back.

Masters slowly rose to his feet and moved his jaw back and forth. His lip was bleeding. "Jesus, Saint. I thought she was free territory."

"You thought wrong." Brady's voice held the same lethal tone as before. And a second later, their comments hit home.

"What the hell do you mean, 'free territory'?" She settled her hands on her hips. Brady snorted. She rounded on him. "And what do you mean by your comment, buster?"

Instead of taking her seriously, Brady laughed in her face. "Don't worry about it, sweetheart." His gaze shifted to Masters. "Are you telling me you came sniffing around here because of her? Not because of the legend of the Snake King?"

Masters grinned, but then winced and touched his lip with his sleeve. "What other reason would I have? You know me. I don't go after anything unless it's a sure thing."

Anger simmered. "A sure thing? A *sure thing?*"

"Easy there, sweets, you're repeating yourself." He turned to look at Masters. "She does that when she gets irritated."

She shot him what she hoped was a withering glance and gathered up her bag.

"Are you ready to go?" She tried her best to hide her anger, but she knew some of it threaded her voice, because Brady smiled at her. Damn jackass.

"And she ignores comments she doesn't like, when she's really pissed."

Crossing her arms beneath her breasts, she tapped her foot and stared at him. Masters stood, and one look told her that he was enjoying himself.

"I'll wish you both luck in your quest." But before he could reach the door, Brady stepped behind him and smacked Masters on the head with the butt of his stungun. Masters collapsed into a crumpled heap, out cold from the blow.

"What the hell did you do that for?"

Brady glanced at her, then back down at Masters. "I know him, worked with him once or twice, but that doesn't mean I trust him. He seems to get out of trouble too easily."

She sighed, and watched as he went through Masters's pockets. When he found nothing but some money, he pulled open the door. After peeking out, he gestured for her to follow him. She did, carefully stepping over Masters's prone body.

As they left through the backdoor, she thought about her reaction to Brady and his strange territorial behavior.

Maybe asking for his help wasn't a good idea.

* * *

Brady set the ship on autopilot. Their departure had gone smoothly. Too smoothly, for his thinking. He knew they were being watched. Felt it in his gut.

"That was easy enough."

He glanced at her and tried his best not to remember the encounter in her room. The memory of their first time together was still churning heat through his body. Besides that, emotions he had thought long gone seemed to have sprouted the moment he heard her prissy voice in the bar.

"That's what I'm worried about."

Her gaze focused on his face, and for a second, he lost all thought. She was paying attention like she had years ago.

Looking to him for guidance. Believing in him. Her admiration had always been a sort of aphrodisiac where he was concerned. Hell, she could probably look at him crossed-eyed and he'd have a boner.

He cleared his throat. "I think someone is probably following us."

"Hmm."

"No comment?"

"No. I figured we would have someone following us."

He cocked an eyebrow. She shrugged and unlocked her seatbelt, standing and leaving the cabin.

"This is a pretty nice ship."

He scrambled out of his seat to follow her. When he found her, she was looking in his food cooler. As she bent at the waist, her pants drew tight across her ass, clearly showing off a definite heart shape.

"I'm amazed you could afford something so nice."

Oh, Jesus. She was swinging it back and forth as she rummaged through his food. It took a second for her comment to register. Through his lust-induced haze, he realized in her usual subtle way, she'd put him down.

"What the hell you mean by that?"

She looked back over her shoulder at him. The image of her bending over while he took her from behind was so clear in his mind he was amazed he didn't come right then and there. Libby had always liked sex in that position. Used to drive her insane, if he remembered right.

"I mean that you tend to give things away. I thought you donated everything to museums and the proper authorities."

"I...ah..." What the hell were they talking about? Fuck. "Um, well, I did that teaching stint in New York last year to make some extra cash. I didn't want to depend on hiring a ship." His smile was self-deprecating as he remembered one really bad job. "I think both of us learned that lesson."

She returned the smile. "That excavation in Miradan *was* a shit job." For a moment, the memory of shared history shimmered between them. Familiar heat crawled through him—the dangerous kind, at that. This wasn't just lust, and never had been. They'd both had their hearts involved before or it wouldn't have hurt so badly when it fell apart.

She turned abruptly and started to rummage again. "You have anything edible in here, Brady?"

The deepening of her voice told him she'd felt it too. That heat, the connection, that no matter how many years they'd been apart, the spark was there. She pretended to keep looking for food, but he knew her well enough. The moment her body flushed with heat, she would be raring to go. No one burned hotter or faster than Libby. The woman might look and act like an uptight pain in the ass, but she had no inhibitions in bed.

As desire threaded through his veins, he moved behind her. He placed both hands on her ass and smoothed them up to her lower back. She stilled as he stepped closer, pressing his cock against her. She straightened and shivered. He leaned his head over her shoulder, bringing his face even with hers.

"Ahh, lass."

"D-Don't use that old ploy. I won't fall for the Irish charm this time, asshole."

Her voice shook. His heart jumped at the telltale sign of her arousal. He slid his hands around to her stomach. One descended to cup her sex. Wet heat warmed his hand. His dick twitched against her. Closing his eyes, he hummed. The musky scent of her arousal filled his senses. He moved his other hand to her breast. Gently, slowly, he grazed the tip of her nipple with his fingers.

"I beg to differ with you. And, darlin', your body agrees."

Chapter Four

A hunger she hadn't felt in six years crawled through Liberty, robbing her of logical thought. As Brady's lips moved over her neck, his tongue darting out over her sensitive skin, he slid his other hand to the buttons on the fly of her pants. Slowly, he popped each one, while he took her nipple between thumb and forefinger. His fingers brushed against her skin.

Liquid heat poured through her. Brady could always do that with just a touch. A word. The man had some secret skill for seduction. He never had to work hard when it came to her. She tried her best to shake her head, clear her thoughts. But the rising tide of arousal swept over her, through her, and she felt her control slipping. From their history, she knew she was helpless to resist once she started going under. He murmured something against her skin. She couldn't understand the words, but the sound of his voice, low and unmistakably aroused, danced down her spine.

Once he had the last button freed, his fingers slid beneath the fabric and caressed her slit. His touch was feather-light, a caress, subtle pressure, and had her moaning his name.

"Hmm." His teeth grazed her earlobe, and his heated whisper shook her to her core. "I think I'm right. Never knew a woman who got so wet so fast."

He removed his hand and pulled her gently away from the unit. With one fluid motion, he shut the door and backed her against it. The metal was cold, but her shiver had more to do with the dark lust she saw in Brady's eyes. Without taking his gaze from hers, he slowly unbuttoned her shirt. He was challenging her, daring her to say no. She choked on the denial she wanted to throw in his face. She wanted to tell him that she didn't want this anymore. Need this anymore. Unfortunately, throughout everything, every problem they'd had, every disagreement, sex had never been a major issue. Most of their fights had been foreplay. Dysfunctional as it was, they'd usually had some of the best sex after those arguments.

It unnerved her that within hours of meeting up, she was in the same situation she had been years ago. Even knowing it was completely wrong, she felt herself falling. *Stupid woman,* she thought, even as her blood flowed like molten lava. It had been so long, longer than she'd want to admit to anyone, even herself.

Pushing the fabric aside, he focused on her breasts. He licked his lips and reached forward, brushing the backs of his fingers against her nipples. She felt the touch all the way down to her toes. Her knees almost buckled.

"So sensitive." His voice was a murmur, darker, deeper, more aroused. The deepening of his voice, the way his accent was now threaded with Irish, sent a delicious swirl of heat to the pit of her stomach. Stepping closer, he slid his hands to her waist and bent his head.

Fire blazed through her as his mouth brushed against her nipple. She looked down. His shaggy dark hair tickled her skin as it slid against her breast. Softer than it looked, it teased her nipple. A moment later, she felt his tongue touch her nipple. As he took the tip into his mouth, his fingers dug into her skin, telling her he wasn't as in control as he appeared to be. Her senses spun; her body throbbed with need. His teeth grazed her nipple, tension coiled in her stomach, and heat seared her veins. Her pussy dripped with liquid. She shifted her legs, trying to relieve the building pressure, and felt his lips curve against her breast. He knew what he was doing, and what he was doing was driving her insane. And, fool that she was, she didn't give a damn. The sensations pouring through her must have made her batty, because all she cared about was feeling his skin next to hers.

He lifted his head. Cool air washed against her breasts, teasing her already sensitive nipples. Before she could react, he was tugging off her boots and pants and was kneeling in front of her. He cupped her ass and pulled her forward, forcing her legs wider.

"Ahh, Libby, you smell so good." He licked her cunt. "Hot, aroused, mine." The last was said with such force, she opened her mouth to argue. But her argument turned into a moan when his slid his tongue between her folds. Over and over he tasted her. He kept one hand braced on her ass while he slid his finger into her. His tongue brushed against her clit, sending another jolt through her. As her muscles tensed, she felt another gush of liquid, and Brady made an appreciative sound in the back of his throat.

He lifted his head as he added another finger. The heat in his gaze held her almost paralyzed. The next instant, he brushed his thumb against her clit, once, twice…and she closed her eyes as the pressure exploded within her.

"That's it, lass, just like that." His voice was rougher, more aroused.

"Brady…" As the sensations swept through her, her bones melted.

Brady removed his hand and came to his feet. She opened her eyes halfway and watched as he tore at the fly on his pants. His hands were shaking so badly, she was amazed he could actually get it done. When he finally popped the last button, his erection sprang free. She reached out and encircled the tip of it with her hand. A drip of pre-cum wet the head, and she licked her lips. Brady let out a strained chuckle.

"Don't even think of it, lass. I want to be inside you."

She caught the drop and spread it around, then pushed her hand to the base and back up again. Brady planted a hand on either side of her on the unit and groaned. He caught her rhythm, flexing his hips to keep time. She felt herself dampen more, and the pressure within her began to build again.

Brady growled and removed her hand. He picked her up by her hips and braced her against the unit. Wrapping one arm around her, he took hold of his cock, positioning it at her entrance.

"Look at me, Libby." She met his gaze and sucked in a breath at the uncontrolled passion, the fires she had unleashed. As he held her gaze, he entered her, inch by excruciating inch. Her lungs seized at the feelings she saw in his eyes. The passion, the tenderness, the undisguised lust—all of them scared the hell out of her. She needed to ignore that and lose herself in the sexual release, but he must have seen her panic, her fear.

"Don't close your eyes, Libby. Wrap your legs around me, sweetheart." Without thought, she responded to his commands. Slowly, he began to move. All the delicious warmth built, her muscles began to tense, and she knew she was on the verge of another orgasm. "Aye, that's it, lass. Oh, damn, you feel so good."

She tangled her hands in the hair on the back of his head and brought his mouth to hers. He tasted the same—decadent, forbidden, delicious. Taking his tongue in her mouth, she mimicked his motions, and felt no small sense of triumph when his eyes slid closed. His thrusts grew faster. He broke from the kiss, her name a shout on his lips as he poured himself into her. One last thrust and he sent her hurtling over the edge again, her body convulsing from the force of her release.

As every muscle in her body slowly relaxed, Liberty was aware of Brady pulling her close and stumbling to the couch. He lay down, positing her on top, and sighed. The sound of it— lazy, contented male—would have normally irritated the hell out of her. Brady was always at his worst when he knew he'd won an argument. But with her body still warm from his lovemaking, she snuggled deeper into his embrace and decided that at the moment, she really didn't give a damn.

* * *

Brady awoke some time later, and it took a moment for him to assess the situation. He kept his eyes closed and inhaled deeply. There was a warm woman on top of him, so it couldn't be that bad. He slid his hand down her spine to her ass and rubbed it. She purred his name. His eyes shot open at the sound of her voice, and the memories of their lovemaking swirled through his head.

Oh, God, Libby. Licking his lips, he could still taste her there. He knew he shouldn't have acted on his impulse, but the woman had always pushed his buttons. Didn't matter what the hell the situation was, he was always ready to slide into her for a nice, long fuck. From the moment she'd let him touch her, he couldn't be within five miles of her and not have a hard-on.

The control panel beeped. Libby stirred, her silky hair sliding around his chest. The scent of their lovemaking mixed with her clean fresh scent. He closed his eyes, trying to ignore the reality of what they faced. Over six years. Six fucking years, and it took less than twenty-four hours before she made him lose control. And dammit, he couldn't go through it again. He was enough of a man to admit he'd almost fallen apart when she left last time. He'd hidden it behind women, booze, and extravagant exploits, but he knew deep down that no matter what, she'd taken a piece of him, a piece of his heart, with her.

"Brady, what the hell is that noise?" He smiled because she sounded like an uptight schoolmarm. She shifted her weight, and he silently cursed his reaction to her.

"I think we are arriving at the Dranirick docking station."

"Oh." She sounded disappointed, and he couldn't help the little jump in his pulse at the thought that she wanted him as much as he wanted her. It took every ounce of self-control to focus on what he needed to get done. He sighed, knowing they needed to find her father before they could even think about sorting out what was between them.

But to make sure he kept her on her toes, he raised his hand and brought it down on her rump. She squealed and wiggled some more.

"Dammit, Brady, that hurt." She rubbed her ass and he laughed.

"Quit being a pansy ass. We've arrived, and you're naked, and I might as well be."

She shoved herself to her elbows and looked around. Her eyes widened as what they'd just done hit her.

"Yeah, don't want to dock at the station in this condition. We'd be the talk of this side of the zone for months."

Chapter Five

Brady had buttoned his pants, finger-combed his hair, and headed back to the controls. Liberty tried to compose herself as she dressed more slowly. This was the reason she hadn't wanted to contact Brady for help. They were always like this. She stepped into her pants and then tucked her shirt in. As she fastened the last button on her fly, she noticed her hands shaking. When she finished her task, she scrubbed her hands over her face. Fear, anger, and the lingering heat of their passion rolled through her.

She had to be better than this, for her father's sake and for sanity. After leaving Brady six years earlier, she'd buried herself in work, pretending to find happiness in her accomplishments. And that was why she had been such an easy conquest for Tony. She'd needed someone to take her seriously, but in the end it had been a disaster of a marriage. And she was to blame. She never loved Tony the way he deserved to be loved.

Glancing at Brady, she thought about her time with Tony and the reason she could never really respond to him in bed.

They had decent sex, but nothing fun, nothing even passionate. For the most part, it hadn't bothered Tony. He was from a family where marriages were often made because of connections and not love. Their marriage had been based on shared interests and mutual respect.

She had been completely bored within a year and held on trying to make it work. But when he had taken over the company, he'd changed, and she couldn't pretend anymore. Their divorce had been polite and amicable. Tony hadn't put up much of a fight after she told him there was no way she could stay with him.

Brady swore when he flipped the wrong switch. He continued to mutter as he fixed the problem, and she felt her lips curve. Brady would never settle for a reserved divorce. He would have fought her to the end.

"Libby, get your ass up here and sit down."

"Oh, be still my heart." Sarcasm threaded her words, but she followed his orders.

He glanced at her. She knew in that brief moment he was taking stock of her. "You're not going to pretend that didn't happen."

Not a question—a statement of fact. Because, she knew, he meant he wouldn't let her. She ground her teeth together as anger lit through her.

"First off, I determine what I want and where I want it." She kept her gaze on the bluish-red planet of Dranirick. "And secondly, I don't like the fact that you would even think I would be a coward about it."

She could hear the voice of the traffic controller murmuring from his headphones. He answered a few questions and then looked at her again. "We have unfinished business, you and I."

* * *

She looked at him out of the corner of her eye. "Oh, really? I thought we just took care of it."

He snorted. "No. I mean from before. And this time you are going to talk about it. About why you felt a need to leave just then."

Because I was drowning. But she couldn't say that. No matter what Brady said in the bedroom, it didn't matter out in the field. He didn't wait for her answer but just went on with landing the ship.

His scruples were just a shade to the right side of the law, but damn if he didn't get close to stepping over the line. Every time she went along with him, broke another one of her rules, she'd felt a part of her soul dying. In the end, she knew she had to leave before she grew to hate him...hate herself.

She knew it was just a matter of time before they would break one of her rules...but this time it mattered. Brady had no problem and would push and prod until she went along with him. And as loath as she was to admit it, she knew it was important. Her father's life depended on it.

* * *

Brady pressed his thumb on the identification machine and then stepped back for Libby to do the same. As she brushed past, her scent drifted to him, and he had to resist grabbing her and taking her back on the ship. His nerves were already raw, and being on Dranirick was going to make it worse. Most of the planet was an unmapped rainforest. They'd had many species on the planet, but the most serious threat came from the Funkai. Funkai were actually a group of humans from Earth whose sexual preferences included abduction and rape. When too many of their members had ended up in jail, they moved to Dranirick because it had been wide open for settlers, no laws.

They pretty much kept to themselves, but rumors were always whispered about people who accidentally crossed their path. And he knew the way Sterling had gone would be right through their damn territory.

* * *

"Brady. You can stop looking at me that way. I'm going whether you like it or not. He's my father."

He narrowed his eyes and shot her a dirty look but didn't say anything. "Let's get going. We have a few hours of good light, and I want to get to the other side of the river before nightfall."

He turned on his heel and stalked out of the station, knowing he was behaving like an ass. It was the only defense he had against her at this point.

"Brady." He stopped and looked over his shoulder at her. She had her hands fisted on her hips, her eyes sparked with anger, and he'd never wanted to jump her bones more than at that moment. Shit.

"I hired you."

Before she could continue, he whipped around and strode toward her. "Listen, sweetheart. There are people on this planet who would like to get ahold of you." His gaze raked her body. "And they ain't gonna want you for your expertise in archeology."

Her face flushed, but she didn't back down. "Brady, we went over this. I'm coming with you. You know I can take care of myself."

But I want to take care of you. He thought the words before he could stop himself. There it was, laid bare for his mind to contemplate. He'd always had a protective attitude around Libby, but now, since she'd stepped back into his life, the protective instincts took control. And it wasn't just to keep her safe. Without even trying to deny it, he knew he needed this woman by his side. From the frown on her face, she might object to any suggestion in that area.

"Listen. I know you're smart." She rolled her eyes. "Smarter than I ever was. And the best damn partner I've ever had." Her expression softened, and he knew he was winning the argument. "But you have been ensconced on Earth in your safe surroundings for how many years? You've never had a problem with letting me take the lead before." She nodded, stiffly. But she'd agreed, and that was all he cared about.

"Let's get on our way. I want to be hunkered down before night."

Even as he turned his thoughts to the trek ahead of them, anticipation jumped along his nerve endings. A room, a bed, and Libby—a man couldn't ask for more than that.

Chapter Six

Libby took another gulp of water out of her bottle, and sighed. A dribble of sweat gathered between her breasts and then slid down her stomach. Her legs ached, her head hurt, and she hadn't been this freaking hot in years. Brady was right— she'd grown a little soft around the edges. A few years ago, she was able to keep up with him without a problem. Today, she knew he'd slowed down more than once to accommodate her. It had shamed her, but she hadn't thanked him, knowing he would deny it. And really, a woman had to have some pride. Especially after screwing a man's brains out.

"The second sun should be setting soon."

His voice was businesslike, abrupt. If there was one thing she could count on, it was Brady's dedication to the job.

"How far are we from that outpost you mentioned?"

He glanced down the dirt path. She followed his gaze and studied the blue-green overgrowth that slipped over the edges like spider webs. "About another five minutes or so and we should be there. I know the owner of the inn. It's decent, so we should be able to get a good night's sleep."

Well, damn, she didn't want to sleep.

Where the hell had that come from? She needed to get away from those thoughts. Sex with Brady was great, but keeping her thoughts on their mission was more important. Last time, the web of his seduction had almost made her compromise her principles. She had to keep her head about her so she could cut herself loose at the end.

"We better get moving." Brady's gaze raked over the trees that lined the road. They varied in height, with yellow bark and fuchsia leaves. Dense with green vines hanging from the limbs, it was impossible to see anything that might be lurking. The hair on the nape of her neck stirred, and a chill ran down her spine. Brady's stride increased and hers did the same. Leaves rustled behind them. She kept pace with him and forced herself not to turn around.

By the time they reached the fork in the road, they were running. Brady pulled out his stungun and grabbed hold of her upper arm. His fingers dug into her skin as he propelled her to the side of the road. She fell to the ground, feet first, sliding across the dirt and the gravel. She landed in a ditch, hard on her ass, and small rocks bit into her palms as she halted her descent. Brady landed beside her with a grunt and immediately rolled onto his stomach. She assumed the same position and pulled out her gun.

The overgrown brush on the side of the road would hide them if their pursuers hadn't seen where they'd slid. A rush of footsteps went by them. Both of them breathed shallowly, trying their best not to be detected. As a dribble of sweat rolled down her temple and the side of her face, fingers of apprehension crawled up her spine. Besides their guns, she knew Brady had a least four knives to her two. But it wouldn't be enough to fight more than three or four people. If they were found out, it wouldn't be pretty. She drew in another shallow breath and fought the urge to sneeze. The putrid scent of rotting leaves filled the heavy air, bringing a wave of nausea each time she smelled it. She licked her lips and looked over at Brady, whose gaze never left the path.

The murmur of conversation drifted to her, and she realized they were probably human from the speech and accent. *Bounty hunters?* Oh, shit. If they had prices on their heads, they were in trouble. Especially on this planet. She strained to catch any of it, and the one thing she did hear was her name and her father's. Then the two words she hadn't thought she would hear.

Emerald Project.

Chapter Seven

Brady felt Libby stiffen next to him and wondered at her reaction. He'd heard them say something about the emerald project, whatever the hell that was, and then they walked off, their voices fading into the night. Waiting several moments to make sure they really were alone, he allowed his breathing to return to normal. His heart still thumped hard against his chest and his nerves were raw. That had been damn close.

Slowly, he inched his way up the incline and peeked out from behind the overgrowth. Thankfully everything seemed clear.

"They're gone?" Libby's voice was reed-thin from terror, not what he expected. She had a bigger set of balls in situations like the one they'd been through than most men.

There was something going on here, but he knew they couldn't get into it out here. Within five minutes, they would be safe at the outpost.

"Yeah, they're gone. Let's get going. Just a few minutes and we'll be able to relax."

He climbed up first, then extended a hand to help her out. She winced as he grabbed her hand and pulled her out of the crevice. After looking around the area, he reassured himself they were safe, at least for now. The dim light made it hard for him to make out every little detail, but he knew his predators had the same disadvantage.

"Let's get going."

She nodded and fell in behind him. Not five minutes later, the smell of wood burning, signaling the outpost was near, allowed him to relax a bit more.

"Are we near?"

He nodded but didn't turn around. Keeping his senses alert was important because muggers liked to hang out near outposts for easy prey. They walked a few more minutes until the road widened, and he smiled.

The outpost was a variety of smaller shacks built close together, looking like something out of a medieval tale. Instead of the steel and glass structures of Earth and some of the more developed quadrants, this one was made of local lumber, sturdy but definitely unsightly. It didn't seem like much, but Brady knew on this planet that places where one could sleep inside and halfway safe were few and far between. He stopped, and Libby stepped up beside him. Scanning the area, he decided to go in the back way. Their pursuers had probably headed here for the night. Not even kick-ass cutthroats like them would want to be caught out in the open at night.

"Doesn't look like much." Libby stretched her arms over her head. "But at this point it seems like a palace."

"Let's go around the back."

She nodded and followed. There was one thing about Libby—she followed orders when on a job. Sterling had raised a woman who could handle a dig and could understand the need for orders.

When they reached the backdoor, he rapped it with his knuckles, knowing that John Hunter wouldn't take kindly to the two of them stepping in uninvited. Even if they were friends. The door opened slowly, the scent of cooked meat seeped through the small crack.

"What the hell do you want, you Irish bastard?"

Brady couldn't see him, but he recognized Hunter's sarcastic voice immediately. Usually he enjoyed a few verbal exchanges with him, calling into question each other's manhood. At the moment, though, his neck prickled. He felt as though they were being watched…stalked.

"Open up the fucking door, Hunter. I need a place to stay tonight."

His tone was sharp. Hunter, apparently recognizing his mood, opened the door immediately. Brady stepped back and let Libby go through the door first. As he stepped in behind her, he noticed Hunter's attention was on Libby. Actually, Libby's ass. He curled his fingers, his nails biting into his palms, and fought the urge to smack Hunter. The predatory look Brady witnessed in the other man's eyes pissed him off. Because, although he had no right to her, he couldn't help feeling possessive. And, dammit, he should have a right. Biting back a growl, he slammed the door shut and caught Hunter's gaze. His amused look did nothing to dampen Brady's anger.

"What are you doing in these parts, Saint?" His upper crust British accent was in full force tonight, thought Brady. Hunter used to be an arms runner. The best in the biz. He stood about the same height as Brady but outweighed him by at least fifty pounds, all muscle. He'd grown up with money and rejected it and the role his family had wanted him to play. Something they had in common. But Hunter had actually been a true bastard by birth, the product of a high-ranking British aristocrat and his middle-class black mistress. His father's aristocratic bone structure with Hunter's mocha-colored skin, not to mention his dark, brooding presence, made him a favorite of many females of any species.

"Looking for Sterling. Have you seen him?"

Hunter glanced at Libby, who was now leaning against the counter of the makeshift kitchen. Brady could tell Hunter knew exactly who Libby was.

"About three months ago, he and that friend of his…Dracon…came looking for men to help them on some damn-fool quest."

"Damn-fool quest?" Libby asked. Her voice was calm, but Brady could feel the underlying tension in her query. "Did it have anything to do with the legend of the Snake King?"

Hunter nodded. "Yeah. Bought a few men, and then they left the next day. Haven't seen him or the men since."

Libby sighed, and her shoulders slumped as if the weight of the news had added another five pounds to her load. Anger sparked in his stomach. Dammit. The woman shouldn't have to chase after her father like he was a five-year-old. When he got ahold of Sterling, he was going to give him a good thrashing. Libby should be off living her own life, pursuing her career, or having babies.

That thought almost knocked him on his ass. He'd never asked if she'd had children, but he knew Libby, and she would never leave her children behind, even for Sterling. And just why the hell was he thinking about Libby and babies anyhow? Wasn't like he wanted anything to do with kids. His childhood was screwed up beyond anything by the time he ran away, and he knew he wasn't father material. And just why the fuck was he thinking about it now?

He shook his head to clear his thoughts and moved on to safer subjects.

"Have you seen three, four men show up here in the last thirty minutes?"

Hunter nodded. "Yeah. They came in, loaded to the teeth. They rented a couple rooms."

Shit. He should have known. They could trek on to the next outpost, but it would get dicey traveling at night. He looked at Libby, who looked like she was ready to pass out. "Got another room for the two of us? Preferably not close to our friends?"

Hunter's eyebrows shot up. "One room?"

"Yes, one room. What the hell is your problem?"

"Brady, calm down," Libby said, embarrassment threading her voice. "Aren't you going to introduce us?"

"No."

Hunter threw him a measured look and then smiled at Libby. She smiled in response, and Brady wanted to smack both of them.

"I'm John Hunter. Owner of this fine establishment. And you are Liberty Wainwright. Very nice to meet you." He offered his hand to shake, and Libby, stupid woman that she was, did just that. But Hunter placed his other hand on top of hers. "I read your article about the new data retrieval machine you helped create. It was truly fascinating."

Even in the dim light, he could see her face flush under Hunter's attention. Irritation crept up Brady's spine.

"I thought that after you have had some time to refresh yourself, you could join me for a discussion on it." Hunter's voice was low, coaxing, and made Brady want to wrap his fingers around the man's neck.

Libby, instead of noticing what a player Hunter was, giggled. Actually giggled like a fifteen-year-old with a crush.

"Well, that would be—"

Before it could go any further, he stepped forward and grabbed Libby's hand. He wrenched it away from Hunter. She shot him a withering look, then turned back to Hunter.

"I would love to, but it's been a very long day, and I just want to get to bed." She was rubbing her palms and she winced.

"Did you do something to your hand?" Hunter's voice had turned so freaking solicitous, Brady wouldn't be surprised if he announced he was running for office.

"Well, I think I have a cut or two."

Hunter stepped forward to take her hand again, but Brady stopped him. "Just show us to our room; I think we can handle it from there."

The amused look on Hunter's face told Brady he'd just been fucking with him. "Sure."

Minutes later, they followed Hunter down a dimly lit hall to their room. He unlocked it, then stepped aside.

"Thank you so much for the help tonight, Mr. Hunter."

Hunter's teeth flashed bright in the dark corner. "Just Hunter, Ms. Wainwright."

She nodded, then went into the room. Before following, Brady caught Hunter's attention. "Let me know if those men leave before morning."

"Will do, Saint." Without another word, Hunter strode back in the direction of the kitchen.

Brady made sure the door was secured and then turned to survey the room. This was only the second time he'd stopped in on Hunter since he'd exiled himself to this godforsaken planet. This was a much better room. It included a private bath, a couple of bedside tables, and one big-ass bed. He guessed he would forgive Hunter this time.

Libby sat down on the side of the bed, dropping her pack on the floor. Knowing her hands needed attention, he set his pack on one of the tables and looked for some antibiotic strips.

He squatted in front of her and took a look at her hands. They weren't that bad, just a few minor scrapes, but this place had all kinds of weird plants that caused allergic reactions in some humans. She didn't say a word as he opened the strips and applied them to her hands.

"So, you want to tell me what those men said that scared you shitless?"

Her head swung up, and her eyes were wide with something akin to panic.

"I have no idea what you're talking about."

"They said something, you looked like every drop of blood in your face drained in one second. There's information you're holding back, lass, and that won't help the situation."

She sighed. "Emerald Project."

He was finished with her hands so he sat on the bed next to her. "Go on."

"This was something that Tony and I ended up getting divorced over."

"You divorced your husband over work?" He didn't even try to hide the sarcasm in his voice. And why wouldn't she? She'd left him high and dry when she'd decided their way of working just didn't gel.

"Not just that." She licked her lips and looked at the floor. "I have no idea what the project is, but it was top secret and was draining a lot of money from the company. It's been around for years. I was working on a plan to do an excavation in the Eruidite quadrant. I got the money, started making solid plans, hired people, got the visas. Then the whole thing was scrapped for the Emerald Project."

"What is it?"

"That was my question. I'd worked there for three years and never heard of it, so I asked Tony. At first he played dumb. Then he got downright nasty. I figured out later that whatever it was, it was illegal."

"Why would you immediately think that?" And just why the hell had she been married to him if she didn't trust him?

"Before taking over the reins, Tony had often said that his father had his hands in a lot of pots." Brady snorted. She shot him a repressive look but continued. "When he moved into the job, he...changed."

"How?"

"Worked all the time, and he became agitated at the simplest things." She shrugged one shoulder. The move was listless, almost resigned. "After that, our marriage went downhill. When he refused to tell me what the project was about, I left. And that's all I know."

"Well, these men must know your husband."

"My ex-husband. I've got to take a shower, clean up."

He nodded and watched her grab her pack and head off to the bathroom. As soon as the door shut, he thought about everything. Sterling, the ambush, her ex. Something was linking it all together, and he would bet that one way or another, it was going to go downhill from there.

He worried his lower lip and almost bit it when he heard the water start. Just the thought of Libby naked, the water sluicing over her body, dripping from her nipples…

Groaning at the image in his head, he tried to convince his body to ignore it. But once it was there, it was no good. His blood was already heating at the thought of slipping into the shower behind her, stroking her wet skin…

Damn, he was hard as a pike. It was either join her, or wait until she came out. The temptation was too great, and knowing that Hunter would be alert to any problems, Brady decided to take advantage of this one night they would have uninterrupted. He walked to the door and tested the knob. It turned easily, and Brady took that as a good sign.

* * *

Libby massaged her head as she lathered her hair, hoping to get rid of the sticks and debris that had become tangled in it in their travels. She remembered now why she'd always kept her hair short while she'd worked the field.

The hot water relaxed her muscles but not her mind. It was jumping from one thing to another, and she really didn't know if she'd ever get anything straight. She knew her ex was involved in this someway…but how? It wasn't helping to have

Brady around, tempting her at every turn. When he'd shown the slightest of possessive feelings, she'd felt an undeniable thrill. Which was not good. She was her own woman. She didn't need a man to be complete and happy.

Of course, there'd been a time she'd been happy to give it all away—her freedom, her independence—to be near Brady. She'd always been the one to walk the straight and narrow. There had been once or twice…

"Libby, for once in your life do you think you could forget the rules?"

Brady was frowning at her again. He always did when she pointed out what he wanted to do was slightly illegal. And it was happening more and more these days.

"Forgetting the rules could land you in confinement. You know how the Obiscian are about their segregation laws. And we are not allowed to drink here. There are laws forbidding it."

He crossed his arms and stared at her. Those blue eyes sparked with defiance, and his frown deepened. It should piss her off that he was even thinking of doing this. Breaking into a store to grab a bottle of wine, in a sector of town they were forbidden to be in. But all she could feel were the telltale signs of excitement heating her blood. Her pulse accelerated, her nipples hardened. Dammit, there was something really wrong with her if she got off on this kind of thing. She was not a thrillseeker.

"Come on, Libby, live a little."

She ground her teeth at her father's familiar saying.

"I live. I live to pick up the mess you and my father leave behind."

He rolled his eyes. "I think you're afraid."

"That's not going to work this time, Brady."

"Really?" He quirked one eyebrow, and his full lips turned up into a seductive smile. "Maybe you're right. You're not afraid."

She nodded, but she knew better than to trust his placating tone.

"I mean, all we'd be doing is sneaking into town, grabbing a bottle of wine. Nothing to be afraid of."

*"I'm not afraid. I'm smart." But with each sentence, he was chipping away at her resistance. She could feel it slipping out of her grasp.

"Smart. You're sure that. Of course, you'd have to be pretty intelligent to figure out that you couldn't do it."

"What?"

"You can't do it. I mean, I know I could get in there and out without being detected. You must know that you'd be the liability."

Even though she knew what he was doing, it was hard not to rise to the bait.

"I can do it. I just don't want to."

He chuckled as he began to walk around her. *"Of course you can. I mean, I know that I can do it, get out free, but you must think that you're lacking in some way."*

Indignation had her talking before she could think. *"I can do it."*

"No, Libby, I think you should stay behind. Don't want to be a liability to me, get me in trouble."

Her anger soared. She knew what he was doing. Knew it all by heart because it worked all the time, but Libby couldn't stop her mouth. "Shut the hell up and let's go."

An hour later, with the militia on their tail, Brady led her down a series of alleys until they knew they had made it out without being identified.

Both of them were laughing so hard they could barely breathe. Brady lifted her with one arm; his hand held the cheap bottle of wine they'd set out to get, and he smacked her on the lips.

She laughed louder, thinking she'd never felt that free.

The bathroom door opening brought her back to the present. Brady opened the stall door and stuck his head into the shower, then pulled the door open. Her breath stalled in her lungs when she saw him. Lost in the memories of their past, she'd forgotten just how potent he was in the flesh. Especially when he was naked. She glanced down at his erection and felt her nipples tighten, already aching for his touch. Her pulse drummed in her head, her body already quickening for him.

One side of his mouth curled up, and his gaze traveled from her head down to her toes. By the time he returned to her face, her nipples were hard and his eyes had darkened with intent.

"Got room for one more?"

Chapter Eight

The moment he stepped into the bathroom, the clean, fresh scent of Libby clogged Brady's senses. In the thick mist of fog, he could see her body outlined on the shower-stall door. Need crawled through him. But this was sharper, more powerful than just his usual sexual urges. It had always been that way with Libby. There were plenty of times he'd cursed the affliction that drove him to possess her. It was heaven and hell. Knowing that they were never going to settle their differences didn't matter. He pulled off his clothes, dropping them on the floor beside hers.

Anticipation skated along his nerves and sent another rush of blood to his cock. He glanced down, smiling wryly at his erection. Hard and already aching to have her, he should be embarrassed by how much he wanted her...needed her. It wasn't an option to lust after her. It was a primal urge that drove him. Something in him knew that whenever she was near, he had to have her or go mental, especially from the lack of blood in his brain.

He grabbed the door and opened it. His breath caught in his throat. Damn, she was beautiful. He pulled the door open all the way. She glanced at his raging erection, and he felt it like a lick. Knowing that her sexual appetite marched along with his made it all that much harder to resist her.

A lot of people looked at Libby and saw the archeology nerd. Her hair was a tangle of wet tresses and suds, reaching halfway down her back. She turned to face him. His heart about leapt out of his chest as his gaze traveled down her body. Water dripped from her nipples, making his mouth go dry. He continued his perusal, taking in the soap still clinging to her rounded stomach, her bare pussy, and her long, sleek legs. Knowing what they felt like wrapped around his waist made him feel lightheaded. His pulse soared. By the time he reached her feet, his balls ached with want. Catching her gaze, he smiled, although even that hurt.

"Got room for one more?" His voice was thick with desire. Jesus, if he didn't have her soon, he'd probably come just looking at her. And what other woman did that to him? Only Libby made him feel like an eighteen-year-old, ready to burst at the slightest provocation.

She swallowed, then nodded. Turning her back to him, she stepped forward to give him room. After closing the door, he reached around her and grabbed the bottle of soap. He squirted some on his hand and rubbed his hands together after dropping the bottle on the floor behind him. The herbal scent was as familiar as the woman in front of him. He stepped closer. His dick brushed against her wet skin. He closed his eyes and groaned. Just that one touch shot straight to his balls. Capturing her hips, he held her still as he pressed his body against hers.

Brady slid his hands to her breasts, her slick skin and his soapy hands making it easy.

"I already finished washing, Brady." Her voice was husky with a touch of humor.

"Really?" He opened his eyes and took each nipple, tugging gently. She jerked in reaction. "There seems to be a few places you missed."

Bending his head, he skimmed kisses along her shoulder and then moved to her neck as he continued pulling on her nipples. Libby moved her hands to the shower wall, but said nothing, showed no other reaction. He smiled. Libby loved to play games. She saw foreplay as a way to engage in a battle to see who would crumble and beg first. Was it any wonder he had to have her any chance he got?

"See." He moved one had down to her pussy. Her breathing hitched. "I'm sure that one or two places might need some extra-special attention."

He rubbed his cock in the cleft of her buttocks, almost coming from that one motion. Lord, he wanted to sink into her pussy, lose himself in the feel of her muscles clamping tight around him, draining him. As he continued to move against her, he slipped a finger into her. She was slick, hot. Not able to help himself, he groaned. Damn, she was always like this. From their first time together...her first time...she was always wet and ready for a good fucking.

He added another finger and moved his other hand back to her hip. She moved in rhythm with him. Each time he withdrew his fingers, she pushed back against him.

"Brady." Her voice was filled with need and surrender.

He nibbled her earlobe, and she groaned his name again. "Whatcha need, baby?"

She drew in a deep breath, and he knew she was fighting an inner battle. She wanted him, but she wanted to hold out, push both of them to the point where they couldn't stand it. To help her make up her mind, he flicked his finger against her clit, and she bucked against him.

"Oh, yes, like that, Brady. Ohhh."

Her muscles tightened against his fingers, and he knew she was close. Damn, he wanted to have his cock buried inside her when she came this time. To draw out the pleasure, he slowed his motions, and she cursed.

"What's the matter?" he challenged her with a teasing voice.

"I—I was really close, Brady."

"You want to come, baby? Want it bad?"

She bucked again, and another gush of liquid wet his fingers. The movement caused him to jerk against her. Shit. If he didn't get inside her soon, he wouldn't make it.

"You know you want it. Just tell me. Tell me what you want."

Pushing back, she tried to increase his tempo, but he wasn't going to allow that. He held her hip steady with one hand and tortured her with his other. But with each passing second, his control was slipping, and he knew he was just a moment away from begging.

"I want you. Now, oh, Brady."

He wanted to tease her, push her further, but the desperate plea burned through his blood, and he knew if she begged again, it would push him over the edge. Stepping back, he pulled her legs wider.

"Bend over more, Libby." She complied immediately, her body fairly quivering with the need for her release. He took his cock in hand and pushed at her entrance, just letting the tip enter. Her muscles teased and tensed around him and he closed his eyes. Damn, that felt good. Slipping into her was like heaven every time. She wiggled, apparently irritated with his slow movements. He knew he might be able to hold out a little longer, but the need clawing at him took over. In one thrust, he planted himself fully inside her. She clamped down hard around him. For just a moment, he held still, enjoying the feel of her sweet pussy. But soon, his body begged for more—for release.

He withdrew and began to move in controlled, measured thrusts. Libby continued to moan his name, her voice so husky he could barely hear it above the water. Each time he shoved into her, his stomach slammed against her ass with a loud smack. He reached around to tease her clit. One…two…and she exploded, her vaginal walls clamping tight around him, pulling him deeper. Her orgasm spurred his. His balls drew tight. After two more thrusts, he came, groaning her name, his voice echoing off the walls of the shower.

Moments later, he leaned back, his cock still inside her, and slid his arms around her body. He kissed the side of her neck and she gave a little contented sigh. He was helpless to fight the warmth that curled into his heart when he heard the little sound. It was if she had never left, and he knew truthfully she hadn't. She'd been right there all along.

* * *

They'd made it to bed finally and gotten a decent bit of rest. Brady had awakened her sometime during the night with his mouth on her, her body humming for release. She woke this time with a start, knowing before she opened her eyes she was alone in the bed. Rubbing the sleep out of her eyes, she glanced around the room and noticed Brady's pack on the floor by one of the chairs and relaxed. He might have thought about leaving her behind for her own safety, but he wouldn't do it. Because he knew she would hunt him down and hurt him.

She stretched her arms over her head, trying to work the soreness out of her muscles. It'd been a long time since she'd used a lot of them. She sat up and swung her legs over the edge of the bed. And some other muscles she hadn't used in awhile, she thought with a wince.

The door opened, and Brady stepped in. When he saw her sitting on the bed, he smiled. Her heart did a flip-flop. Oh, Lordy, he was gorgeous. He closed the door and approached the bed.

"I wish we didn't need to leave so soon." The devilish look in his eyes let her know exactly what he was thinking of doing. It was then she realized she was sitting there naked as the day as she was born.

Libby wasn't a prude, and she definitely had never been shy about her body. Still, her face flushed.

"Jesus, Brady. Can't you think of anything else?"

She got up with a huff and he chuckled. He grabbed her arms and pulled her into his.

"Not where you're concerned, lass." The heat in his voice did funny things to her stomach. He leaned down and kissed her, never closing his eyes. Arousal darkened the blue, but there was something, something that scared the hell out of her. A rush of goose bumps prickled her skin. She could feel his erection against her stomach. Her nipples hardened and warmth pooled between her legs. She wanted to close her eyes, but she fought the urge, or maybe he willed her not to break the connection. Her heart was now doing somersaults.

Before she could sort out the feelings—hers and his—he broke the kiss. He released her and took a step back. He swallowed, hard, and then looked away from her.

"Why don't you get dressed?" He drew in a deep breath. "We...ah...we need to get out of here before those bounty hunters know we're here. Better to be ahead then..." He glanced at her, his gazed roaming down her body. "Do you think you could get *something* on?"

The unsteady feelings that had left her breathless just moments before vanished. She giggled, she couldn't help it. He sounded so put out that she was standing there naked.

"Sure, Saint." She drew out his name, and his eyes narrowed. She bit her lip, trying not to laugh.

"Woman, you don't know who you're messing with. Get in there and get ready."

He turned on his heel and left. The moment the door shut, she dissolved into another fit of giggles. But as she dressed, she was surprised when a sob erupted and she felt tears well up in her eyes. Stress. That was all it was. Her father, the search, fighting to get Brady to help. It had nothing to do with the fact that she was still in love with Brady. She sat with a thump on the bed.

Aww, shit.

* * *

Libby had been quiet since they'd left Hunter's outpost. Normally it wouldn't bother him. Women often talked too much and aggravated him to death. Libby had always been different. Sterling had trained her to be silent in the right situations, and she'd always been a quiet girl. But this was different.

From the moment he returned to the room after she dressed, he sensed there was something wrong. She'd been crying, which was very un-Libby-like. He'd thought about the situation and decided that maybe the stress was getting to her. Worry about Sterling, not knowing where he was or if he was alive—that could wear on even the strongest individual.

Two hours later, he wasn't so sure anymore. There was something distant in the way she talked to him. She wouldn't meet his gaze. There was something going on there. It wasn't the sex. He knew better than that. Libby had never been a prude. Even if she regretted what they'd done, she wouldn't act this way. Or would she? A ball of irritation burned in his stomach.

The second sun had risen, bringing with it unwelcome heat and a rise in the humidity. They were gaining altitude also, and their trail grew to a narrow overgrown path that they had to clear sometimes to get by.

"Where are we headed today?"

It was her first unprompted comment since they left, so he readily grabbed it as a lifeline. "I think we can get to an area they call the Funkainian sector. Problem is, we have to avoid the Funkai."

"The perverts."

He shot a smile over his shoulder. "To each his own."

"There's a difference between sexual preference, and abduction and rape."

"I agree." He faced forward again. "And that's why they came here. There weren't that many people settled here. So they could come up with their own laws."

"Of course." Her sarcasm wasn't lost on him. He agreed. They were scum, but debating whether they should be hunted down by the Intergalactical Strike Force and imprisoned wasn't important right now. Getting across the area undetected was.

"I think they should be hunted down and castrated."

Leaves rustled behind them. "Shut up."

Her footsteps stopped. *Shit.* Now she wanted to talk. His neck prickled with awareness, as if someone was stalking them.

"What did you say?"

He turned and stalked toward her. "Listen. I know someone is here. Someone—man, alien, or beast—is following us for some reason. I can feel it in my gut." Her eyes widened and she nodded. Before he could turn around, footsteps sounded behind him.

"Now, what do we have here, Joe?" asked an amused male voice. Apprehension curled in his gut and stole his breath. Looking back over his shoulder, he noticed three men, all of average height, wearing what looked like loincloths. All of them were heavily armed. He counted at least two knives on each of them. Their chests were bare, and all of them had tattoos on the right shoulder.

Shit. Funkai.

Chapter Nine

The tension between the group of men and Brady crackled. Libby wanted to step in and try to talk their way out of it. Brady would get pissed. Besides—she glanced at the newcomers—she figured they wouldn't be happy with her meddling. Tall, but not as tall as Brady, the three men were barely clothed. Their bare chests glistened with sweat. All three of them had hair down to the middle of their backs, and each one was barefoot.

They had to be Funkai. *Crap.* As the silence grew thick as the air around them, she tried to think of everything she knew about the sect. Yes, they supposedly had strange sexual practices, but most of it had never been proven. The sexual laws on Earth in the early twenty-second century had left them ostracized. A couple years after they left, most of the restrictions had been repealed. What she did know was that they were monogamous. Once a couple had paired off, they stayed together, and no one encroached on either's territory. A plan was forming in her mind, but if Brady got pissed and screwed it up, they'd end up in a heap of trouble.

"We're just passing through." Brady's voice wasn't as casual as the comment implied. There was an edge there, as if he knew they were in for a fight. She looked at the men again. He was probably right.

"You need our permission." This was said by the tallest of the group. He broke eye contact with Brady and smiled at her. Blond hair, pale green eyes, and a muscled body made him an attractive man. She found herself returning the smile. Brady stepped in front of her.

"Mine." His voice was deep and threatening.

The leader's smile vanished. "We'll see about that."

Brady bristled at the tone, but she knew he would lose a fight with the three men. One-on-one, he could take each of them; but even with her help, they still had another one. He wasn't thinking straight, because he was worried about her.

She leaned forward so she could whisper in his ear. "Brady, it'll be okay. Trust me."

For a second, she thought he might fight, but finally he relented with a curt nod. Two of the men walked forward and tried to separate them.

"I think you need to think twice about touching her."

Both men looked toward the leader and he nodded. Brady allowed her to go in front, and he followed as the two other men flanked him.

The leader slowed so that she could walk beside him. They were of the same height, especially with her boots on.

"My name is Walter." His voice was a charming purr. She almost laughed in his face. First of all, he was acting as if they were getting acquainted under regular circumstances. Maybe they were for him, but this was beyond absurd. But then, when she was in Brady's company, anything could happen. The second thing she thought of was that Walter was not a name a man wearing a loincloth and walking barefoot would be called.

She cleared her throat. "It's very nice to meet you, Walter. My name is Liberty."

His eyes widened. "Liberty Wainwright?"

"Y-Yes."

"Your father's named Sterling?"

She nodded. Her heart fell to her stomach.

"Have you met him?" She couldn't keep the desperation out of her voice.

"Yes, two...three months ago. Was looking for some legend." His voice told her he didn't think much of her father's pursuit.

"Was he with anyone?"

He frowned. "I would rather talk about you."

"I haven't seen my father. Brady and I are looking for him. He's been missing."

"He had an older gentleman with him. And a young man. I remember they argued over something, but they all left together the next morning."

"A younger man?"

He pursed his lips, apparently not happy with her question. "This man you are with. Did he speak the truth?"

She sighed. Men were all the same. Once their dick was involved, they had a one-track mind. "Yes."

"Then why do you need to know about this younger man?"

"My father has been missing, and anything we can find out is important. It could lead us to him."

He nodded, his eyes sparkling with admiration. "Are you sure you're with him? Smart females are hard to find around these areas."

She bit the inside of her lip. It was that or scream at him. "Yes, I'm with him. Now, the younger man?"

Sighing, he glanced at Brady, then looked back at her. "Yes, he was a bit of an ass. I have a feeling that he'd never been on a trip like this one. He complained all the time about the weather, the food."

Her pulse accelerated, her mouth lost all moisture. A shiver of dread crawled down her spine.

"Anthony Freemont."

* * *

As they rounded a bend in the road, Brady noticed a few scattered buildings. The structures were modern, resembling many of the homes on Earth. It seemed odd that a bunch of men who dressed like cavemen lived in probably the most modern village on the whole freaking planet. Just their luck.

He scowled at his two friends and then at Don Juan, who'd been kissing up to Libby since they started off. His gut burned. If he thought it would do any good, he'd stomp up there and push his way between them. He knew the two men on either side of him would lay him flat on his ass if he even tried. And from the look in Libby's eyes, she had a plan.

She laughed at something Don said. Brady curled his fingers into his palms. Dammit. What the hell did she think this was? Prom night?

The man on his left chuckled. "Our friend here is worried Walter is charming his woman."

Figured they would be captured by a barbarian named Walter. He snorted. Libby turned and gave him a warning look, then turned back around. What the hell was up with that? Did she think he was some little boy who couldn't behave? Like he would get them in trouble because he was jealous?

Shit. He *was* jealous. Even while they were together, he'd never had a problem with jealousy. Not because he thought no one was interested in Libby, but he'd been so sure of her love that he knew she would never cheat. She laughed again. The sound of it usually sent his body humming. This time, however, his blood heated. The urge to grab her by the hair and drag her off so that all of them knew she was his, almost overwhelmed him.

He counted backwards from ten. Walter brushed a lock of her hair back over her shoulder. This time he counted backward from twenty. He knew she had a plan and charming Walter was part of it. It didn't make it any easier to watch some jackass manhandle his woman.

As they walked into the village, there was little activity except a few stray children playing. Of course, they stopped and stared at two strangers being led through their isolated community. The Funkai usually kept to themselves, unless you trespassed on their land. And he'd avoided the area on his other visits to the planet. They just didn't have time to waste.

They walked up the steps of the largest structure in the center of the village. Large Roman columns lined the front of the building, which gave it a look of being a city hall in any US city. Once inside, they were led down a hallway that was lined with offices. As several people passed them, he noticed they were dressed as if they'd just walked out of an office anywhere on Earth. Business suits, dresses…they looked normal.

They reached a set of double doors. Walter leaned over to whisper in Libby's ear, and she nodded. He slipped through the doors. She turned and walked toward Brady.

"This is rather odd, isn't it?" When she noticed his guards were paying attention, she flashed them a smile. Brady would be amazed if they didn't drool. "I'm so sorry. I didn't mean to sound rude. But everything I've read about your civilization is that it's primitive. It's odd to be captured by men in loincloths and then be led into a modern village."

"You have read what we want the world to think."

She started and turned. Brady looked over her shoulder. Their newcomer was a man in his forties, dressed in a tailored suit. Unlike their friends, he wore his hair short, and if Brady had seen him anywhere else, he'd think he was just a normal businessman. He was tall, and his dark hair had threads of gray. His bearing told Brady this was someone important.

The newcomer studied Libby, then moved toward him and his guards. The smile he shot Libby was filled with sexual interest.

Brady stepped forward to stand beside her. He half expected their captors to grab him, but they didn't do anything.

"You must be Liberty Wainwright. Walter was right—you are beautiful." Brady glanced at Libby and noticed the blush. Was every freaking man here going to be after her?

"Yes, I am." She extended her hand. The man took it and kissed her hand before releasing it. Her face turned a brighter shade of pink.

"A pleasure. My name is Jason Funkai. I'd say I was sorry that you have been put in any discomfort, but that would be a lie. It is not that often we get such pleasant company."

The man's tone was filled with lazy sensuality. He didn't even bother to hide his interest.

Libby, God bless her, ignored it. "This is my associate, Brady St. James."

The man's gray gaze showed a flicker of acknowledgement of his name, but he kept his attention focused on Libby.

"I've heard of you, Saint. But the impression that Walter gave me was that you were together."

"We are." Libby sounded confused by this line of questioning. Hell, Brady wasn't sure what was going on either.

"No matter, right now. I understand you're looking for your father. There isn't much I can tell you about him. He was here for a night and left the next day. Pleasant man."

Sterling had been here? Brady shot her a look, but she wasn't paying attention. All her attention was for Funkai. She showed no surprise, leading him to think she might've known about her father being here. Why hadn't she told him?

"Now, why don't we go in and meet the council. With these developments, there might be a longer discussion on the outcome."

"Outcome?" Brady asked.

"Yes. Walter gave me the impression that you two were together, but since you are just working together...well, there will be some discussion about Ms. Wainwright's future with the Funkai."

Funkai smiled at Libby, and Brady knew that he'd meant that he wanted to keep Libby for himself.

Well, crap.

* * *

Libby shifted on her chair and sighed again. She glanced over at Brady, who was still pouting about her slip-up earlier. The mistake wasn't going to be easy to untangle, but if he would talk to her, they'd have a plan. Instead, he'd told her she was an idiot and refused to say anything else since they'd been led into a waiting room.

Even though she silently berated herself for the mistake, she thought Brady was being completely unsympathetic. The news that her father had been here, and been with her ex-husband, had thrown her for a loop. She'd wanted to get Brady alone to tell him, but now he was sulking like a little boy. And, really, what was she supposed to say when they asked her? She had no freaking idea what Brady was. Other than a pain in the ass.

"You know, you could have let me speak."

She looked over at him. His arms were crossed over his chest, his gaze straight ahead, and he was frowning.

"So, you're speaking to me?"

He shot her a derisive look. "I know what you're thinking. You're thinking that you should be in charge. Well, in this area, you are dead wrong, lass."

He was really angry. He hadn't raised his voice, but his Irish lilt had slipped into it. That only happened when he was aroused or angry. Very angry.

"Oh, and you were doing such a good job of it."

"These people are different. They expect the man to wear the pants."

Anger lit through her. "So I was supposed to let you fuck it up."

"Fuck it up? *Fuck it up?* What do you call this?"

"A minor setback. We'll be on our way tomorrow."

He shook his head. "No, lass. They mean to keep you."

She'd suspected that, but she knew she could get them out of it. It would require Brady to not act like an ape. She glanced at him. They could be in some trouble.

Before she could say anything, Walter came through the door. She blinked. The loincloth was replaced by a conservative suit, his hair bound at the base of his neck.

"Ms. Wainwright." He glanced at Brady. "Saint. Mr. Funkai and the rest of the board are ready to see you now."

Libby and Brady stood to follow Walter through the door. Brady placed his hand on the small of her back to usher her through the door. The room they entered was round; a large horseshoe table sat in the middle and was occupied by ten gentlemen. Jason Funkai sat in the center. There wasn't much light in the rest of the room, but the table seemed to be under some kind of spotlight.

"Ms. Wainwright. Saint. Please come forward."

As they walked forward, Brady took her hand and pulled her closer to his side. He leaned down. "Go along with me on this one, Libby."

She nodded because she knew that he would have to take charge. The Funkai seemed to have built the illusion they wanted the world to see, but there was one thing that wasn't a lie—this was a male-dominated society. Years in the field had taught her to respect their hosts, unless it was a matter of life or death.

Funkai took charge of the meeting. "We've been discussing the issue of Ms. Wainwright." His gaze dropped to their joined hands, and she could feel the tension spike another notch. He didn't like what he saw. "There are several interested parties who would like to court her."

"Court her?" Brady's tone was derisive. "You call capturing women and keeping them against their will *courting?*"

Several of the board members shifted restlessly, unhappy with Brady and his comments.

"This is not our way. Yes, we have been known to bring women here, but they are never forced to do anything they don't want. But we do give our men a chance to convince them to stay. We've been known to return women, but we like to keep up the idea that we are barbarians, to keep others out."

They were hiding something. The only reason to keep people from coming into their community would be to hide something. But what, if not their strange sexual practices?

"Really? I hear you're sexual deviants."

This produced some grumbling from the board.

Jason held up his hand and it stopped. "Yes, we do practice some bondage. That is it. But we are not here to discuss that. What we are here to discuss is Ms. Wainwright's immediate future."

"She's with me."

"She said she was your associate."

Brady's lips stretched into a humorless smile. "You know women; they like to think they're in charge."

Funkai smiled. "Well, be that as it may, since she is without a partner, we feel she should stay and get to know a few of our men."

She inched closer to Brady, not liking this conversation at all. The modern, educated, independent woman in her wanted to scream that she could take care of herself. But there was another voice that just wanted Brady to take care of it all and get them the hell out of there.

"She's mine."

"I understand your conviction, Saint. But the truth is, we have had people do this before, and later we find that it was merely a ploy to get the woman away." Funkai studied him, then glanced at her as if coming to some decision. "I think we can let you go."

Giddy relief poured through Libby. They were going to be free. Each minute that ticked away was another minute that her father could be in danger.

"You think?"

"You say that she is yours." Brady nodded curtly. "And all we ask is that you prove it."

Chapter Ten

Brady sat drinking some sort of wine that tasted like elderberry, and studied his host. Once Funkai had an agreement from the board, Libby had been whisked off to prepare, and he'd been treated like an honored guest. More and more, these people confused him. Or it could have been the wine. Since his second glass, he'd lost count of how many he'd had, and his head was floating five feet above his body. There was also a hint of sexual tension humming through him.

"Your Ms. Wainwright was not happy when she left." Humor laced Funkai's words.

Brady grunted. "Libby likes to run the show."

"Yes. She is a managing woman."

There was no derision in his voice, as Brady would have expected from a man who lived in this society. He studied the man, taking more note of his appearance. He'd been right about his age, somewhere in his mid-to-late forties. He ruled the clan here with an iron will that Brady had to admire. Even if the dickhead had been after his woman.

"I would think that would be a drawback."

Funkai's lips curled. "There is something to be said about a spirited woman." *Good God, was there ever.* "And you're gullible if you believe all the stories."

"You admitted to practicing bondage."

His smile deepened. "Well, there is also something to be said for having a woman who likes to be tied up and spanked." The image of doing just that to Libby sent a roll of lust rushing through him. He set down his wine. "But we perpetuate that image to keep people out."

The wine had clouded his thoughts, and the thoughts of spanking Libby weren't helping, but he started to piece things together bit by bit. "You're hiding something valuable."

"A way of life."

"No. Something that makes you rich."

Funkai laughed. "I'd heard you were a smart one. Yes. Saint, you are talking to one of the wealthiest men this side of the zone. And all of us here share the money. My grandfather had been an important man on Earth—rich, powerful. But when they started to restrict sexual practices, trying to legislate personal lives, he knew he had to leave." He leaned back in his chair and took a sip of wine while his gaze became unfocused. "When he happened on this area, he found a metal that was so precious, he knew people would pay a fortune for it."

"Naper steel? You are the people behind Naper steel?" The metal was one of the strongest ever forged, but no one seemed to know from where. There were agents who handled the sales, but where it originated had been a secret since it hit the market.

"Yes." His gaze focused on Brady again. "We take from this planet, but we do not destroy. If people found out, if this leaked, they would destroy this planet. They would tear down the forests, killing God knows how many species just to make their money."

Brady nodded, thinking of the destruction of the rain forests on Earth in the late twentieth and early twenty-first centuries. They were still trying to battle the effects of their greed today.

"So you let people think you're barbarians, that you'll steal their women and kill them if they trespass."

Funkai's smile returned. "Yes. And it helps that if someone becomes a member of the community, they have to agree to cut off all ties."

"How do you keep it secret if you tell everyone who comes through?"

"We don't. I tell you because I've heard of your integrity. I was hoping I could convince you not to tell people you were here."

"Mr. Funkai." Walter approached them. The frown he'd been wearing since the order of the board was still in place. *Too damn bad, dickhead. The woman is mine.* "I've been alerted that Ms. Wainwright is ready."

"Thank you, Walter. I will take Saint there myself."

Although surprise lightened Walter's eyes, he showed no emotion on his face.

Funkai stood. "Shall we?"

Brady nodded and followed the older gentlemen out of the room, trying hard not to smirk as he passed the very disapproving Walter.

They walked side by side down a series of hallways. "I envy you, Saint. Ms. Wainwright is an extraordinary woman. You've known her long?"

"Since we were kids. Her father trained both of us."

"Ahh. I won't say I contemplated overriding the decision of the board and kicking you out, but I had a feeling there was history there. I thought the woman would protest. "

"The lady would have your balls for breakfast."

Funkai laughed as he walked up a flight of stairs and stopped when they reached the end of another long hallway. "Now, you know the rules. There are cameras. But, just so you know, there is no sound recording. That would be intrusive."

"And watching us have sex isn't?"

Funkai just smiled and shook his head. "There is a phone in there that will connect you to the kitchens. There should be plenty of wine and refreshment, but just let them know if you need anything. Good luck."

Nodding at the guard stationed at the end of the hallway, Funkai pulled out a key card. He slid it into the lock and then, with a smile, turned and left him. The door slid open. Brady stepped in and stopped dead in his tracks.

Jesus. It looked like something out of a harem. Pretty much everything was draped in red. Red silk hung from the walls; red sheets coved the king-sized bed. The bed looked like black wrought iron, and he didn't doubt there were some extra-special toys to go with it. The only thing that seemed to stand out was the wood-like floor.

"Don't just stand there with your mouth open."

Libby's voice came from the right side of the room. It was then that he noticed her standing in a doorway that he assumed led to a bathroom. His heart jumped to his throat and almost knocked him senseless. What the hell was she wearing?

Her hair had been let loose and was a wild tangle of curls down her back. They'd applied makeup, not to overwhelm but to enhance her features, drawing on her quiet beauty. But the outfit...holy mother of God. His blood churned and he lost all moisture in his mouth. Damn, she looked good in black.

It barely covered all the important parts. The halter-like top consisted of a piece of soft fabric that had been looped around her back and then crossed over her breasts and tied behind her neck. Her midriff had been left bare by the low-riding genie-looking pants that were cinched at her waist and her ankles with bits of gold fabric. She walked toward him, and he almost fainted. As she moved, the pants did. The voluminous fabric was transparent enough to leave little to his imagination. His gaze roamed up her body, stopping at the gold choker around her neck.

She was a wet dream come to life.

"Can you believe that they trussed me up like some harem woman?"

He swallowed, trying to think of something to say, but each time she gestured with her arms, her breasts moved. The fabric was soft, and he could just make out the outline of her nipples. He licked his lips.

"Brady?"

"What?"

"What the hell is wrong with you?"

"Lass, I can't think straight."

She humphed and then crossed her arms beneath her breasts. The edge of the fabric inched closer to her nipples. He groaned as another wave of heat shot straight to his dick.

"I would have never taken you for a man who needed a woman dressed like some prize."

Why was she talking? She looked at him like she expected him to carry on a conversation. That was hard because all his blood had drained from his brain, which was spinning from images of slowly divesting her of that outfit.

"Libby, darlin', it isn't that I have to have it. But I've never been known to look a gift horse in the mouth." His voice had thickened, and his Irish accent became more pronounced as the images grew sharper, more real. Hell, he could hear her moans, taste her on his lips as if they were already making love.

Her eyes widened. He could see that her body was already responding to his, in the way her breathing deepened. Swallowing, she looked down his body.

"H-How can you think I can do this?" She caught his gaze, and her earnest expression put a halt to the idea of jumping her right then and there.

He closed the distance between them and pulled her into his arms. She tucked her head beneath his chin and sighed. The scent of her, Libby and something musky, wild, filled his senses. It took every ounce of self-control he had left—and there wasn't much—not to attack her.

"Libby, we don't have a choice. We wouldn't get far if we tried to get out of here, and there's no way in hell I'm leaving you behind with this pack of slavering idiots. I can't believe the way they all drooled over you like you were theirs for the taking. Jesus."

"Brady, for a man who is supposed to be putting me at ease, talking about why he couldn't believe people are attracted to me isn't the way to go."

He sighed and hugged her closer. "Sorry. I'm not thinking straight."

She pulled out of his arms and a wave of cooled air chilled him. He didn't like that one bit. He wanted in her in his arms, under his control.

Whoa, where the hell had that thought come from? He shook his head, trying to clear it.

"These people are watching and listening to us and expect us to jump on the bed and go at it like a couple of minks."

He chuckled at her analogy, and she shot him a dirty look. "They can't hear."

"What?"

"They can only see." His blood was humming with the need for sexual release, but he needed to take this slowly. Libby might not have many inhibitions, but having sex with hidden cameras in the room would not be her bag of tea. He noticed a table with wine, cheese, and fruit. "Let's have a drink and relax."

He would have laughed if he didn't think it would hurt. *Relax.* The only way he would relax was after he'd buried his cock deep inside her. Libby trailed after him to the table, and he poured her a glass.

"You're not having any?" She sipped it, and apparently finding it to her liking, took a larger drink of it.

"Funkai and I were drinking while you were changing clothes."

She sighed. The fabric drew tight over her breasts. He couldn't stop the impulse to reach out and brush the backs of his fingers against her nipple. Her startled eyes shot to his. She bit her lip as he felt her nipple harden beneath his touch.

"I like to see that." His voice had grown huskier.

She closed her eyes as he stepped in front of her. He leaned forward and nipped her earlobe. "They can see, but they can't hear us. I know that isn't much of a consolation, but I don't see any way out of this. Just forget they're there. It's just us back in that cave in Yentalen, and you've seduced me with your body, your smile...your heart."

"Brady..." His name came out as a moan when he pinched her nipple.

"You know what you do to me, lass. Jesus, I feel like my blood is on fire." Even he heard the slight tremble in his voice. Heat licked along his nerve endings, and the very fabric of his soul screamed for him to conquer her, to take what he thought of as his. "Think about it. Doesn't it make you feel just a little bit naughty to know that someone is watching?" He nipped at her chin. "That maybe, just maybe, they're turned on by watching you. Watching you get hot...gets them hot."

He kissed a path from her neck to her mouth. Cupping her chin, he leaned forward and brushed his lips against hers. Her eyes slid closed as he settled his mouth against hers. She immediately opened and he dove in.

His head spun as the taste of her filled his mouth. The tangy wine flavored the unique essence he associated with Libby. Sweet as chocolate, hot as a pepper, she pulled him deeper into her spell. As he continued to kiss her, he slid his hands down her body, brushing her nipples, then around her waist to grab her ass. He almost came on the spot when he felt her bare ass beneath the fabric. His dick twitched as he drew her tight against him. Something clattered on the floor and he didn't give a damn what it was. Her hands cupped his chin. He lifted her off the floor, and she wrapped her legs around his waist.

He broke away from the kiss and headed to the bed. She scraped her teeth against his earlobe, then licked it. The touch of her tongue burned a path all the way to his cock. She was grinding her sex against him, moaning his name. Never in his life had he seen her go up so fast.

Reaching the bed, he tumbled onto it, but Libby barely seemed to notice. She molded her hands to his head and pulled him down to her lips again. His body was screaming, telling him if he didn't get out of those clothes right then, it wouldn't wait. He truly didn't want to embarrass himself on camera, so he pulled away. It took him a couple of tries, but he got out of his shirt. He threw it over his shoulder, then slid off the bed to stand. As her legs released him, she rested her weight on her elbows and watched him disrobe. He almost fell down as he hopped on one foot then the other to get rid of his boots. Next he shucked off his pants, leaving him completely naked.

He moved to join her back on the bed, but Libby stopped him.

"No." She slid to the edge of the bed, bringing her mouth level with his cock. "Beautiful."

She rubbed her thumb over the tip. A drop of pre-cum wet her finger. Capturing his gaze, she licked his cum off her thumb. His balls twisted as she closed her eyes and moaned.

"You taste good, Saint." Her voice whispered across his skin, and he felt his dick unbelievably lengthen more. "But, then—" Her lips curved. "—you always did taste good."

She leaned forward and licked another drop of moisture. Then she licked down one side and up the other. As she cupped his balls in one hand, her other slid to his ass, massaging and squeezing.

He watched as her eyes slid closed and she took his dick into her mouth. Curling his toes, he fought the urge to grab her head and fuck her mouth in earnest. Her expression was as if she were a contented kitten licking up the best cream. She was in charge, and he was glad to let her take the lead. He watched, mesmerized, each time he disappeared between her pink lips, pulling him closer to the edge but not so close he fell. Just enough to tease him beyond all thought.

Each time she drew to the top of his shaft, she twirled her tongue around the tip of it. He closed his eyes as she began working on him in earnest. Her rhythm increased as the sounds of her licking and slurping grew. One hand on his balls and one on his dick, she hummed against his skin. Unable to help himself, he grabbed her head and back to keep tempo with her. Each time he pushed himself between her lips, his body drew tighter, edging closer to completion. His balls drew tight as his blood rushed to his groin.

With regret, he pulled her away and tumbled her back onto the bed. Desperate to be inside her, he clawed at the waist of her pants, trying to figure out a way to get the damn things off.

"There's a slit in the crotch." Her voice was edged with the same kind of sexual tension he felt shooting through him, and it almost pushed him too far. She was as close as he was, and he had barely touched her.

He pushed her legs wider and slid one hand between her legs. He found the opening, thankfully, and slid his finger into her tight, hot pussy. Oh, Lord, she was wet. Her liquid fairly flowed over his fingers as the musky scent of her arousal filled the air around him. Without further preparation, he pulled his hand back and then entered her in one fast thrust. For a moment, he stayed still, enjoying the feeling of being inside her.

Nothing had ever felt as right as when he had his cock inside of her, connected to her. Then she wiggled and he was lost.

He lifted her legs to his shoulders and began to pump himself into her. She was close, her body quivering with the need for release. Each time he pushed back into her, her inner muscles clasped tighter, drawing him deeper.

"Come on, Libby." He looked down at her. Her red curls spread out over the bed in disarray, her eyes were closed, and her moans increased in volume with each of his thrusts. "That's it, lass. Come for me."

"Brady." At the sound of his name, he felt his body explode. He continued to pump into her as his hot seed spurted. She began to convulse, her inner muscles pulling him deeper, drawing more seed from him.

"Oh, God, Libby."

Moments later, he gently moved her legs from his shoulders and rolled over beside her, drawing her into his arms. She tucked her head under his chin and threw one arm over his stomach. At the sound of her steady breathing, he knew she was asleep. He kissed her temple.

As she snuggled against him, he knew that nothing had ever felt this right. His world had been cold and bleak without her all those years. Knowing that, and convincing her, was going to be the problem. She'd left for some reason, something she found lacking in him, in their relationship. He had to find out what it was, what made her run, and fix it. If he didn't, he wasn't too sure his heart would survive her leaving this time around.

* * *

Libby woke several hours later and snuggled closer to Brady.

"You awake, kitten?"

She looked up at him; his eyes were half closed, and a lazy sensual smile curved his lips.

"Just when did you start calling me kitten?"

"Hmm, I think it was about the time I had an image of you as one licking up cream."

Her face flushed. She wasn't a prude, but just the thought of the things they had done in full view of other people was embarrassing. And very arousing.

"You liked it, didn't you?"

"I love oral sex. You know that."

He chuckled. "No. You liked the fact that you were doing something, and other people were watching."

Her body quickened as his comment, but she kept mouth closed. She knew it had turned her on, but that didn't mean she liked the effect it had on her.

"Ah, come on, Libby. I won't tell anyone." He rolled over in one fast move, and she was on her back, with him on top. His cock was hard and ready against her mons. "You liked it, didn't you?"

Desire flamed in her belly at the sensual heat in his eyes. But it was the warmth, the love she saw that was her undoing. He had a beautiful body, a quick mind, but it was his eyes that always got her. Clear, dark blue, and all too perceptive. Every time he looked at her like this, she felt that he could see all the way into her soul.

"Brady...I still can't believe..."

"That it made you cream to think of people watching you. Common fantasy."

"Well, I lived the fantasy; that was enough. And we have things to discuss. We have to decide where we go from here."

He reached behind her neck and undid her top, pulling it away from her body. Bending his head, he licked first one, then the other nipple.

"How about we try being naughty just once more before we go? Hmmm? They aren't going to let us go for a few hours, and well, we do have this big bed..."

She chuckled. "Brady, you're insatiable."

He began inching his way down her body. "Only with you, lass." She thought he looked like a pirate with his long black hair and his Irish accent threading his voice. He settled his mouth on her pussy, his tongue darting between her lips, and all thoughts of plans drifted away as she gave herself up to the pleasure that only Brady could give her.

* * *

Brady was packing up the rest of his gear as Libby came in dressed in her regular clothes. He was sad to see the harem girl disappear, but they both know they had things to accomplish before they figured out just how to be together. That was one thing he had determined in the early morning hours while she'd slept—she wasn't shaking him loose this time. Somehow, someway, he would figure out a way to keep her by his side.

She threw the outfit she'd been wearing onto the bed. He grabbed it up.

"What are you doing?"

"If you think I'm giving that thing up, you've got to be out of your mind, woman."

She snorted but continued gathering up her things and nibbling on the breakfast they'd been given. "So, which way are we going?"

"We keep on the same path."

She sat on the bed to pull on her boots. There was nothing sensual in her movements, no flirting, but he couldn't take his eyes off her. He knew he would never get tired of looking at her.

"You think Sterling was on the right path?"

"I don't know if he was, or if there's even anything to claim, but from what Funkai said, he continued the same way I was planning on going."

She sighed, her mouth turned down in a frown.

"Hey, love, we'll find him." She shrugged. Oh, Christ, she was losing faith in him. That was not good. Panic welled up in his throat. He swallowed it back and squatted between her legs. "Libby, sweetheart." He took her hands in his and willed her to lift her gaze to his. When she did, he continued. "We'll find him. I promise you that."

"What if he doesn't want to be found? What if he can't be? What if..." *He's dead?* That's what she wanted to say.

"Don't worry, it will work out. Trust me?"

She nodded and sniffled. The door slid open, and Funkai entered, Walter and his friends hard on his heels. All of them were dressed in suits, as if going to a business meeting. A definite change in appearance from the day before.

"I trust you were well taken care of?" He asked the question of both of them, but his attention was fixated on Libby. Brady rose to his feet and blocked their view.

"Yes, we were. You have my weapons?"

He nodded and motioned for Walter to give them back. Walter did so begrudgingly.

"Do you need anything else?"

"No, we'll be on our way." Libby stood and took her weapons from him, storing them.

"Ms. Wainwright, I hope you find your father soon. I didn't like that young man with him."

"Young man?" Brady knew his voice was sharp, but ignored the strange look Funkai shot him.

"Yes." Funkai frowned. "They fought constantly; I have no idea about what."

"What was the man's name?"

"Tony Freemont."

Chapter Eleven

Brady marched along the path, not looking back once in the last thirty minutes, but Libby was sure he wore the same scowl he'd had since he found out about Tony. Jesus, he looked at her as if she'd lied to him. She hadn't. She'd forgotten, but he didn't want to discuss it.

Since then, he'd been silent as a tomb, and as pleasant as having your teeth drilled. She continued on behind him, sweat dribbling down her back. Without stopping, she pulled out her water and began drinking. She was tired. Very tired. Not only were her muscles sore from walking, but they ached from their activities the night before.

"Are we stopping for lunch?"

He grunted a response.

"Is that a 'yes' grunt or a 'no' grunt?"

"We should be there soon."

"There, as in the place where the legendary emerald—"

"Yes."

"Listen, Brady, I forgot about Tony. Walter told me about him, and then they had that meeting and... Are you listening to me?"

He grunted again, and she lost her temper. She stopped walking and took a deep breath before she started shouting.

"Listen, you jackass. I forgot." He stopped and turned, his eyes narrowed in agitation or anger. She didn't give a damn which. She was hot and tired and just wanted to go home and sleep, but she had to find her father. And he wasn't making it easy. "It wasn't foremost in my mind when the damn freaks back at that place started telling me that I had to have sex and be observed while doing it. Did you think I was thinking of my ex-husband then? Jesus, Brady, I was worried you were going to start fighting them and then they would kill you. Why the hell I love such a pigheaded jackass, I'll never know. My father said you would be a pain in the ass, and he was right. I have no idea why—"

He closed the distance between them. Without saying a word, he pulled her into his arms and kissed her. She pulled back from him, and he tried to follow.

"Brady, we don't have time for that."

"Lass, the woman I love tells me she loves me, I have to kiss her." His voice was thick with emotion, and the sound of it made her eyes sting. "I'm sorry I was such an ass, but I was worried you were trying to protect your ex-husband."

"I would never protect Tony. Anything that happens to him, he deserves."

He smiled. "We have a lot of things to discuss, you and I, like why you felt the need to leave all those years ago. But right now we'll find your father, and then get the hell out of here." He sobered. "I do love you; you know that, don't you, Libby?"

"Yes."

"How very touching."

They turned their heads simultaneously, and Libby gasped when she saw her ex-husband surrounded by three large ruffians. All of them were armed to the teeth.

"Tony Freemont, I take it." Brady released her and shoved her behind his back.

"Brady St. James." Tony nodded in Brady's direction, stepped forward, and punched Brady in the jaw. Not ready for the punch, Brady fell back on his butt.

"Tony, what the hell are you doing?"

"He deserved it, the son of a bitch."

Brady came to his feet ready to attack, but she stopped him. "Brady, you'll never win. They have more guns, more knives, and more muscle." He glanced at the other men and nodded curtly.

"What do you mean, he deserved it? He's done nothing to you."

Tony's pale gray eyes narrowed while he studied them. He'd always been a lean man, but he looked almost gaunt now. His cheeks were caved in, his bones more pronounced. His hair was thinning, and his general appearance was of a man who was unwell.

"What did he do to me? You stupid bitch, you know exactly what he did to me."

Oh, God, she'd forgotten about that mess. "Really, Tony. That wasn't Brady's fault. And I am sure you don't want everyone to know about that."

Tony glanced around at everyone watching with rabid interest. "Well, I guess you will save me from that one humiliation, huh, Liberty?"

"Where is my father?"

"I have no idea, but it doesn't matter." Calm, cool. The tone in his voice irritated her. It was as if they were discussing a missing golf club.

"It matters to me."

"He's not the one I need." He looked over her shoulder at Brady. "But I'm so glad that you brought me exactly who I *do* need."

"Brady?"

She glanced over her shoulder at him, and he shrugged.

"Yes, Brady. Jesus, don't you know who you've been screwing like a freaking bunny for the last few days?" A smiled stretched across his lips, but there was no humor at all in it. "Your *Saint* is just the man I need. A direct descendent of Irish blood—royal, at that. He must go into the cave to retrieve my emerald."

* * *

They were taken down a deep incline into a cavern, one of the thugs in front, Tony next, then Libby and Brady. Libby had never seen that look in Tony's eyes, and she was really frightened. Truly. He seemed to have gone over the edge. He really believed in the power of some damn emerald.

She glanced at Brady, who was grinding his teeth. She knew he was itching to fight Tony, and really, it would only take one punch and Tony would be out for a day or two. A bruise was forming on Brady's jaw where Tony had hit him.

They reached the bottom of what looked like a dried-up riverbed. The guards stayed behind them, and Tony looked around the area.

"You'll be happy to know, Liberty, that your father was well last time I saw him. Of course, he left me to fend for myself with only one bottle of water. That's why I had to hire some help." His voice was as calm as if he were ordering a salad or conducting a business meeting.

"What was the disagreement about?" Brady asked the question in just as cool a voice.

"Sterling thought we should turn the emerald over when we found it." He picked a piece of lint off his jacket. "I didn't."

"You're saying you did nothing to him?"

"Yes. Last I saw of him was his backside. Now, are you ready to go in and get the emerald?"

"I've decided I don't like caves, make me uncomfortable."

"Oh?" Tony's gaze moved to the men behind them, and one of them grabbed her. He put a stungun to her head. "I think that should convince you to get over your problem."

* * *

Brady inwardly cursed. He should have seen that coming. But really, he hadn't thought Freemont had the balls to order the murder of his ex-wife. Apparently greed and insanity helped him come to that decision.

"You know, I understand a stungun to the head is a particularly painful death." Freemont's voice was sickly sweet.

Every instinct told Brady to hold back, play it cool, but inside, anger churned his gut as he watched the blood drain out of Libby's face. He'd waited six fucking years, long years, waiting and wondering if he would get her back again. No punk-ass corporate shill was going to take her away from him now.

He swallowed his rage and stepped forward. "What do I have to do?"

"Nothing much. The legend says that one of pure Irish blood must enter the cave to retrieve the emerald. Once you leave the cave, you can give it to me, and you're free to go with Liberty."

"How do I know you won't do something to her while I'm in there?"

"You don't. But your choice is take a chance or stay here and watch her die."

He curled his fingers into his palms, trying to fight the urge to wrap his fingers around the bastard's neck. "You can come with me." It was a spur of the moment idea, and one he hoped the jackass was stupid enough to take him up on.

Tony thought for a moment, his pale eyes studying Brady. "I guess I could. Nothing says that I can't be there, just that the only person to bring the stone out should be Irish." He turned to his goons. "If you hear anything, or if he comes out alone, kill her. Ready?"

Brady nodded. He looked at Libby and fought the anguish that had him wanting to roar. She wasn't in pain, and she wasn't falling apart. Not his Libby. She was tough. But he could see the rise and fall of her chest as her breathing hitched every now and then. He knew she was fighting her own fear...for him...for herself.

"You touch her, harm her, even think about her, I will hunt you down and castrate you."

They didn't say a word, but he could tell that they understood he meant every word.

"I'll follow you, Saint."

Brady walked into the cave, trying his best to fight the overwhelming sense that they were heading for a disaster. He just hoped he'd stalled long enough to give Libby some time to come up with a plan.

* * *

Libby drew in a deep breath and tried to fight the fear that clogged her throat. She didn't trust Tony; he'd gone completely over the edge. Never before had she seen anything so cold, calculating, or downright crazy in his eyes. He really believed all the crap about being able to rule the universe while in possession of an emerald. She was trying her best not to scream from the pressure. She wasn't sure how the guards would take it.

It was just her rotten luck that she finally figured out that taking chances and letting loose wasn't all that bad, and her whacked-out ex-husband had to show up and screw up the whole damn thing. She'd laugh, but she wasn't so sure she could keep from crying.

The guards had let her sit on a huge rock near the side of the entrance to the cave. She rubbed her arms as a cool breeze blew across her skin. The second sun was starting to set, and the dampness in the air made it seem even colder. Trying not to draw attention to herself, she studied her guards from beneath her lashes. There was no way to overpower them, but there might be a way to outwit them. As she jumped from idea to idea, she heard the rustling of leaves behind her. She glanced over her shoulder. A murmur of voices drifted toward her.

Before she could blink, the area was swarming with men dressed in black suits. She couldn't make out one from another, but she knew they were human. They came in, stunguns drawn. There was a lot of shouting and scuffling, but soon the guards had been subdued, unarmed, and surrounded by a sea of black.

Two men separated from the group. Both wore the same fitted black suits as the other men, but these men she knew. Robbie Masters and John Hunter walked toward her, both of them with expressions that looked like they wanted to kill someone. She just hoped it wasn't her.

"What are you two doing here?"

"Saving your ass, and Saint's," Hunter said. "Where the hell is he?"

"In the cave with Tony."

"Shit." This came from Masters.

"What do you want to do?" John asked him.

Masters studied her, then looked at John. "If we go in, he might freak."

"Too late for that."

Both men shot her a silencing look.

"Why do you say that?" John asked.

"Well, for one, he's slipped over the edge. I mean gone completely insane."

Masters nodded. "I have to agree. We've had him under surveillance for months. His behavior is erratic. We just have to figure out what to do."

"I can go."

"You?" both men said together.

"Yes, me. He hears you all, he'll freak out and maybe kill Brady. He isn't expecting me to pop into the cave, but he sees me as less of a threat."

"Hmm, it could work," Masters mused.

"Masters, Saint will kick your ass, you take her in there."

"Do you see another way?"

John sighed and shook his head. "We'll back you up." He handed her a stungun, and she shook her head.

"Knives. I'm really good with knives."

* * *

"According to this passage—" Freemont held up a printed sheet close to his face, trying to read it. "—it says that you should find the emerald in the pool of water behind you."

Brady looked around the dim cave and tried to repress a shudder. The only thing he hated more than heights was dark, enclosed spaces. It smelled of mold and salt. Strange, but he figured the pool Freemont was talking about was from an underground saltwater spring. This area of Dranirick was known for its salt lakes.

He ambled over to the pool while trying to fight the clawing panic inside of him. They were so far in the cave he couldn't hear what was happening on the outside. And that terrified him more than climbing mountains. He prayed he would make it out before anything else happened to Libby. He had to distract Freemont while he thought up a plan.

"So, what was it that you hit me for, Freemont?"

He peered over the rocks to look into the pond. It looked like a hot spring, steam rising off the water, but the scent of salt was almost overwhelming.

"You mean Libby didn't tell you?"

"Uh, we haven't been doing much talking."

"Figures. The damn woman was cold as ice every time I touched her. Nothing I did in bed would please her." Brady fought a smile and lost. He looked over his shoulder at Freemont, who was glowering at him. "See anything?"

"No. So, that's it. That's what you hit me for?"

He didn't answer for a few seconds. "No. I hit you because the last time we made love was the first time she ever climaxed."

Brady frowned. "And?"

"She called out your name."

He turned and looked at Freemont, who was frowning again. He couldn't stop the laugh that erupted.

"Oh, man. I deserved that hit. Damn, I'd be ready to cut your balls off if she had done that to me."

Freemont's hand tightened around the gun. "Just get the fucking emerald, and you can have your precious Liberty back. Just hope that the men out there don't think that maybe they want a little taste. "

Brady bit back his panic, looked into the water, and saw nothing but blackness. He knew the legend was a hoax, but there was no way Freemont was going to believe him. With each minute that passed, he knew Libby was in danger a minute longer. But he couldn't lose control. If he did, he would fall apart and wouldn't be able to keep Libby safe. And once they were free, he didn't care if she wanted to spend their lives together making schedules and spouting off about ethics. As long as they spent it together—that was all he cared about.

"Do you see it?" Freemont's voice had tightened in anticipation and was edging toward hysteria.

Think. There had to be something to distract him and get the stungun away from the bastard. Then it came to him in one blinding flash. He reached into the water, cupping his hands.

"Freemont! Come look. It's beautiful."

A flurry of footsteps approached him, and when he knew Freemont was close enough, Brady turned, splashing his face with the salt water.

Freemont screamed. "Ahhhh, my eyes!"

"Brady!" Libby called from somewhere behind Freemont. He swung around, still not able to see, and lifted his stungun. Brady was on his feet and jumping on him within seconds, but not before Freemont got off a shot. He landed on top of Freemont, the stungun flying out of the man's hands and skidding across the stone floor.

Brady lifted his head and was on his feet before he could think. Libby lay on her back, a burn on her shoulder. Real, mind-numbing terror rushed through him. Jesus, no. He knelt beside her and couldn't think of what he should do next. She wasn't moving.

"Brady."

He looked up at the sound of Hunter's voice, but he couldn't think.

"Does she have a pulse?"

Right. Pulse. He felt for one, and relief edged away the fear as he felt her heart beat steady and strong.

"It looks like just a flesh wound, but I want to put some salve on it," Masters said as he leaned over as if to pick her up.

"Don't touch her. I'll carry her." His voice was hoarse with anguish. Both men stepped back. Hunter went to gather up Freemont, who Brady heard blabbering about the emerald.

Gently, he slid one arm behind her neck and the other beneath her knees. He rose, and she murmured something against his neck. The warm breath against his skin made him want to sing.

"Brady."

"Yeah, love."

"My shoulder hurts."

He chuckled. "I know, love."

"Next time, you're taking the hit, Brady."

A lump clogged his throat. "You got it, Libby."

Chapter Twelve

Hot, blinding pain burned Libby's shoulder and radiated through her body. She tried to sit up, to walk off the pain, but something was holding her down. Struggling, she slapped at the barrier holding her down.

"Libby, love. You have to stay still so Hunter can apply the medicine to your wound."

She tried opening her eyes, but she didn't have the strength to lift her eyelids.

"It hurts." She couldn't keep the pain out of her voice. "I just don't want to deal with it anymore."

"Hunter is going to take care of you. You'll be just fine."

"Brady."

"Yes, love?"

"I wanted you to know, just in case I die—"

"You are not going to die." The vehemence in his voice comforted her. She sighed.

"Even so, I wanted you to know that I love you."

"I love you, too, Libby."

She tried to smile, but she felt tears gather in her eyes and slide down her face.

"I wanted you to know that I left before..." She sucked in a breath when another shaft of hot pain radiated from her shoulder. "I wanted to say that I left because I was afraid. You...me...different."

He chuckled, although for some reason it sounded watery to her. "We are at that, lass. Well, to make it up to me, you have to marry me."

"Sure, Brady, anything you say." Warmth spread through her, relaxing her muscles. She figured John had given her something for the pain. That was her last thought as she drifted off into nothing.

* * *

Libby ground her teeth together and decided that maybe, just maybe, she should have left Brady in that cave.

"Brady, I'm not an invalid."

"Doc says bed rest."

"Hunter is *not* a doctor."

He stared at her, blinked once, and turned his attention back to his handheld ebook reader. It had been three days since she'd been hit, and he had been driving her crazy. He treated her like glass. She didn't like it one bit.

Sighing, she looked at the ring on her finger. He'd held her to her promise, but she'd insisted on a fast wedding. At least, after they sorted out the mess of what had happened. After the dust had settled, they'd found out that both Masters and John were agents for some agency, although neither of them were forthcoming about just who they worked for. But they'd been watching Tony for months as he embezzled thousands of dollars from the government.

"You never did explain what that nonsense was about being royal Irish blood."

He shrugged. "My family is distantly related to the English aristocracy."

"You're royal, and you didn't tell me?"

He looked up, surprised by the irritation in her voice. "We don't think much of it; and really, Libby, you know my family and I don't talk anymore. But I guess you could say that I have some blue blood in me."

Dismissing her again, he went back to his ebook reader. She sighed and looked around the room. She had nothing to do. Brady wouldn't even join her in bed. She'd tried to convince him just a few moments earlier, even offered to put on the genie outfit, but he'd refused. If she heard him utter the words "Hunter said so" one more time, she was going to punch him in the nose. Hard.

"Isn't there something I can do? Why don't you get me a book, too?"

He looked up, frowned but nodded, and went to do her bidding. Before he reached the door, loud voices sounded down the hall and the door burst open.

"What the hell have you done to my daughter, Saint?"

She blinked. "Daddy?"

She jumped out of bed, ignoring Brady's reprimand. "Daddy." She threw herself into his arms. Taller than her by three inches, and muscled, without an ounce of fat on him, he could easily lift her off the floor. He hugged her close, and she closed her eyes, enjoying the familiar scent of peppermint that she always associated with him. He kissed her cheek, and the whiskers from his beard tickled her face.

"What did you do to yourself, Libby?" His voice was gruff with emotion, and she felt her own eyes sting with tears.

"What she did was risk her life to save your sorry ass, and you don't even appreciate it."

Slowly, her father set her aside and faced Brady.

"And what did you do? Let her go off running around. You're supposed to protect her."

"I did protect her, but the ass she married tried to kill me so he could have some fictional emerald. And another thing—"

"You didn't do a very good job of it."

Both of their voices had risen to the point where she winced from the sound bouncing off the walls.

"Shut up."

Both of them looked at her as if she had grown two heads.

"I can take care of myself." The men looked at each other and smiled. "You're going to piss me off."

"Never mind that. You're safe, and that's all that matters. Hunter says you're good to go. Get your things and we can hop on out of here. I have some meeting down in New York City in a couple weeks, so we have to get going if I'm going to make it."

"First of all—" Brady grabbed her arm and pulled her over to his side. "—she's not going anywhere. And second of all, what the hell happened to your quest?"

"Not going anywhere?" Sterling looked at both of them, his eyes sparking, his face flushed with anger. "And just why do you have some say-so in that?"

"Because I'm her husband, and she's staying with me."

Her father's eyes widened and then a smile curved his lips. "Well, now, that's more like it. When did this happen, and why couldn't you wait? I wanted to walk you down the aisle."

She smiled. "I didn't want to wait, and we did a quick civil ceremony. Neither one of us wanted a big ceremony."

"Ahh, Libby, that's okay. Fantastic, in fact."

Brady stopped his celebration with a question. "Sterling, what the hell were you doing running around after the legend of the Snake King?"

"Oh, that." Sterling shifted from one foot to the other. "Well, see, Libby was unhappy, and I had been researching things, and…it was a good plan."

"Plan?"

"I knew I made a mistake about Freemont, Libby. And I knew you'd never stopped loving Saint. So I figured out a way to give him to you."

For a moment, she couldn't speak. This was beyond anything her father had pulled before. "You mean you concocted this story, put my life in danger, and yours and Brady's, to get us back together?"

She heard Brady chuckle and shot him a dirty look.

"Ahh, love, you know your da does nothing in a small way."

"So you think I should just forget about it?"

"Well, it did turn out well."

"Brady St. James, you know if we let him get away with this now, it will only keep getting worse."

"He did get away with it."

She turned and realized her father had slipped out the door. "Dammit."

Brady pulled her back into his arms. "Ahh, love, it turned out perfectly."

She sighed. "I guess so."

He leaned down and brushed his lips against hers. "Your father is safe, your ex is in jail, and we're married."

She felt his erection against her stomach and her body responded in kind. "Saint, you know that you're easy, don't you?"

He smiled, his dimples in full force. "Only where you're concerned, love; only where you're concerned."

Melissa Schroeder

Born to an Air Force family at an Army hospital, Melissa has always been a little screwy. She was further warped by her years of watching Monty Python movies and her strange family.

From the time she read To Kill a Mockingbird in the seventh grade, she dreamed of being a writer. After years of struggling, trying to write short stories filled with angst, she finally listened to her college writing instructor and allowed her natural comedic voice to shine through. She counts Jayne Ann Krentz, Jenny Crusie, Stephanie Laurens, Julia Quinn, and Lori Foster as influences in her writing.

She is a military wife and mother to two military brats and an adopted dog daughter, and lives wherever the military sticks them. Which, she is sure, will involve heat and bugs only seen on the Animal Discovery Channel. In her spare time, she reads, cooks, reads, travels, reads some more, and dreams of living somewhere the bugs die in the winter.

Be sure to visit Melissa Schroeder on the Internet at http://www.authormelissaschroeder.com/

CARTE BLANCHE

Camille Anthony

carte blanche

NOUN: *n.* Inflected forms: pl. cartes blanches: kä*r*t blä*n*sh', kä*r*t' blä*n*sh')

Unrestricted power to act at one's own discretion; unconditional authority

ETYMOLOGY: French: *carte*, ticket + *blanche*, blank.

In the days before the world burned, the original definition of the term "carte blanche" literally meant "blank ticket." If one could obtain a blank letter or ticket stamped with the king's seal, one could write whatever they wished upon the paper. Many such papers were secured and sold for a price to ruthless men of power. Many people disappeared—some into the dreaded prison called the Bastille and others into the murky waters of an undisclosed and unmarked death. And so carte blanche came to be known as limitless power and authority. The years passed, and in the latter days of the kings of Great Britain, men took mistresses as they always did. Also as always, the women who captured the lusts and interests of such men demanded something in return for their favors. The bargaining was intense as the doves negotiated everything but a wedding dress. The highest any kept woman could aspire was to be given a home of her own and a blank ticket of credit.—Ananda, ship's librarian Diaspora *a.p. 194*

Prologue

One of the last original colonists from Old Earth, Liana stood on her balcony, eyes narrowed against the hot rays of Paradyse's afternoon suns. One hand shading her face, she gazed out over the verdant, teeming jungle of New India. The huge orange sun that was the primary solar light shone down on the pale blue expanse of trees and underbrush, highlighting the turquoise fronds of the fur tea plants—so named because the leaves of the indigenous plant were clothed with a soft, velvety covering that resembled the fur of some Old Earth animals. The smaller dwarf sun, blizzard white and dying, bathed everything in double shadows.

Liana sighed. Sometimes she missed Earth with a pain that threatened to rip her heart apart. Green trees and grass, blue water and skies... Lord above, she missed the simplest things. Closing her eyes against the memories of a long-dead reality, she drew in a deep breath. She missed her parents, who had not been among those rescued.

She, of all her family, had been the only survivor of Earth's death throes. She had grown to maturity aboard the colony ship, ironically looked upon as one of the leaders. Her visions had given her a place of authority. After all, she had been the first to sound the alarm, though no one had heeded her. Amidst the turmoil of terror, the people had turned against all scientists, claiming rampant technology had stripped them of the atmospheric protection Earth had needed.

Liana's lips quirked up in a sardonic sneer. Never mind that scientists had been telling people for decades that they were destroying the stratosphere...that the ozone layer grew dangerously thin... At that point, the people weren't looking for answers—they were looking for scapegoats.

She'd lived through the time of panic and horror, hoping never to be involved in such again. Now, she sensed a disturbance, dreamed a disorder, a glitch in the rightful order of things. Something was stirring; something evil and insane rode the winds, targeting the family she'd adopted as her own. Targeting her new world.

I am an old woman, retired and forgotten. I have earned my peace. What have I to do with the trouble coming upon this place and these people?

Liana shook her head, her grizzled curls brushing against her thin cheeks. She had seen the end of civilization, had seen the old world burn. Just like then, she knew herself incapable of ignoring the danger to those she had come to love. She couldn't stand by and neglect to give a warning; much good it would do. Against her will, she recalled the emotional devastation of that long-ago time.

Long before Earth's sun had exploded, she'd dreamt of the great conflagration over and over again. Telling her parents had been futile. They wouldn't believe the flighty child she'd been, didn't believe such powerful, important visions could flow through her. The other adults had responded in the same vein. A melodramatic dreamer, they'd called her, idly brushing off her warnings and dire predictions. Nearer the end, they'd all believed, all listened, but they'd waited too late to take meaningful, effective action. During the chaotic days just before the end, they'd managed to save only a pitiful few. There were times when she still wished she hadn't been among those chosen to occupy a berth on one of the seven colony ships sent off before the massive nova destroyed the sun. From their vantage point light-years out from Earth, they'd watched in horror as the sun flares engulfed the planet, instantly killing those who'd had no other means of escape...

Throwing off the memories that haunted her still, Liana turned her back to the world outside. There was much she needed to do to prepare for the threat that drew nearer every day. Evil's stench surrounded the figure of the father, and she feared it might be beyond her capability to aid him. Even if she succeeded, the attack against her father would devastate Chastity, and she would need her old *ayah* in the days to come.

Liana tightened her lips. She'd sensed the seedling talents of a visionary in the girl years ago. Accepting the position as her *ayah,* she'd trained the young child. During those formative years, she'd grown to love the intelligent youth as the granddaughter she'd never had. This new world couldn't afford to lose the talents of a budding seer. Chastity must be protected at all costs.

Gliding over to her storage chests, Liana began packing for a prolonged visit. She just hoped she wouldn't arrive too late to do what little she could.

* * *

The loud retort of a shot rang through the air, startling Chastity out of a light doze.

"What the hell—?" *That sounded like it came from Father's rooms.*

The book she'd been reading fell from her lap as she jumped up from the divan. Rushing out the library door, she tore through the corridors separating the duke's private quarters from the rest of the house. Her scandalous pantaloons—held in oft-reiterated aversion by Papa—gave her the freedom of movement she needed to reach her father's side as quickly as possible.

Heart pounding from the double rev of exertion and fear, she exploded around the last corner and skidded to a halt. Lungs laboring, she frantically dragged in enough air to shout, "Father!" as she burst through his bedroom door.

Sheer curtains fluttered at the bank of tall, open windows. Beneath one screenless opening, her father lay sprawled, his bloodied chest draped half out the low marble sash.

"Oh, my guardian angel-serpents! Papa!"

Chastity dropped to her knees beside her father, fingers scrabbling, pressing against his carotid in hope of finding a pulse. Her hands shook badly, hindering her efforts. A curse and a sob broke free as she took a deep breath and held it, fighting to steady herself and her hand.

"Powers Above...help me!" she pled, trying again for a pulse, this time at the wrist. Recalling a bit of medical trivia, she made sure not to grip with her thumb. A faint, thready beat pulsed against her forefinger and she collapsed in a weak huddle, thankful tears raining down her face.

She slid all the way to the floor and cradled her father's head in her lap. "Why would someone shoot you, Father? What enemy do we have that I don't know about?"

Just then, the thud of retreating footsteps sounded on the cobbled flagstone walkway, followed by the jingle of a harness and the whinnying of a horse. An outraged yell, a cry of pain, and the sound of clanging metal rang in the stable yard. She listened to the clattering hooves clip-clopping down the long dirt drive and ground her teeth. Anger seethed within. Torn between wanting to catch the person responsible for harming the most important person in her life, and staying to see him out of harm's way, Chastity cursed the unknown person but chose to remain with her father.

The perpetrator may have escaped today, but she would see the villain captured and repaid if it were the last thing she did in this life.

* * *

"Oh, hell, no, Liana, I refuse to go! How could you expect me to just up and leave while my father is still struggling to survive?"

Liana sighed at the truculent look marring the earthy beauty of her former charge's face. She'd raised this turbulent child and knew better than most what that expression presaged. If she wanted Chastity to walk the only path of safety she could design, she'd have to present her with logical, overwhelming reasons for going against her deepest instincts.

"And if you don't go, who will catch your father's would-be killer?"

The arrested glare was all she could have hoped for. Those velvety brown eyes went vague as the young woman's focus turned inward. Her shoulders slumped. "Just the thought of having to deal with so-called 'polite society' turns my stomach. I don't have it in me to sashay around like a weak reed, leaning on strong, protective men. I am a capable woman and I—"

"Of course you are capable. You are also a *smart* woman, and smart women know when to bend."

"Bend?" She threw up her hands, her frustration and angst obvious to her old nurse. She'd never liked being confronted with a situation she had no control over. "Don't you mean break, *ayah?* How far am I supposed to bend, Liana? If I go there pretending Father is...has died...Uncle David will believe he is my guardian. I haven't turned eighteen, and by law, he will have control over me until that time. You know how greedy he is. What if he tries to marry me off?"

"Really, Chassy, why build mansions out of servants' quarters? You need only insist any betrothal last until your birthday. Once you reach your majority, you have but to refute the match. Think, girl! Where else can you ferret out our culprit? It is up to you to give your father the time he needs. Our enemy can't learn the attempt at eliminating the duke didn't succeed. The next plan will definitely be more lethal."

"Why can't we tell my uncle and let him help?"

"Didn't you just bring up your uncle's greed? Unfortunately, your mother's brother has always coveted wealth and power. I cannot dismiss the fact that he might be involved some way. If he felt he could gain control of your family's wealth through controlling you..." She shrugged and shook her head. "We won't take that chance."

"I feel so torn. On one hand, I want to find my father's enemy, but on the other, I dread not being here if he should need me."

The fear in Chastity's eyes hurt her. If it were in her power, her former charge would never have to deal with the pain of losing a parent or loved one before the ordained time. Unfortunately, those kinds of resources belonged to Beings of higher elevation than herself.

Sighing, she laid her palm on Chassy's cheek. "Child, if I could go for you, I would. I give you my word—I won't allow further harm to come to your father. I have grown to tolerate him over the years. I will guard him for both of us. Go to your uncle. Find out what you can."

"What if I find...*him?*" Fear and anticipation warred in her voice and expression.

Liana chuckled, refreshing amusement momentarily displacing the dread she'd felt since before arriving at the duke's plantation. "I don't doubt that you will. It is fated, after all. I suspect what you are really asking is, 'How should I respond to the man who has been haunting my dreams for the greater part of my young life?' and my answer is: honestly and courageously."

"Huh! I'm no coward! I fear no man."

"I didn't say you did. However, you *do* fear giving in to the emotions of love."

"Love weakens a woman, steals her autonomy, and leaches her power. Once a man claims a woman, she becomes less in his eyes. I've seen it happen too many times to doubt my conclusions. Much as I love my father, I remember how he treated my own mother. She died of a broken heart."

"Chastity, you must stop allowing the past—and someone else's past, at that—to influence your future. Grab your destiny with both hands and wrestle it into a shape you can live with. Do not bow your neck to strictures, but in the same vein, do not allow fear or bitterness to color your decisions so that you reject the one thing that can fulfill you."

Chastity sneered. "You think I need a man to fulfill me? Are you saying a woman cannot reach fulfillment without a big strong man to lean on?"

"I'm not saying that at all. I'm saying that *you* need love to fulfill you. Do not be so focused on not allowing any man to dominate your will that you allow yourself to be blinded by prejudice." She placed a gnarled hand on Chastity's tense shoulder and squeezed. "Take my advice, young one. Don't be like your old *ayah* Liana, who passed up the most glorious opportunity of her life and has lived to regret it."

Chastity wandered over to the window, eyes roaming the contours of her family holding. "It has been years since I've journeyed away from this plantation." She turned her head and met Liana's gaze. A small laugh escaped her. "My heart pounds at the thought of leaving these familiar surroundings, my home."

Over at the stable yard, the grooms were saddling two celebeasts. The two women watched the giant steeds prance and stamp, their six huge feet shifting and moving in the odd pattern they used to produce the smooth gait they were so prized for.

Chastity swung back to face her old nurse, a frown on her face and accusation on her lips. "All right, I'll go. But then, you knew that, or the grooms wouldn't be settling the celebeasts in preparation for a journey."

"You give me too much credit, little one. The grooms are preparing to travel to my home and fetch back my healing supplies. I'll be here longer than I had thought, since I plan to remain until this is all over. Besides, the celebeasts are better suited for country riding. You'll be taking the ducal flitter into the city."

As she spoke, the air was gently displaced as a smooth, multi-windowed, cylindrical coach glided up to the main drive and hovered silently two feet off the ground. The door whooshed open, and a liveried chauffeur stepped down and out and stood beside the craft, awaiting orders.

Chastity hugged her mentor and teacher. "I'm only doing this because you'd never give me a moment's peace otherwise," she teased, knowing it was usually the other way around.

"Report to me often," Liana begged. "And watch your back. Trust no one. Don't let anyone know you suspect foul play."

Jaw hardening, Chastity nodded. "I'll take care. You make sure to keep me up to date on Daddy's status. Let me know immediately if he—" She broke off on a shaky breath. "—takes a turn for the worse."

"I will, dear."

The maids came out with her luggage and loaded it into the cargo section of the hovering vehicle. One maid remained in the transport. She took a seat facing a window, hands folded calmly in her lap. With a last goodbye embrace, Chastity entered the flitter and motioned for the pilot to take off.

The plantation fell away below, the panoramic view well-known and well-loved. Chastity had a fleeting notion to order the flitter about and return home. A frisson of fear slid down her spine and she knew—as clearly as if she'd seen it in a vision—her life was about to change.

Chapter One

Well, this is certainly not the way I'd choose to celebrate my birthday! Hunting for would-be assassins and breaking the stupid engagement my uncle has forced upon me.

Standing beside her soon-to-be ex-fiancé on the wide landing of the lofty, ornate stairway, eighteen-year-old Chastity Tilson glared at the long queue of aristocrats lined up to make her re-acquaintance. Pert breasts riding high in a barely there bodice with no visible means of support, she managed to look both demure and daring in shimmering, glowing yards of shifting silver chiffon and lace.

Wasting half the evening greeting the stuffy upper crust of society was the last thing she wanted to be doing. She needed to be following the few clues she'd been given, not hobnobbing with people who all hated what she stood for: female independence. She refused to be at the beck and call of any man. Bowing and scraping didn't suit her. She'd never done so and had no intention of starting any time soon.

Her uncle may think himself her guardian, but he and his handpicked puppet would soon learn better. Only her father had ever tried to boss her around, and he'd ceased that exercise in futility before her eighth birthday.

On her other side, Alicia, the marchioness of Avondale, leaned over and hissed at her to *please* smile. Chastity glanced around and up, a sneer curling the right corner of her mouth as Alicia's quiet plea sounded in her ear. She felt so much older than her cousin; it was always a surprise to realize the woman towered over her own petite frame.

"I have no intention of being polite to this pushy, nosy rabble."

"Great gad, woman! Can you never act as you are supposed to? You disgust me."

"How nice to hear you say so, Bernard. In fact, I'm pleased. I believe the little surprise I've planned for you later this evening will more than meet your expectations."

The marchioness took a faltering step back, head whipping to and fro between the engaged couple. As their sniping continued, she began to look faint...and panicked. "Lord Karmon, Father expects such uncivilized actions of Chastity; however, he would be shocked to see you behaving so before our company."

Bernard's face turned red and he looked away, lips drawn tight with anger, body tense with the effort to control his temper. "You are correct, of course, Lady Avondale." He gave a stiff bow. "My apologies. As usual, I lost my temper around your cousin."

Chastity hid her grin at Bernard's chagrin. Patting Alicia's arm, she gave the hostess of tonight's extravagant gala a pitying glance. "Poor Ali, forced by your daddy to play chaperone to your wild, New Indian relative. This re-entry into polite society isn't working, and it's obvious you've realized I am slated to be this season's most spectacular failure."

"Would you *please* stop snarling at your guests and *behave?*"

"*Your* guests, cuz," she returned out the side of her mouth, lips barely moving, "yours and Bernard's. I didn't invite any of them, so my behavior has been exemplary...relatively speaking."

Alicia's shoulders slumped. She did dejected well and managed to make Chastity feel guilty. After all, her quarrel wasn't with her cousin. Truthfully, she had always liked Alicia best of all her relatives.

"Doing it a little too brown, dear," she whispered.

Lowering her head, Alicia slumped more.

Chastity threw her hands up in surrender. "Oh, very well, I'll try to act *civilized...*for your sake." She laughed at Alicia's exaggerated, relieved sigh, but the next guests had her wishing she could take back her rash promise. Gritting her teeth, she gave a curt nod and begrudgingly acknowledged the duke and duchess of Pettibone.

Slim to the point of scrawniness, Pettibone towered over his stout lady wife, his sour expression stealing what little handsomeness he had. Completely ignoring her, he greeted Alicia and Bernard, leaving his wife to trail along behind him.

Fighting back the wicked urge to do something to shock the spit out of the dour-looking aristocrat, she settled for batting her eyelashes at him as she snatched up his hand and vigorously shook the limp appendage.

The duke's appalled expression pleased Chastity to no end. He was trapped by his own interpretation of socially acceptable behavior. He couldn't retrieve his hand without committing a gross social gaffe.

She smiled full in his face. The duke froze in place. His eyes widened then flared with sudden heat.

What? Why do men always get that look on their faces when I smile? Yuck! Deciding she needed to stop smiling, Chastity shrugged off the incident and reached to shake the duchess's hand. She, at least, looked friendly.

The pale green eyes that met her brown ones held no censure, and the generous mouth curved in a motherly smile as the dimpled woman squeezed her hand. Unwinding a bit, Chastity gave the short woman a real smile in return. The duchess startled her by drawing her closer and furtively whispering, "My name is Lucynda. You need to come to me at the earliest opportunity, dear."

Already acknowledging the next guests crowding behind the royal couple, Chastity nodded absently. Trying to pay attention to names and titles and figure out what the duchess of Pettibone's secretive exchange had been about started a pounding headache behind her eyes. She gave up both exercises, content to have Alicia prompt her with names.

"His Royal Highness the Grand Duke of Archer and Her Royal Highness the Grand Duchess of Archer."

Now, here were people she delighted in seeing.

Chassy's curtsey to the royal couple was deep and respectful. The king's brother and his wife had always been true friends.

"Chastity," the grand duke began in his powerful basso voice, "we were so sorry to hear about your father's demise. He was a good friend. We shall miss him." His voice never cracked, but she read his sincerity in the hooded look he shared with her.

"Thank you, Your Highness." She bowed again. "My father always held you in high regard, as do I."

"Has the murderer been apprehended yet?"

Chassy's lips drew flat, her eyes narrow. "Not yet, sir, but you can rest assured I will find the person or persons responsible for separating me from my father."

"Not now, Archer!" The low reprimand reminded Chassy she was not in a private place.

"Your Highness," she whispered, sinking into another deep curtsey.

Duchess Eileen pulled her up from her genuflecting and hugged her, pressing a warm cheek against hers in a sign of affection. "It is so good to see you out of mourning, Chassy. Life must continue, but we understand how you still miss him. Feel free to call upon us for any need, darling. You are like a niece to us."

Their words melted the shield of animosity she'd erected, and tears stung her eyes. She cringed, not willing to expose her true worry to the crowd of vultures comprising most of the evening's guests.

"Yes, indeed, you may call upon us, child." The grand duke curled his index finger under her chin and lifted her face. "Losing a loved one is hard, *liebchen,* but this is not the place to let others see your pain…or your anger." His low-pitched words were for her ears only.

Grateful for the support, Chastity nodded, letting him wipe away the evidence of her pain with his finger.

"Smile for me, now. Let me see that vaunted appeal others have mentioned," he urged with avuncular humor.

Obeying, she flashed the couple a wide grin and was shocked to see the man she thought of as an uncle stiffen and flinch back. The grand duke stepped back and reached blindly for his wife's hand, curling his fingers about hers as if he held on to a lifeline.

Unease roiled through Chassy. The smile fell from her face. She didn't want to understand his reaction, but was glad beyond words she hadn't seen lust glittering in his gentle eyes.

"That is a mighty weapon you wield, young woman," the grand duchess murmured, mouth curved in a wry grin. "Use it wisely."

Huh?

She pondered the grand duchess's words while the royal couple passed on. Another took their place, with another and another lined up behind those. Growing more frustrated by the minute, Chastity fidgeted beside her momentary fiancé and her cousin. "When does this interminable ritual end?"

Bernard drew away, distancing himself physically as well as emotionally. His nonverbal disapproval was biting and acerbic. "It ends as soon as the last well-wisher is greeted, and not before. *Cretin,*" he finished, muttering under his breath.

His pompous attitude irked her, and she twitched her skirts to the side. He wasn't the only one who could convey disgust and dislike with a gesture. Giving him her back, she resumed greeting and smiling at the guests, her emotions as frozen as her fake smile.

Her uncle had done exactly as she'd prophesied, forcing a dynastic betrothal upon her almost as soon as she'd arrived. The duke of Eathrington was a familial martinet, holding the reins of his household in a tight, controlling fist. His wife and children all toed the line or faced the threat of disinheritance. He pretended he acted in Chastity's best interests, but he lied to himself as well as to her.

Bernard, Lord Karmon, was the only son of the neighboring aristocratic family. Lord Eathrington had long coveted the rich lands that marched along his northern borders and saw a way to ensure they would come into his hands. By offering Chastity's vast ducal lands as bait, he'd managed to get the family to agree to deed over the contested land. As soon as the marriage went through, the lands were his.

Little did her uncle know she had no intention of falling into line and being one of the quiet, retiring, brainless social butterflies he'd turned his own daughters into. This betrothal would end tonight. She would finally be able to rid herself of Bernard's possessive posturing and snide male attitude of superiority.

The party wouldn't really get started until midnight. When the clock struck, Alicia would have a huge cake rolled out, and the guests would wish her felicitations. Bernard planned to announce the date of their wedding.

Chassy'd made plans contrary to theirs. She could hardly wait. A few more guests to greet...a few more hours 'til freedom.

Tremendously bored, she barely noticed the last few people she greeted. A handshake, a curtsey, a regal nod of the head, depending on the social status of the ones presented to her. And then a commotion at the door distracted her. Gaze wandering toward the front door, she glimpsed the new arrivals.

She froze in the act of clasping the hand extended toward her. Mouth falling open, Chastity gaped at the tall gentleman passing beneath her elevated position at the top of the flaring staircase. Her spice-brown eyes followed his path, greedily drinking in the unadulterated male splendor.

"Great guardian angel-serpents...just look at him!"

Under the glittering light of a thousand flickering candles, the man's darkly tanned skin was a dramatic contrast against the pristine white of his neck linens. The tailored cut of his formal black tuxedo and skintight breeches emphasized the powerful outline of his magnificent build. The close-fitting cloth indecently hugged his body, highlighted the heft and jut of his sex.

"My god!" Chastity gasped, ignoring the shocked expressions of the bewigged nobleman standing before her, hand still outstretched for the acknowledgement she'd failed to make. He huffed, insulted when she absently shooed him out of her line of sight, and then literally pushed him out of the way when he didn't move fast enough.

Head a-swirl with the giddy rush of sudden arousal, she leaned over the banister for a longer, more focused look, craning her neck to keep *him* in view. She couldn't drag her eyes away.

"You are insufferable!" Bernard snatched her arm, pulling her away from the railing. "You're making a fool of yourself."

"Look who's talking," she snapped, baring her teeth and yanking her arm away. "Touch me again and I'll garrote you. I was going to save this for later, but since I can't stand your hands on me another moment, I'll tell you now: This betrothal is over!"

Bernard grimaced, distaste etched in every line of his face. "You don't have any say in ending our betrothal. Your uncle set it up, and he is the only one who can nullify it."

She brushed her hands together, ridding them of the slimy feeling of having touched Bernard, and shook out her skirts. Lifting her head to meet his gaze, she glared at the man who thought he owned her.

"Lord Karmon, I have officially gained my majority…and my independence. My money is not subject to my uncle's control after tonight. *I* am not subject to my uncle after tonight. And I choose not to be subject to *you,* ever. Now get out of my sight; you're obstructing my view."

"You won't be so saucy once your uncle hears about this," he sputtered, face red with anger.

Ignoring his blustering, Chassy turned her back on him, no longer concerned with anything he might have to say. Moving to the stair rail, she also ignored the gasps of those who had gathered around to eavesdrop. Leaning over the side, she searched the crowd until she again sighted her prey.

"Ah! There you are, you handsome hunk, you." She sighed dreamily as the man paused to speak to an acquaintance. As the two men spoke, he shifted until he was facing the stairs, giving her an unobstructed frontal view.

The man was gorgeous. No male should be built like that, endowed that well… If that bulge behind his pantaloons represented his cock at rest, she couldn't wait to see it in full erection.

Perhaps he follows the current fad and stuffs padding in his small-clothes. Even as the thought crossed her mind, Chastity chuckled, shaking her head. Somehow, observing the fluid shifting of honed muscles as he maneuvered effortlessly across the parquet floor, she just knew there was nothing false or artificial about his athletic body. That bulge was all him—every long, thick inch of it.

Liana had been right, as she usually proved to be. Fate had caught up with her tonight...and what a fate. Forgetful of her audience, she groaned deep in her throat, a gruff, sexy sound she'd never made before. Pressing both hands against her chest, she attempted to contain her thudding heart, her thundering pulse. Mind racing, she blinked drooping lids, striving to clear her racing thoughts.

Just the sight of him energized her, made her see colors where the world had been black and white. Her nose twitched as aromas assailed her—the sweet, cloying miasma of a hundred different battling perfumes almost overwhelmed her. Beneath it all, the scent of him, sharp and green, like new growth in a primal jungle, reached her, driving a spear of lust into her brain.

The knowledge of him thrummed in her blood. Since early girlhood, she had dreamed, had chased an elusive form through fantasy landscapes of recurring nightly visions. At first, they'd been frightening, disturbing, dark and mysterious. Over the years, the dreams had morphed into erotic fantasies that made it easy for her to reject the pale imitations of manhood surrounding her. None of her would-be swains could measure up to her dream lover.

Without having ever met him, she knew this man loved peas, but never touched liver. Knew he kissed divinely, liked his tea cold, and his sex hot and sweaty.

Certainty warred with confusion. How could she know such intimate details about the man, yet not know something as simple as his name? With no effort on his part, this man had already captured her attention. If she weren't extremely careful, he could end up stealing her heart.

Hands shaking, she turned back to her cousin and gripped her wrist, intent on gaining some information about the man. "Ali, quickly, you've got to tell me who that gorgeous man is."

"I don't think I'd better. You're already too starry-eyed over this man. He is dangerous with a capitol D." Alicia leaned away to murmur an absent acknowledgment at some late-arriving guests.

Gnawing her bottom lip, Chastity waited impatiently while the young marchioness completed her hostess duties so she could get back to their conversation. She couldn't help but notice how her cousin dealt with each of her guests, the important ones as well as the not-so-important. Everyone was treated as if they were special.

If one didn't know better, they'd think Alicia loved hostessing. In fact, Chassy knew she abhorred these elaborate social events, but would do anything for her adored and adoring husband, Monty...Montgomery, marquis of Avondale, held political aspirations.

Ali's father, the duke of Eathrington—acting as Chastity's new guardian—had agreed to sign Monty's Indigent Bill if he would allow his wife to host this party. Of course, Monty had agreed, his hopes of political advancement winning over his dislike of his cousin-by-marriage.

As soon as Alicia finished her duty, Chastity spun her around. "All right, now give! Tell me everything you know about that man."

"You know, Chassy, I've always liked you. It isn't your fault that you had to spend the majority of your formative years in the uncivilized wilds of New India with eccentric Uncle Cedric."

"Gee, thanks, cuz."

Ali raised her eyebrow at the sarcastic note in Chassy's voice. "You're welcome. Watching your outlandish behavior, while frightening at times, has been very entertaining. I wouldn't dare behave like you, but I'm actually enjoying this gala. At least, I was until you went ga-ga and your eyes popped over the one man you should never have seen."

"Who is he?" Chassy gritted her teeth. "I swear, Ali, if you don't tell me, I'll go ask him myself."

Alicia shook her head and tsk-tsked at her charge's threat. "I believe you would, too. Very well, then, his name is Darian Acer, second son of the earl of Chesley. He's since been disinherited and is now known as 'Dare-the-devil' Acer— 'Dare' for short."

"Darian..." She tasted it on her tongue. "I like it. It's a strong name, fit for a strong man."

"I wonder how he got in," Alicia mused aloud. "I certainly did not invite him." She faced Chastity and placed both hands on her shoulders, forcing her to pay attention. Dropping her voice to a whisper, she hissed, "Listen to me, Chassy... Dare may be beautiful to behold, but unfortunately, he is not safe. He is *not* the kind of man a woman like you should pursue."

Chassy disengaged herself from her cousin's hold. "A woman like me? Shall I tell you what kind of woman I am, Ali?" A practiced flick of the wrist set her dainty fan in motion, too late, trying to shield her expression. She hoped Ali didn't see the avid gaze she directed toward Darian Acer. "I am the kind of woman who wants Darian Acer."

Humming softly, Chassy twisted her neck and visually followed the gentleman's leisurely progress across the crowded ballroom, watched him saunter about with the unconscious grace of a Bengal tiger.

Women paused and stared when he entered their sphere. Conversations lagged and petered out until he passed by. The feminine attention he garnered didn't surprise her. She'd never seen such luscious eye candy, and she was sure the other women had just as good taste.

"It cannot be. You are the daughter and niece of dukes. He is the disgraced, disinherited son of the earl of Chesley. Since his family threw him out, his behavior has been notorious, and I don't like the way you are blatantly ogling him."

"I shall soon do more than ogle, believe me."

"I feel a sinking sense of impending doom here." Ali clutched at her chest. "I've never seen you so bemused. Are you bewitched? Father will have apoplexy when he catches wind of the excessive interest his wayward niece and affianced ward openly displayed for a man he holds in abhorrence."

"After tonight, your father's sentiments will have no bearing on what I do."

"Posh! He'll never countenance an alliance there, darling."

"You mean *marriage?*"

At her cousin's nod, her lips curled up. She couldn't help it—she laughed. "First of all, I repeat, his desires no longer concern me; and secondly, one does not need to *marry* to enjoy such a magnificent animal! Just *look* at him..." She followed her own advice and returned to doing so. "He is a fine specimen of prime male flesh."

In a day when men wore their locks short and restrained or confined beneath stiff wigs, he allowed his black locks to flow in a wild sweep down over his broad shoulders. No ribbon confined the silky tresses that many women would have clawed eyes out to have as their own. Chassy giggled excitedly, licking her lips at the thought of getting her hands into that sleek, abundant fall of storm-dark hair.

"Shush! Do not even jest like that!" Alicia gasped. She glanced about, hoping no others had heard her cousin's bold comments.

"It is so like you New British to restrict yourselves when it comes to sexual matters."

"That's a bold statement, even for you, cousin. Recall that *you* are also a New Britain noblewoman, and expected to act like one!"

"Pooh! Who was jesting?"

Alicia drew back. "Your attitude makes my heart pound. I feel trouble gathering around like acid thunderclouds. If you continue to refuse to be governed by what you call the 'staid strictures of our shallow society'...I wish I could have gotten my hands around Uncle's irresponsible neck."

"Why? Because I've been raised with all the freedom of a boy-child, allowed to roam free in the jungles of Newer India with the children of servants? Trained to think?"

"That's a start. The unorthodox beliefs you espouse are the direct result of your exotic upbringing. It doesn't help that you openly scoff at society's strictures, constantly courting censure. Your antics are keeping polite society in an uproar."

Chassy raised her eyebrows. "Really, Ali. I cause uproar because I think nothing of flitting neck-and-nothing in Hyde

Park, or of visiting Hookman's library unaccompanied by a maid?"

"Not just those instances, though they were bad enough, but what about when you went into the slum-infested area of Whitechapel to find the home of that little chimneysweep?"

"He was injured cleaning the chimney in my rooms."

"That's the attitude I'm talking about. If you weren't the daughter and niece of a duke and filthy rich in your own right, you would be a social pariah. Instead, you've been deemed an original, and every unattached male of any consequence was courting you before Father announced your betrothal."

"My popularity shall be on the rise again when word spreads that I am once more available."

"I doubt even your unrivaled popularity could withstand the rumor of a romantic association with Darian 'Dare-the-devil' Acer," Alicia cautioned. "Everyone knows he compromised his own brother's fiancée. When she was found increasing, she drowned herself, and the brother—their father's heir—hanged himself two days later. His father publicly accused him at the double funeral, and cast him off when he offered no defense. His poor mother died in a fire less than a week later. Some say she set the blaze herself, driven mad from the loss of her sons. His father had Darian turned away from the church. He wasn't allowed to attend her funeral."

Her voice dropped to an intimate whisper. "Since then, he has become naught but an amoral rakehell, flaunting his sexual excesses in society's face. On top of that, he is poor as a church mouse. It's rumored he has only his winnings at the card tables with which to support himself."

Chastity's fingers closed on her fan until the thin wooden boards threatened to snap. "What did people expect? That he would crawl into a corner and hide? He is not that kind of man!"

"How would you know what kind of man he is?" Alicia demanded, her eyebrows winging high in skeptical inquiry. "You haven't even met him yet, Chassy. Do you claim to be an expert on his innocence or guilt, or on how he would respond in any given situation?"

"I-I just know. I don't believe he is guilty at all," Chastity replied after a moment's startled reflection. "And as for making his acquaintance... There is no time like the present!" Laughing gaily, Chastity gathered up the voluminous drifts of her spangled skirts and sprinted down the wide staircase.

"No, Chastity! Wait!"

She didn't wait; she sped up, easily outdistancing her cousin, who no doubt thought her mad, courting a looming social disaster. Joy spun through her. Feeling light and buoyant, caught up in the excitement of embracing her fate, she raced through the ballroom, her laughter trilling out behind her.

In the widening distance, she heard Alicia's hushed cries as she hurriedly tiptoed after her. Sparing a thought for her poor cousin's fashionably shod feet, she hoped her dogged relative would stop following her before those teetering heels landed her flat on her face. Besides, nothing she could say would stop this reckless tumble into scandal.

Chapter Two

Where the hell are you, Crofton?

Angry and impatient, Dare stopped a waiter and deftly exchanged his empty champagne flute for a full one. He swept the crowded ballroom with a jaded black glare. Lifting his glass, he tossed back the high-priced bubbly, barely tasting it, his disregard an insult to the years spent in perfecting its exquisite bouquet.

His ire grew. Crofton had begged and pleaded until Dare had finally agreed to meet him at the Avondales' party, but he was nowhere in sight, and Dare's legendary temper was in danger of exploding.

Snagging another full glass, Dare gulped its contents down. He hated these debutante events, and never attended. Being here made him antsy, aroused buried memories. He preferred they stay buried.

He curtly refused a fourth flute from a hovering waiter. There wasn't enough champagne in the house to drown out the clamoring voices of the past. He needed something stronger...scotch or a good fuck.

Since an excess of scotch always left him with a headache, he decided on the latter. He swept the room again, this time with a darkly sensual intent to his midnight gaze.

Years of debauchery had honed his senses where women were concerned. His chest rose on a deep inhalation. He could smell the subtle aroma of sexual arousal a room away, even when masked by the strongest perfume. He knew—and played on—the allure his salacious reputation held for these bored women of the upper ten thousand. He had but to wink and the majority of them would fall over themselves climbing into his bed. There was no uncertainty, no longer any delight to the chase or thrill of victory.

What chase? He'd grown weary of their eagerness long ago. Lately, it seemed the ladies' lust outstripped his. Emotionally, he was a deadened husk, and that was just the way he liked it. What did emotions have to do with lust?

Fucking was a matter of hips and lips, friction and heat, cocks and cunts. Contrary to rumor, he didn't accept payment for fucking. He considered the act a mutual scratching. Both parties received what they wanted. He made sure of that. No woman had ever claimed he left her unsatisfied, but once finished, he showered and left. He never slept with the women he'd pleasured, never took them to his quarters.

This place held any number of likely bed-partners and he had no intention of going back to his quarters alone. Let's see...whom would he choose, which lady would partner him tonight? *Lady B—?* No. He'd had her early last year, and while she had been an acceptable toss, he made it a firm rule never to go back for seconds.

Lady S—? Uh-uh. Groverton claimed she was a bed banshee; left teeth marks and scratches all over the man. He preferred his skin intact, thank you. Young *Lady C—?* Hell, no! The chit had "marriage mart" written all over her. Marriage! Ugh! It was enough to make a man's cock wilt.

"Dare! Glad you could make it!" A boisterous greeting accompanied the hearty slap to his shoulder.

Darian abandoned the amusing pastime of choosing tonight's lover to glower at his erstwhile friend and secret brother. "Where the hell else would I be, seeing as you badgered a promise of attendance out of me?"

Chezann Crofton, earl of Rotham—C.C. to his friends— grinned. Smiling, he looked too innocent to be friends with the notorious Dare Acer. His dark morning-glory-blue eyes and his fair complexion were a gift from his mother. So was the thick blond hair, gleaming with highlights of platinum, that tumbled over his high brow and cascaded down his shoulders to be caught back in a thin black leather ribbon. But the chiseled profile, the cleft chin, the full, perfectly curved lips were the genetic legacy of his publicly sanctimonious father, the earl of Chesley. Even his height and muscular physique was a match for Dare's, and those with discerning eyes easily saw the familial resemblance. Chezann was a golden, angelic copy of the darkly demonic Dare.

People who knew him—like his brother and their cronies— knew his looks were deceiving. Dare wondered for the hundredth time how they had come to be so close.

The unacknowledged son of his adulterous mother's noble lover, Chezann had been raised as another man's heir, with all the trappings of wealth and position that came with the lie. Upon his beloved stepfather's death, he had used that wealth and social power to implement his long-awaited revenge. His first act had been to put his mother out of his family seat and cut her allowance to a bare minimum. Further, he barred her from ever stepping foot in any of his numerous dwellings, with the threat of cutting her funds totally. His next move had been to befriend his disgraced half-brother to annoy and toy with his "natural" father.

At twenty-seven, C.C. was as profligate as his elder half-brother, if not more so. He trusted few, especially the fairer sex, and callously used his spectacular looks to practice his amorous wiles.

"All right, C.C. Why am I here?" Dare asked, his low voice an irritated growl.

"I want you to meet a young lady," his brother replied, glancing about the room almost nervously.

"Dammit, C.C.!" Dare's thick brows came down over his glittering eyes. "Tell me you didn't have me cooling my heels for over an hour to meet a debutante."

"Not just any debutante, Dare," C.C. protested. "Wait till you meet her. I tell you, she is nothing like the usual fare. This woman has spirit! Imagination! Verve!" His eyes lit up when he spied Chastity already coming toward him. "She's making her way over here! I swear to you, Dare, this might be the woman I could give up all the others for!"

"I take it you haven't fucked her yet," Dare quipped, sure his brother's unusual enthusiasm was merely a case of sexual anticipation and frustration.

Chezann drew himself up to his full, impressive height. His narrowed eyes bored into his brother's. "It is not what you are thinking, and I will thank you not to speak of her like that." His low voice carried a cold warning.

Dare was taken aback by C.C.'s vehemence. "I suppose I must see this paragon," he said, the playfulness falling away, "if you are serious about her." C.C. was the only person left in his life he held in affection. "As your elder brother, I must determine if she is worthy of you. Do you mean to offer for her?"

The question gave the younger man pause. "I-I haven't gotten that far yet," he stammered, throwing out his hands. "But I do like her…a lot. Please, just keep an open mind."

"You know how I feel about debutantes and their infernal search for husbands," Dare reminded his smitten companion. "However, as you ask it of me, I will…attempt to be civil."

"That is all I ask." C.C. grabbed Dare's sleeve. "Here she is! Chastity, allow me to introduce Darien Acer, my bro…er…ah…my best friend. Dare, Lady Chastity Tilson, 'Chassy' to her friends."

Dare turned to greet his brother's new interest and time stopped. The world went away. At six feet, six inches, Dare was used to feeling like a giant around the ladies, but this goddess's autumn-highlighted curls didn't even clear his shoulders. He would have to bend far to meet her moist pink lips. Better to lift her up to him.

He closed his eyes and saw her still. Saw her held against his bedroom wall while he pushed his thick erection into her small, tight sheath. He could almost feel the kiss he shared with her in this waking dream, taste the sweetness of her lips, savor the slickness of her pink little tongue…

He opened his eyes and she was there, staring back at him with a boldness that said she knew where his mind had gone. She was a concerto in fall colors—rich brown hair, brown eyes. But what browns! Streaks of gold glinted among the dark mahogany strands. Her eyes sparkled, the lightest brown swirled with darker specks of…gold? Cinnamon? They were alive with humor and sexual awareness.

"Chastity," he croaked. "What misguided fool named you so inadequately? You should be called Persephone…Aphrodite!"

The vision smiled, revealing a deep-seated dimple in her left cheek. "I am pleased to meet you at long last, sir," she said, extending a gloved hand. "Aphrodite? Wasn't she the goddess of love?"

"She was…and Persephone was a golden-eyed goddess beautiful enough to tempt the lord of the dead."

He took her hand and held it for an inappropriate length of time, noting she made no protest. Turning her hand palm up, he deliberately brushed an openmouthed kiss on the exposed skin of her wrist above her glove, tasting her with the tip of his tongue. Smiling against her skin, he felt her gasp, felt the involuntary press of her hand against the caressing movement of his lips.

"But you said…'At long last.' My lady…?" he queried, unable to tear his eyes from her speaking gaze.

"I despaired of ever finding you," she informed him, her words coming low and airy, as if she could not catch her breath. Beneath the veil of her evening gown, her chest rose and fell, her breasts quivered, and her nipples sharpened against the confines of her tight bodice. "For years, I have seen you in my dreams—"

"Are you sure you do not mean nightmares?" Chezann snapped, anger cracking his voice. His harsh words shocked Dare back into a realization of their surroundings. He lifted his head and met his brother's gaze.

The young earl glared at him, his handsome face sullen with anger at his brother's betrayal. He snarled. "I did not mean her for *you,* Dare!"

"I know, C.C.," Dare answered softly, turning his head to address his brother, but keeping his eyes locked with hers. "Yet, she is...*mine.*" As the words left him, he realized he spoke the truth. His hand tightened on Chastity's slim fingers and felt hers squeeze back in an unconscious statement of reciprocal possession.

"So you *do* make a habit of stealing women?" The soft-voiced taunt was a vicious attack, designed to hurt. It did.

"Oh, Chezann," Chastity cried, "how unworthy of you...and unfair. I warned you. I told you I could not love you."

The young earl had the grace to look shamefaced. "You told me you could love no New Britisher!"

Chastity nodded. "True, but Darian always appeared so dark...I did not know he was New British."

"What is happening here?" Chezann demanded.

"Damned if I know," Dare admitted wryly. Running his left hand through his gleaming tresses, disarranging their ordered fall, he struggled against the tidal wave of desire surging through him for this woman. "C.C., I would not hurt you for the world, but...I cannot back away from this, from her. Not even for you."

Dare's eyes met his brother's, and the look in them caused the earl to suck in a shocked breath. "You bastard, you talk as if you know each other, as if you have a prior claim, yet I *know* you have never met. This is insane!"

"No. This is a miracle," the woman whispered, an enigmatic smile softening the lush lines of her mouth. She turned to

Alicia, who had just come up, and her lips curled in a soft, dreamy smile. "Dare and I are going for a walk in the garden. Don't wait up..."

Chapter Three

Dare led her down the marble steps into the shadowed realm of leaf and flower. He drew her into the heart of the garden where a maze—its walls the dense, interwoven strands of tall bushes trimmed into fantastical shapes—would shield their tryst.

Wandering deep into the interior, they strolled until the sounds of the party faded away, and the crickets' song was heard above the gurgling of a small fountain. She sank down onto a cool stone bench and spread her skirts, demurely covering her slippers.

"Who are you and where are you from, angel?" Dare asked, walking over to her. "I cannot believe I could have missed you had you been here long." He smiled at her. "Besides, you have a faint accent—?"

"I was raised in New India. But that is of no real interest to you," Chastity challenged, turning to him and placing one gloved hand on his arm. "You want to know what my lips feel like...what I taste like."

"Yes!" Dare agreed, dropping down beside her and sweeping her into his embrace. Bending her pliant body backwards, his lips dipped into the hollow of neck and shoulder, skimming the smooth exposed skin. He opened his mouth on her, repeating his earlier caress of tongue against warm flesh.

She flung her head back, arching her breasts into the solid expanse of his chest, offering up the banquet of her body. He eagerly accepted her invitation, heart beating out of sync as he skimmed the tops of her breasts.

With breathless anticipation, he pulled back long enough to tug off her gloves. He wanted to feel her skin-to-skin, and the gloves were a hindrance.

With a sigh, she sank her fingers into the thick, black mass of his vibrant hair and he reciprocated, combing his fingers through her silky strands, glad she'd gone against fashion and worn it down.

"I have felt your phantom lips on mine forever, but you always left me wanting. Let my feel you now. Kiss me...kiss me..." she urged, using her hold to tug his head down to hers.

With a groan of excitement, Dare resisted her, determined to make her wait, make her as hungry as he. Stealing little nips and sips of her flesh, he nibbled his way up the column of her throat, his hands busy at the bodice of her gown. Triumph swelled through him when his hands at last touched warm, pliant flesh, and his fingers opened and closed over the full mounds of her breasts, plumping them, rubbing his thumbs over the rising crests.

A frisson of heat unfurled low in his belly when Chastity moaned with need and growing arousal. Her hand lowered to boldly cup the steely length of his penis, her fingers testing the rampant surge through the sturdy cloth of his pants.

Dare melded their mouths in a fiery kiss, his tongue speaking within the sweet, dark cavity of her mouth. It was an ancient language promising dark delights and endless ecstasies.

Beneath his studied assault, Chastity mewled and moaned and melted, drenching the fingers that had forged their way up the smooth flesh of her thigh to pry open the pouty lips of her sex.

He found her wet and creamy. "Oh, gods!" he groaned. "You are so responsive!" His praise was muffled against her swollen lips. He swirled a finger high up inside her tight passage. "So drenched and juicy...I want a taste, need to see if you are as sweet as you smell. Will you let me?" he asked, introducing another long finger into her honeyed depths and stirring, stirring.

Chastity squirmed on his hand, her inner muscles spasming on his marauding fingers. "I shall explode!" she warned him, her breath coming faster, harsher. "I feel as if a tumultuous storm is battering me from the inside out."

"No storms yet. This is too sweet to rush."

Dare eased his movements, backed down the pleasure, lengthening it, drawing it out. He eased his fingers out of her and stripped off his coat. Spreading it on the broad bench, he settled her back and went to his knees beside her.

She bit her lip as his hands coasted up her thighs, lifting her skirts. He met her eyes as the material bunched around her waist. Even in the dark he could see the wash of warm color change her face from white to pale pink cream. He stretched up to caress her mouth with his, tongue dipping and sliding along the slick surface behind her lips.

With a rough groan of need, Dare moved back down. His hands went before, pressing against the top of her thighs, widening her legs so he could fit between them. Against the soft, smooth, protected flesh near her womanhood, his face and hands felt rough and clumsy.

Brazen and bold, he opened her, his thumbs pressing the feminine lips apart. Leaning close, he took a deep breath, inhaling the sweet, musky aroma of her feminine scent. "Mhmm, you smell divine—creamy...and hot...and mouthwatering. I can't wait any longer. I have to have a taste..." He bent to her, his mouth hungry and hard against her tender skin.

She moaned, fingers burrowing through his hair to tug at his scalp. He loved the feel of her hands on him, urging him on. He nibbled on the sweet knot of flesh exposed by his unveiling hands, and her hips bucked. Tightening his hands on her, he held her down and fluttered his tongue in her welling juice, thrilling at the liquid proof of her desire.

"You taste delicious, darling. I'm going to slurp you up."

Gasping, Chastity grabbed her skirts, flattened them so she could watch him feasting on her, lapping the length of her weeping opening, taking her tender labia into his mouth.

"Guardian angel-serpents, that feels good!" Her body undulated, unable to hold still under his ministrations. She eased herself back on her elbows, bringing her legs up to clasp his head between her knees.

The sweet smell of her aroused flesh drove Dare beyond control. Hands palming her bottom, he lifted her hips, brought her to his mouth, and thrust his tongue deep into her churning passage.

A groan welled up in Chassy's throat, the sound rising like pleasurable agony. The vibration of her extremity rumbled in his chest, and he attempted to devour her, to drown her in sensation. He tongued and bit and drew and nibbled until she writhed beneath him, whimpering as she fell into a grinding completion.

He felt the explosions under her skin tightening her tendons and bowing her back. Her belly muscles rippled and she screamed her release, falling boneless beneath his ministrations.

Reluctantly, he dropped one more kiss on her quivering pussy before moving up to cover her lips with his, cutting off her scream before others could hear and investigate. Leaning his forehead against hers, he drew in several deep breaths, fighting to control the almost overwhelming urge to open his pants and release the huge hard-on throbbing behind the tight cloth.

His earlier need to fuck had transmuted into a need to be within this one woman. His body wanted no other. He greatly feared she'd just ruined him for any other woman.

* * *

"You didn't enjoy that as much as I did," Chastity said when she regained her sanity. "Let me ease you," she offered, placing her small hand on his still rock-hard penis.

Dare captured her hand, held it prisoner against his begging erection. "This is not the time or place." He groaned, clenching his jaw, grinding his teeth at the tight, hot pressure compressing his cock. Her hand around him felt beyond good.

"Much as I would enjoy taking you up on your generous offer," he whispered with a wry smile, wishing he dared take advantage of her willingness, "we've been gone too long. I'm surprised some chaperone hasn't already come looking for you."

Unable to believe he'd actually refused the chance to have his cock sucked, he shook his head while he eased Chastity's skirts down, assisted her in righting herself, and helped her to her feet. And was there to catch her when her legs gave way, his strong arms supporting her slight figure.

With a shaky laugh, Chastity clung to him. "See how you make my knees weak?" she teased, trailing a hand down his chest to his groin and giving his penis a generous squeeze. "You were miraculous. Thank you."

Groaning, Dare took her rounded derriere in both hands and pressed her into his jutting hardness, trapping her hand between them. He took her mouth in a desperate kiss that swept them both into a dark, climactic paradise. He felt her shiver, felt her melting, reforming around his jutting hard-on. He felt her in his soul. "I want you...need you..."

She gasped into his mouth. "I want you, too...so much!"

"Come to me soon! Tonight," he demanded.

"How and where?"

"Come to my rooms. I'll make the arrangements. Will you come?"

Chastity leaned against him and gave a shaky laugh. "I already *have* and no doubt I shall again!"

His laughter joined hers. Entranced with her, bewitched by her, he was amazed at how she lifted his dark spirits. Simply by existing, she had changed his beliefs about debutantes and marriage in less than an hour's time. She was right. It *was* miraculous. *She* was miraculous! "Chastity—"

She placed a hand over his lips. "Call me Chassy."

"Chassy...Aphrodite...Persephone...my goddess! May I ask you an important question?"

Chastity's eyes lit up. "Before you ask, will you permit me to ask something?"

"Of course, my dear, whatever you wish." Dare smiled reassuringly. She had probably heard the rumors about him. He had never before attempted to defend himself. His pride hadn't allowed it. But for her, he would put the old stories to rest. And he could assure her she needn't worry he would continue to keep mistresses after their marriage. With her generous and passionate responses, she'd convinced him her erotic fire would supply all the warmth he would ever need.

Chastity eased out of Dare's arms. "I've heard the rumors about your brother and his fiancée—"

Ah, just as I thought. He reluctantly let her go. "I can expla—"

She held up a restraining hand when Dare made to interrupt. "I do not believe a word of that silly story." Her brisk, matter-of-fact words convinced him of her sincerity. Before he could thank her for the gift of her trust, she continued.

"I know about your resulting financial situation. I'm an heiress. I can make things easier for you, if you'd let me."

Taking a deep breath, she clasped her hands in front of her. "The solution to your dilemma is simple. All you have to do is accept my offer of carte blanche."

Chapter Four

Body still so sensitive that her clinging nightgown was an irritant, Chassy flopped on her bed, fulminating thoughts running through her head. She was too heated and sexually frustrated to sleep, too angry at Dare for leaving her like this. How could he refuse her? How could he leave her aching and hurting like this?

With a disgruntled sigh, she rolled over and onto her feet. Tossing off the nightgown, she went to the window and pushed the casing wide, letting the night breeze in to caress her hot skin. It didn't help.

She'd hoped for something more exciting, but she would make do with her own hands. She'd learned to masturbate at an early age, driven by the erotic dreams of a phantom lover who touched her with hands of fire. There were times when she burned, melted from the scorching heat of lust. Sometimes, the weather itself seemed to goad her into recklessness. Lying back on the bed, her hands moved in tandem with her memories...

In New India, during the seasonal heat, the land sweltered under the two suns of Paradyse. The damp, clammy air pressed close and heavy against her skin. At such times, she took to her room. Stripping off her clothes, she'd sluice her skin with the cool, room-tempered water in her washing basin.

The water always felt silky and slick running over her heated flesh, cooling her and heating her at the same time. Hands cupped, she would lift her bounty above her head and allow the coolness to flow down her face and over her shoulders. Each shining drop glistened in the afternoon lights, lending the sheen of diamonds to her skin.

After she'd rubbed the silken moisture into her thirsty skin, she would bring the basin to her bedside and again dip her hands in the basin. Lying back, she'd spread her legs and bring her dripping fingers to the hottest, aching part of her. Fingers swirling, she would dip and rub, dip and rub, working the cool into her tight folds until the heat swallowed up the coolness. Liquid met liquid, and she smoothed the slippery fluid over the small knot of nerves that rested at the apex of her thighs.

Languid minutes would pass as she pleasured herself, rising on a drifting cloud of sensation that threatened to dump her into a cauldron of boiling delight. Fighting for breath, she would bring her knees up, hugging her hand between her thighs as she stroked and stroked, fingers slipping in the wet delta of her sex. Hips responding to the cadence of her pistoning hand, she lifted into her circling movements, melting as the summer heat invaded the room, crawled under her skin.

When her breasts swelled and nipples tightened, she lifted her hands to the pouty tips and twisted. Sharp spikes of sensation burned through her veins, connected the diamond-hard tips of her breasts with the pulsing core of her clit. When

*the crisis came, she crested with a smothered scream, her balled
fist stuffed in her mouth.*

Her climax blasted through the memories. Shivering in the
aftermath of her climax, she pulled her drenched fingers from
her pussy and brought them to her lips. Rolling onto her belly,
she drew the covers up over her head, buried her face in her
pillows, and wept.

Dare had ruined her body for anyone but him. Her orgasm
had been nothing close to the one he'd given her in the garden.
When she came for him, she'd screamed aloud, the sensations so
overwhelming she hadn't cared who heard or even saw.

Chastity blinked her tears away. Body still aching, nipples
still stiff and full, she firmed her jaw. There was only one thing
she could do. She'd present her offer once more. This time, she
wasn't going to take no for an answer.

Chapter Five

"You did *what?*" Alicia fell back against the mound of pillows, her cup of chocolate wobbling in her hand.

Chassy sighed. "I tell you, I thought the man would drop dead from a stroke, he grew so angry. I never suspected he'd have such tender sensibilities." She shook her head. "I don't understand what I said to anger him so. Don't all men want the freedom of sex without the ball and chain of marriage?"

"Surprisingly, not all do. I know a large number of men who revel in the married state. Once they get past the hurdle of the actual proposal, they settle down quite nicely."

"He hadn't proposed. In fact, he asked me to come to his rooms so we could finish what we started."

"Well, technically, he couldn't honorably ask you to marry him when you hadn't officially broken your betrothal with Bernard."

Chastity went over to the chocolate pot and poured herself a cup of her cousin's favorite brew. Snagging a handful of scones, she walked over to where Alicia was lying. "Scoot over."

Alicia drew her legs up and made room for Chassy at the foot of the bed. "Don't keep me in the dark; what else happened?"

"First, let's get back to what you just said. You know...that statement about how Dare is honorable? Is this the same guy you were warning me about last night, the guy who is supposed to be bad for me, a social pariah?"

The marchioness fluffed her pillows and threw herself back on them. "Everything I said is true. He's all of that and then some. I think it's worse that he can exhibit honor at times and still act so dishonorably when it suits him. Now give...tell me what he did after you dropped that bomb."

Chassy took a sip of her chocolate. She kept her head down when she answered. "He turned me down. Flat. For a moment, I thought he would hit me. Then he left. That's when I came back into the ballroom and made my public 'hell-no-I-won't-go' speech to Bernard. He took it well, by the way, don't you think?"

Alicia smirked. "As well as one of Father's lapdogs could take it, knowing he'll have to give the great man bad news." She sat up. "All kidding aside, Dare is a dangerous man. Angering him like you said you did could have seriously scary repercussions."

"He should be worrying about the repercussions I'm planning," Chassy hissed. "Do you know how much it hurts to be left primed and ready, and then have the man walk off in a huff?"

"If Monty did that to me, he'd be sleeping in the nursery for a month!"

They laughed together.

When they subsided, Ali asked, "So what are you going to do now?"

"Make him change his mind, of course. I don't want to be a virgin anymore, but since I met him, I don't want anyone else to be my first. It has to be him."

"You're in love with him."

She stiffened in her seat. "I am not! I'm in lust with him, yes, but not the other 'L' word."

"I think you're lying to yourself, cuz. I've never seen you like you were last night."

Chastity stood up and placed her empty cup back on the tray with a little snap of her wrist. "When are you getting up? I want to go shopping."

"I'm still sleepy. Monty kept me up late last night, celebrating Father's name on his petition. His spirits were...shall we say...very elevated!" She brought a hand up to cover her giggles.

"I really don't want to hear about you hitting the jackpot when I crapped out. Get your lazy butt up and out of that bed and get dressed."

Alicia threw her covers back and swung her legs out of the bed. "You are such a tyrant. I'll go, but I get to drive the flitter this time."

"'Oh, hell, no,' she said to the kamikaze flitter pilot. The last time you were at the controls, we were ticketed seven times."

"Monty fixed them."

"In seven minutes."

"No one told me they had changed the speed limits there."

Chassy raised her eyebrows. "They didn't, Ali. They've been subsonic since the landing."

"What can I say? I like to go fast."

"What can I say? You're not driving!"

Ali pouted while she signaled for her maid. "You are such a flathead when it's anyone else but you acting up."

"News flash! I may 'act up,' but I never endanger anyone by my actions. You can't say that about your driving techniques. Get your bath, dress, and hurry up, or I'll leave without you."

Ali paused on her way to the bathing room. "And I want to go with you... *why?*"

Chassy poked out her tongue. "Because I'm going to flit around 'til I find Dare's hangout, and your nosy ass will miss all the action."

With a laugh, Ali skipped into the disrobing room. "I'll be out in ten minutes. Don't dare leave without me."

Chassy kept the smile on her face until the door closed behind Alicia. When she heard the snick, she sank down on the side of the bed and buried her head in her hands.

Ali thought they were going to find Dare so she could proposition him again, pressure him into an affair he'd already said he didn't want; but she needed to find Dare and apologize, to ask him if they could start over again. Her mind shied away from the memory of how badly it had hurt when he'd turned her offer down.

Pain had flashed throughout her system, burning along her nerves like carbolic-acid-etched steel. The scary part had been realizing her pain had very little to do with still being horny as a celebeast in heat, and more to do with fearing he was walking out of her life before he'd walked into it.

Why did she only remember what Liana said when it was too late?

* * *

The men rushed into the apartment, Dare shooing away the last of the persistent angel-serpents that clung, fluttered, cooed, and groomed him every chance they got. Going outside in the daylight hours always ended this way. Thank the gods the angel-serpents weren't nocturnal beasties—he'd have no social life at all.

"Damned persistent things won't leave me alone."

"You aren't aggressive enough with them." His brother never took his eyes from the flash of iridescent colors. No one could ignore the beautiful, winged, snakelike creatures. Their presence drew fascinated stares and wishful thoughts of being accepted as a companion. In all of Landing history, no one had ever drawn a cloud of them the way Dare did.

"They know you don't mean it when you shoo them away."

"Oh, I mean it, all right. I just have no intention of accidentally angering one and dying a quick, horribly painful death."

C.C. picked up the decanter of bourbon before glancing over his shoulder. "I don't think you have to worry about that. Those serpents are highly protective of you. I've never seen the like. In fact, if we went according to legend, you couldn't possibly be guilty of anything, because the angel-serpents only flock to those they've judged pure in heart."

Dare snorted, amusement lighting his countenance. "I wasn't feeling very pure in heart last night, I'll tell you. After being propositioned by the woman I planned to make my wife, being pure was the last thing on my mind. I wanted to fuck her to within an inch of her life and then beat that last inch out of her."

Chezann's eyebrows twitched together. He tilted his head to the side and studied his elder sibling, a confused glint in his eyes. "You never came back into the house. I saw Chassy, and she looked like she'd been run over by an out-of-control celebeast. I wanted to ask her what happened, but when I got close enough for conversation, I saw her eyes..."

Dare jerked around to glare at his brother, quick panic running up his spine and jangling along his nerve endings. "What was wrong with her eyes?"

"They were lifeless. Dead. She looked traumatized." C.C.'s voice held censure and disapproval. He flopped down on the long settee in the drawing room. "She didn't deserve whatever it was you did to her. I didn't defer my interest in her for you to mistreat her."

"Mistreat her? Mistreat *her?* Hell, I was ready to offer her marriage, and she offered *me* carte blanche!"

After a moment of shocked silence, C.C. threw himself back on the settee, convulsed with laughter. "You've got to be kidding! She really offered you carte blanche? Oh, to have been a fly on the wall—"

"She really did," Dare snapped, his words clipped and surly. He still couldn't believe it. He had found the woman of his dreams, and all she had been thinking of was turning him into her gigolo!

"Well, what were the terms?" Dare's younger brother could hardly get the query out without choking on his giggles. "I mean...was it a generous offer?"

"You find this funny, Chezann?"

C.C. sobered at the warning chill radiating from his elder brother. Dare only called him by his full name when he was beyond irked at him. But he could only maintain his sober mien for a moment before his grin broke out again.

"Well, yeah, but I can see you don't." Laughter erupted, and it took several tries to get his words out. "But you should, Darian, you really should," he gasped. "The situation is hilarious!"

"You think so?"

"Look at it from anyone's point of view but your own. The most notorious lady's man of New Britain falls in love for the first time, and, before he can propose marriage, is propositioned as a mistress."

Dare's empty tumbler sailed past C.C.'s head to shatter against the far wall. Teeth clenched against renewed pain, he stalked over to his brother. "We connected last night. Even you had to have seen it. It wasn't a figment of my imagination. Was it?"

"No, you didn't imagine it. I've never seen anything like it."

"Thank you for that." Dare clasped C.C. on the shoulder, gave a squeeze. "Anyway, when I saw her, everything clicked, fell into place. For the first time in a long time, my life felt right. You know, these last eight years people have clothed me in guilt until my innocence felt like an ill-fitting coat. No one believed it belonged to me."

No longer able to sit still or talk calmly without *moving,* Dare began to pace off the confines of the studio. "She took one look at me and saw straight to my soul. She *knew* I was innocent. Do you know what that meant to me? How it cleansed me?"

Dare inhaled and held the breath for a long time, then let it out slow and easy. His voice dropped. "Do you have any idea how I've felt all these years, knowing women spread their legs for me not because they think me innocent but because they believe I'm guilty? They fuck me for the nasty thrill of trysting with a murderer, a deceiver, a man with no honor or brotherly love. Society thinks I whore for money and labels me a gigolo. I used to deny the term, but what else do you call a man who allows himself to be used like that?"

"I call him brother."

Dare turned and looked at the only one who had expressed faith in him during the last eight years. His face relaxed and his lips quirked in a soft smile. "You saved my life, you know. I was at the lowest point when you came to me—ready to put a gun to my head and pull the trigger."

Chezann nodded at him as he rose and went to the bar. He poured them both another drink. "I kinda thought that might be the case when I approached you. I wasn't sure you'd allow me to help you."

Dare sighed and thankfully accepted the tumbler of golden liquor. "You offered me something inestimable that night. Your trust gave me back the love of a brother."

"I have never felt cheated. Over the years, you've returned whatever I gave a hundredfold."

Dare held up his glass and gazed into the amber depths. "You know what she did to me, to *us?*" He didn't wait for an answer.

"She took what was growing between us, took something fragile, sacred, and fine and turned it into something crude and sordid. While I was dreaming up ways to offer her love, honor, and fidelity, she was busy mapping out terms for a tawdry affair.

"For being ready to service her whenever she feels the need, I will have a fashionable townhouse fully furnished and staffed; a monthly allowance of three thousand pounds; and in addition, she will pay off all my outstanding debts. Oh, I forgot to mention she is a virgin," he snarled. "If I *initiate* her without pain, the monthly stipend doubles."

Chezann's laughter dried up. His eyes widened at the insult Chastity had served Dare. As he watched his older brother storm about his bachelor digs, his stance grew wary and cautious. "I'm glad she refused my suit," he admitted. "I don't think even *I* am up to handling a situation like this. Since I haven't heard any uproar, may I assume you hid the body?"

"I haven't killed her…yet!" Dare growled, angry again after verbalizing the chit's boldfaced terms. "I'm more tempted to whip her curvy ass. That wild little tumbleweed has gotten her way far too long. She needs trimming back."

"So what do you plan to do about it?"

Dare came to an abrupt halt, a smile widening his mobile lips, his eyes narrowing with some wicked intent. "I believe I shall accept Chastity's offer. In the meantime, I'll teach the forward little baggage the difference between being a wife and a mistress. Only after she admits the error of her ways will I marry her!"

"There's only one problem with that scenario, brother."

"What's that?"

Amid uncontrollable laughter, C.C. got out, *"You're* the mistress."

Chapter Six

The flitter hovered over the entrance of Hookman's Lending Book Store. Inside the leftover technology of a dead world, Chastity and Alicia scanned the crowd, trying to decide where they should begin their search.

"I will never understand why the Touchdowns decided to pattern this world after Regency Britain. I mean, what was the point? Look at us. We might have been thinking to go back to a better time, a gentler time, but we brought their troubles with us."

Alicia looked confused. "I don't understand what you're saying. Our society is stable and—"

Chastity turned a disbelieving gaze on her cousin. "Do you ever listen to yourself? Who was the one who took me to task last night about visiting the *slum-infested* portion of Whitechapel?" She threw up her hands. "Ali, we have the super rich exploiting the super poor. Eventually, if something isn't done, we'll have the same upheavals that tore apart the original society."

"But what can we do about it? We are only two women...how can we expect to change the world?"

Chassy looked grim. "We do it one step at a time. And we can teach our children to do the same. We have a responsibility to the underprivileged in our society. If we abandon them to their despair, we will be guilty of suicide, for our neglect will bring about our ruination."

"Good galaxies, Chassy, I can't wrap my mind around all this gloom and doom you are spouting. Today is too beautiful to spend it speculating on a dreary future that might not even happen. I thought we were supposed to be finding your boyfriend."

"Dare is far from being a boy. There's not a man in New Britain that can hold a candle to him."

"There!" Ali shook her finger at her cousin. "That sentiment is probably why Monty can't stand you. You're quick to point out his shortcomings."

"Hey, what does he care what I think? As long as you can't see his shortcomings, that's all that should concern him."

"Chassy, isn't that Chezann?" Ali tapped the onboard visual screen. It showed a figure walking away from Hookman's.

"Yeah, that looks like him."

"If we can find where he's going, he might lead us to Acer. He can usually be found in his company. But we can't just walk up to him in the street. We'll go to Hookman's and do some discreet snooping."

At the thought of seeing Dare again, Chassy's heart thumped once and then settled back into a slightly faster beat. Her tummy felt hollow and cold. She pressed a hand to her middle, trying to contain the fluttery sensations beating there. "Yes, let's go find Dare. I have many things to say to him."

They exited the craft after setting the control for it to remain aloft and ready for reboarding upon their return. The ramp retracted when they reached the bottom, sliding soundlessly back into the skin of the ship.

The proprietor of Hookman's greeted them at the door, ushering the two women into his establishment with a lot of toadying and scraping. "Ladies, welcome, welcome to my humble shop. Allow me to serve you some tea while you browse our selection. You will find we stock the latest journals and novels. We even have a large section of romantic tales on the back wall."

The cousins exchanged an amused look, the need for words between them erased due to their practice of communicating with a glance or a raised eyebrow.

Once the manager seated Alicia, Chassy accepted the chair held out for her. Leisurely removing her gloves, she tucked them in her reticule before picking up the cup of steaming tea and plunking two cubes of sugar into the fragrant mixture. "We are seeking Lord Rotham. Has he been here today?"

The man wrung his hands, a nervous motion noted by both cousins. "The earl is a great reader. He was here earlier, as he is most days. However, I fear you've missed him. He left shortly before your own arrival."

"What a pity," Chassy purred, sipping her weak tea. "We were desirous of meeting with him." She unobtrusively slid a large-denomination pound note under her saucer, leaving the corner exposed.

"Perhaps one of your servers overheard his direction and can inform us of the next stop on today's travels?" Her fingers played with the bill, edged it closer toward the man.

The proprietor's eyes grew large and avid with lust for the money. She could almost see the wheels turning as he tried to figure out a way he could earn that amount of cash. "I will ask around right now. If anyone recalls something, you may be sure I will return and inform you immediately."

"Thank you," Chassy murmured.

"So kind..." Once the manager left, Ali sat back and sipped at her tea. "Well, so much for that. What shall we do while we wait?"

"Lady Chastity Tilson?"

Chastity looked up with a smile. A woman stood over her. She looked familiar. The smile left Chassy's lips while she tried to recall where she'd seen her before. *Oh, heck, the short, chubby woman from last night...what was her name, again?* "Yes, I am Lady Chastity. Lady...er...ah...?"

Ali came to her rescue. Rising, she dropped a perfunctory curtsey and extended her hand in greeting. "Why, Your Grace, how lovely to see you. How are you this afternoon?"

Oh, right! Chassy recalled now. She was the pleasant-natured duchess with the rude husband. Pettibone, hadn't it been?

"Please, Lady Avondale, call me Lucynda." The sweet-faced woman turned her head and her soft green eyes hardened as she focused her attention on Chastity. "I had hoped to receive an early morning visit from you, my dear." Her voice chilled. "I knew your father...well."

Chastity's mind sprang to attention. This was the second time this woman had alluded to a meeting between them. What could she possibly have to discuss with her? Unless...*perhaps...?* No!

On the face of it, it didn't seem possible that the mild-mannered, pudgy duchess of Pettibone might have information—or somehow be involved with—the person or persons unknown who had tried to kill Chassy's father. What else could she conclude, though?

"How well did you know my father?"

"Very well. We were...childhood sweethearts. I wanted the opportunity to, well...reminisce with you."

Cold spread through Chassy as she looked at this small, nondescript, grandmotherly woman and wondered if she'd been the force behind the blow that brought her father low. She fought to maintain her composure.

...this is not the place to let others see your pain...

The grand duke's words of last night echoed in her mind, gave her the strength to hold on to her control.

"Forgive me, madam. The wound is too new. I am barely out of mourning."

"I understand, my dear." She patted Chassy's arm. "Take your time coming to me, but remember that every day, the time grows shorter."

Chassy exchanged a shocked glance with Ali as the little duchess glided away.

"Your jaw is sagging." Ali couldn't keep the smirk off her face.

Chassy didn't respond, too busy trying to unravel the mysterious pronouncements Lucynda Pettibone seemed so fond of spouting.

She locked gazes with Alicia. "What was *that* about? Take my time, but time grows short?"

Ali shrugged. "Very strange mumblings, if you ask me. I feel like the patron who comes to the play in the middle of the act, incapable of catching up with the action or making any sense of the plot."

Chassy snorted. "You *did* notice she didn't give me a choice about coming, only a choice of when I came."

"And are you planning to go?"

"Oh, I really think I might." Chassy brought her cup to her lips and took a long drink. She didn't set the cup down until she'd drained it. "Let's get back to the flitter. I'd like to—"

"My ladies," the proprietor interrupted, "one of my waitresses overheard Lord Rotham saying he would be stopping over to spend some time at the Landing Museum. If you like, I can send a servant after him."

"That won't be necessary, thank you." Chassy stood and tugged her gloves back on. "The museum is a neutral place where we can accidentally bump into Lord Rotham. Your assistance will not be needed."

The man's whole posture fell. Chassy hid a smile. She'd forgotten the money she'd offered as incentive for his help. "The tea was quite delicious." She gestured toward the bill still sticking out from under the edge of her plate. "Please accept this token of our appreciation."

Stammering a grateful "Thank you, madam!" the proprietor whisked the plates, saucers, and cups off the table and wiped the top down. When he finished, the money had disappeared.

Chapter Seven

"Why, Lord Rotham, fancy meeting you here! I hope we are not intruding upon your contemplation of the antiquities housed here."

A wry smile widened C.C.'s mouth as he bowed over Alicia's outstretched hand. "Good afternoon, Lady Avondale. The intrusion of beautiful women is always a pleasure. Chassy…" He bowed again, deeper.

"C.C."

She smiled at him, but it didn't reach her eyes. It hurt to see her bright beauty. Hurt to know she would never love him or shine for him, never light up from inside at the sight of his face. Not like she'd lit up for Darian the night before. The light in her eyes had been like a thousand incandescent candles, hot and vibrant and burning with lust and something deeper.

"How may I be of service to you, ladies?"

Chassy cleared her throat. "Dare."

C.C. lowered his eyelids, hiding the resentment he knew would be visible if he met her gaze right now. When he opened them again, he caught the cousins exchanging a speaking glance.

"You want Darian." His voice sounded gruff even to his own ears.

"To know his direction, yes," Chassy whispered.

"You want Darian." He repeated his statement, his voice grown hard and implacable. She would admit the truth to both of them, all three of them, if she would have his help.

"Yes." She met his gaze, her brown eyes direct and clear, and no shadows of deceit darkening the smooth surface. "I want Darian."

The lights turned on within her, almost blinding him with her need.

"I will take you to him. But first we will escort Lady Avondale home."

*   *   *

"C.C., why did you insist on Alicia going home?"

He didn't respond for a long time. She was about to ask again when he sighed, then tugged on the reins to turn and slow the celebeast-drawn carriage. He pulled over to the side of the busy street and came to a complete halt.

Turning toward her, he propped an elbow on his knee and cocked his head. "You want the truth?"

"Please and always."

"I didn't think you needed an audience when you met with Dare. I don't know what you told Lady Stanton, but you and I know you aren't going to be taking afternoon tea with my brother."

Shock roared through her. Ignoring his sarcasm, she latched onto the one item of information she never would have expected. "Darian Acer is your *brother?*"

C.C. shifted impatiently. "Oh, for goodness' sake, Chassy, how could you not know? Open your eyes and really *see*. I thought you were more observant than most. You certainly stared at him enough last night to memorize his features."

She blinked. When she looked again, she saw Dare in C.C.'s long limbs and bone structure. The broad forehead and strong jaw, the length of arms and legs, even the shape of the eyes, though the color was different.

One hand covered her mouth. "Oh, my god!"

"No, our father."

She couldn't stop gazing at him, searching for and finding more similarities. "Who else knows?"

He ticked them off on each finger. "Let's see…our mutual father, my mother and deceased father, and most assuredly Dare's mother, the poor thing."

Curiosity swamped her. "Darian is the elder?"

"Between us, yes. I am the younger indiscretion, the unadmitted sin. Darian and his other brother were the classic example of the heir and the spare. Darian was the spare. Only, it wasn't Dare's mother who wandered after the spare was secured, but our lordly father." The sneer in his voice clashed with the playboyish aspect he usually projected.

She nodded her understanding. In most good families, the partners married dynastically. Love rarely came into the equation. After the wife gave her husband two sons, the unspoken tradition allowed her to seek love elsewhere. Her mother and father—well, her mother, anyway—had suffered through the same type of marriage. Society never held the husband to the same standards.

"I don't know what to say."

"Congratulate us. We have wrested victory from the defeat and ignominy heaped upon us by a common enemy."

A half-smile stretched her lips. "Congratulations."

C.C. nodded and flicked the ribbons over the celebeasts' backs, setting them back in motion. "I hear congratulations are in order for you, also."

She bowed her head, finding it hard to meet his eyes. "What do you mean?"

"I hear you are in the market to acquire a new mistress."

Her face flamed. "He told you."

"*Yelled* is more like it." The laugh that rumbled in his chest held no amusement. "I've never seen him angrier. Or more hurt."

The heat of embarrassment burned so hotly her flesh felt inflamed. His eyes when they met hers were a hard, clear blue, fanning the heat to a higher blaze. "You don't approve of my offer to him, do you?"

"I don't approve of you hurting my brother. You are hard on a man's heart, Chastity. I find myself grateful you did not choose me."

Chassy gasped. "You're being mean, C.C."

"You're right. That was unworthy of me, milady. My apologies."

Her heart sank. "Oh, C.C., I don't want to lose your friendship over this."

"We're here." He pulled up on the reins, bringing the carriage to a halt. He jumped down and came around to help her down from her high perch.

He looked too much like Dare. And though he was not his brother, being rejected by him was like taking a knife in the chest. Panic choked her, froze her forward momentum, and scattered her resolve. "I can't do this. Take me home. Take me back."

His hands were on her shoulders, shaking her. "Calm down! Listen, Chassy. Listen to me. My brother cares for you. In all the years we've known each other, he's never refused me anything, but last night he refused to back away from you, knowing how much I wanted you for myself."

He released her and stepped back. A gamin smile lit his handsome face. "So I sulked a bit. What can I say?" He splayed his open hands, lifted his shoulders in a rueful shrug. "I'm used to getting my way, but you haven't lost my friendship, and you won't."

She hugged him tight. "Thank you. You cannot know how much I appreciate that. You're about the only man I know who doesn't expect me to simper and bat my eyelashes like the usual run of silly debutantes. You don't belittle me for trying to better myself."

Chezann laughed low and shook his head. "If I am such a paragon, how can you not love me?"

She placed a gentle hand on his cheek and he rolled his head into the palm of her hand, pressing against her skin. "I do love you, C.C. I just don't lust after you. One day—"

He raised a cautioning hand. "Please don't tell me some day I'll find a woman who will love me as I deserve. I couldn't stand that right now. Just make me one promise."

"Anything."

"If this thing between you and Dare doesn't work out, don't overlook me as a possible replacement."

Chassy closed her eyes and thought about that, thought about missing Dare, needing him, and finding his phantom echo in the lines of Chezann's lithe body. Her soul rebelled against the notion, knowing it would kill her as surely as a knife through the heart. She raised a hand and rubbed the skin between her breasts, feeling the ache on a spiritual plane.

She wasn't aware of shaking her head so frantically her hair broke loose from its moorings and tumbled about her shoulders. Cognizance came back when C.C. rocked her against him, a hand smoothing from shoulder to waist and returning in a calming pattern.

"Bad idea, huh?"

She shuddered, buried herself closer for a moment as she fought to regain her equilibrium. Her hesitant words, when they came, were forced from a constricted throat. "You are so alike...it would be an abomination." She raised her head and looked at him, courageously meeting his deep blue gaze. "It wouldn't be fair to you. Every day, I'd be cheating you because when I touched you, loved you, I'd be touching Dare, loving Dare. It would make you a substitute...and you're worth more than that."

"I wouldn't care—"

She placed a finger across his lips. "Yes, you would. Eventually, you would. We'd end up hating each other. You'd hate me because I used you. You'd hate yourself for allowing me to do so. I'd hate you because you wouldn't be *him*. And I'd hate myself for hurting my best friend."

C.C. sighed. His chest rose and fell under her head. She could feel the slow, resigned beating of his heart. "Best friend, huh?"

"The best."

He sighed again. His arms squeezed tight for a moment, before he released her and took a step back. "I guess I can live with that."

Chapter Eight

Chastity stood on Dare's doorstep, rubbing her aching knuckles and wondering what had brought her to this state. A small, icy snake of fear curled low in her belly, hissing in warning each time she banged on the door. Bold as she usually acted, she'd surprised even herself by showing up on a man's doorstep in broad daylight, determined to apologize for hurting his feelings, only so she could try to talk him into becoming her personal fuck toy.

She didn't want just anyone. Her reaction to C.C.'s advances had proved to her she only heated up for Dare. And right now, the heat within her threatened to burn her to cinders. It wasn't just about fucking. Not really. She hadn't even done that, yet, so it wasn't as if her entire life revolved around sex.

"Hey, lady, you can knock on my door anytime!"

She whipped around to find a crowd gathering. People passing by eyed her with knowing gazes and sleazy grins. Beginning to feel self-conscious, she shifted, hiding her face, and again beat on Dare's door.

Where was he? Why didn't he answer? C.C. had assured her he was inside, yet she'd knocked twice—to her knuckles' detriment—and had received no response.

Hurt welled up; tears threatened to spill. She gasped as chills rippled across her chest and spread down her arms. A lump of ice formed in the pit of her belly, freezing her all the way to her soul. Was this his way of rejecting her...again? *Please, no!*

"Darian Acer! Darian Acer, you open this door! I'm not going away until I speak to you," she yelled at the top of her voice, banging on the door with both fists, determined to get a response. He wasn't going to get away with ignoring her.

The door opened abruptly and her hands, already in motion, landed against a firm, broad chest. Arms grabbed her and yanked her through the portal. "What the hell are you doing here?" Dare stuck his head out and scanned the street both ways before slamming the door shut. Turning to face her, he leaned against the door, his hands tucked behind his back.

"What were you trying to do...ruin your reputation and blacken mine even further? You know better than to show up at a bachelor's digs without a chaperone." He saw her mouth open and raised his voice, continuing before she could get a word in edgewise. "Chastity, you need spanking. Your behavior is unacceptable."

His displeasure scalded her, hurt in a way her father's frequent scolding never had. Her pain quickly gave way to anger. How dare he pass judgment on her when he was no angel himself? "You didn't find it so last evening, when you begged me to come back with you so I could...presumably...*come* again."

He had the grace to look shamefaced. "Don't remind me. That was your fault—"

"Mine!"

"Yes, yours," he accused. "You had me out of my mind with lust."

Her lip turned up in a fine sneer. "Trust a man to blame the woman in these situations. I suppose I tied you down and had my wicked way with you until I rendered you totally under my control."

Long fingers raked a furrow through thick black hair. "Something along those lines, yes," he mumbled, flicking a guilty glance down at her.

"You lie!" Chassy wagged an accusing digit in his face. Stalking over to him, she stabbed her stiff finger at his chest, emphasizing each point.

"First, if I had been in control, you never would have left me last night. Second, I wouldn't have been standing outside begging for you to let me in. Third, I wouldn't still be a virgin…and a hungry one, at that!"

Dare straightened away from the door and loomed over her. His eyes gleamed with a growing fire, an intimate flame that seared the tips of her stiffening nipples and twanged the cord that ran between her breast and her vagina.

"You know, I wasn't going to see you again. Then I thought better of it. Why the hell not? If you want an affair, I'll give you one. After all, I come out ahead in this win/win situation."

He discarded his shirt.

"I get to fuck you any time I want, any way I want, without having to worry about having to marry you. And you can tell the whole world how you tamed bad-boy Dare-the-devil Darian Acer and made him heel at your feet."

His words set her belly quivering with nerves. Her labia swelled and moistened. Chassy backed up, eyes caught, held captive by the sheer power of his black, fathomless gaze. Her tongue darted out to bathe suddenly dry lips. She held up both hands, whether to ward him off or offer up her body, she didn't know. "Dare, you sound angry..."

"Baby, I ain't angry, I'm horny. I've got a boner a mile long I plan to shove up your hot little twat."

A wicked grin on his face, he taunted her with words she'd never heard, promised actions she'd never imagined. "You're getting a good bargain for your money, you know. I have it on the best authority that no one can suckle a nipple like I can. And hot, juicy pussy is my favorite dish. Most men want to cut to the chase—a few kisses, a couple of finger-thrusts, then on to the main meal of fucking. Not me." He winked at her.

She moaned.

He began to stalk her.

"I like to linger over my food. I'll make you come two or three times on my tongue before I'll be ready to mount you. You've never had cock, and mine is on the large side, so I'll be hard—excuse the pun—pressed to *initiate* you without pain, but I'll manage it. Wouldn't want to forfeit that double bonus, you know. I'll have to open you up good, loosen your inner muscles with a finger or three."

She retreated further, never taking her eyes off his advancing form. Oh, god, he was beautiful. Even as menacing as he appeared now, he moved like living poetry in motion. Long legs fluidly, effortlessly brought him closer with every step. The shifting of his powerful thigh muscles drew her eyes to the huge bulge nestled between them. She pressed a hand over her heart to calm the frenzied pounding. Her other hand rested at the hollow of her throat where her pulse raced out of control. She swallowed thickly. "N-now..."

"Yes, now," he agreed, his voice raspy and low. "Once again you have taken control of me. I will not leave you. I am the one begging *you* to let me come in." His sinful mouth smiled at her, his lustful eyes stared into hers. "I will feed you so well from passion's cup that you will no longer be hungry...or a virgin."

The nether lips between her legs actually fluttered. They swelled and pulsed. A wash of liquid bathed her thighs, embarrassing her at how ready her body became by just listening to his provocative words. Conversing proved difficult. Two words trickled out. "Oh, god—"

"On the contrary..." His teeth gleamed in the afternoon sunlight, lips curved wickedly as he reached for the ties of her dress and began to unravel her.

Chapter Nine

The plush, plump cushions of the red velvet settee made a decadent backdrop for her creamy, naked skin and the masses of brunette hair spilling over the side of the retiring couch.

Amidst slow, languid lovemaking, he'd removed ten hair-bobs, plying her with a honey-sweet, openmouthed kiss each time he tugged a shining silver pin loose.

Her body was his cornucopia of delights, her emotions so open and responsive to him. He loved everything about loving her. The way she shifted and moved, moaned and made those little helpless noises in the back of her throat...she made him feel like a conqueror.

"I'm going to savor every inch of you, taste and sample your face, shoulders, arms..." He propped himself up on an elbow and traced her eyebrows with his forefinger. "I want to explore the very veins beneath your skin, trace every rivulet and estuary back to their source."

She moaned and shivered under the caress of his hand, lifting toward the moving digit as it glided down her neck and skirted the outsides of her breasts. "S-s-source?"

He dipped his finger into the shadowed hill of her breast and stroked rhythmically, palmed a straining nipple and pressed down, pinching the tight flesh between his thumb and forefinger. Dipping his head, he put mouth to nipple and suckled, drawing strongly on the tender bit. Opening his lips, he swallowed the stiff morsel, hollowing his cheeks as he worked her determinedly, pulling on her crest until it popped out of his greedy mouth with a loud slurp.

She bucked beneath him. Her high-pitched mewl tightened the secret spots along his spine. The helpless sound hardened his cock and tingled in his balls. He played with her wet nipple, flicking it carefully, giving just enough of a sting to make her lift to him in needy supplication. Taking it back in his mouth, he used his teeth and tongue so devilishly her eyes rolled back in her head.

Not wanting her to crest, he released the tight nubbin and leaned back. His hand coasted down the flat, pale plane of her belly, the silky, unblemished skin a vast contrast to his calloused, rough palm. "Your pelvic bones are your inner shores. They contain a primal sea, a turbulent ocean that seeks to escape the confines of its fleshly prison."

He rubbed his hand over her mound, cupped her sex, and used his thumb to circle her clit. "Can you feel it cresting, the waves breaking inside you?"

"My bones feel liquid...like I'm melting. Too hot...too much..." Her body rippled beneath him, undulating in a sensuous curve that had him gritting his teeth and scrabbling for control.

Moving stiffly, afraid he'd fall upon her and ravish her, Dare lowered himself down her body until his hands and mouth reached the sheltered cove of her sex. Eyes glued on the glorious sight, he reverently parted her labia with his thumbs, exposing the flushed, swollen center that gleamed with the evidence of her desire for him.

"You humble me with your beauty and willingness," he whispered into her flesh, stroking a path of fire up her fluttering folds. "There is a heartbeat in your pretty little pussy. Does it beat for me?"

"Y-yes...oh...*Dare...!*"

Her broken response moved him, melted some of the anger that had built inside him over the years, made him want to cherish her. She was his bright flame, his salvation. He'd lost all desire for others, didn't want anyone but her spread beneath him, accepting his touch and his worship.

Her hands clenched in his hair, tugging at his scalp. The small pain twisted in his gut, sparking an impatience to be inside her. Bending his head, he extended his tongue and lapped roughly at her little button of nerves. His teeth nibbled at her, nipped a sharp warning of coming turbulence.

When he lifted his head, his face shone with her intimate juices. His stomach muscles clenched in need and dread as he watched her swoon under his ministrations.

Her face had gone slack. Her sherry-brown eyes, glazed with the pleasure he'd worked into her body, gleamed behind heavy lids. Her breasts quivered with each unsteady breath. Her rosy nipples stabbed up toward the ceiling in a begging arch. He could chart the waves of her inner sea under the thin skin of her belly.

A growl rumbled low in his chest as he stood and flung off the rest of his clothes. Intemperate, impatient, he kicked off his shoes, snatched at the buttons holding his trousers together, ripping the cloth in his hurry.

Freed, his cock sprang up, ruddy and red and aching, already dripping with the need to be buried in the hot, wet channel he'd stretched carefully with two fingers.

Sighing with relief, he gripped his erection with one hand and cupped his balls with the other, hissing at the heat pouring up his spine from the base of his cock.

Feeling like the greenest youth, he slid his fist up and down the stiff length, desperate to bleed off some of the pressure before he slammed into Chassy and fucked her as if she were a dockside whore. She didn't deserve that kind of initiation. She'd trusted him to see to her deflowering, and he was damned if he'd botch this for her.

His hand moved faster, milking his throbbing hard-on.

Almost there...

A slight noise shattered his concentration. He opened his eyes and glanced up to find Chassy leaning on her elbow, legs wide open, the fingers of one hand buried in her cunt. Her thumb compressing her clit, she watched his frantic movements, her wide brown eyes avid on the steely jut of his cock.

It was almost too much. Biting his lip to distract his rising lust, Dare increased his movements. Running his fist over the mushroom-shaped head, he gathered the slick moisture to ease his way.

"Dare."

He looked at her. "Yeah?" he croaked, cleared his throat. Conversation was the last thing on his mind.

"You wouldn't let me taste you last night. Can I, please?" She gestured at his reddened cock.

His hand slowed and stopped while he debated with his better half.

This time is supposed to be for her!

Yeah, well, she wants to suck cock—who are you to deny her?

And it'll help take the pressure off. Oh, hell, yes. For sure!

Okay, but don't let her swallow this first time. Might put her off.

His cock led the way to the settee, bobbing with eagerness. She didn't waste a minute. Her hand gripped him, brought him to her mouth, and a second later her lips closed over him, wrapping him in silken heat and darkness.

What she lacked in finesse, she made up for in willingness. She ran her tongue down his length, swirled it along the distended vein that ran the underside of his cock. Joy juice dribbled from his slit and she lapped it up, smacking her lips at the taste.

"Yum."

"So *glad* you like," he managed, hands fisted in her hair. He rethought his decision not to spend in her mouth. Nothing thrilled a man more than watching his woman swallow his come. Ejaculating in a tight cunt came a close second, but having Chassy on her knees before him, her mouth working him so eagerly—that won the laurels.

At the last minute, he held to his resolve and snatched his cock out of her mouth. He had to fight her for it. Moving out of reach, he fisted his hard-on and jacked it furiously, aided by the moisture her mouth had supplied.

His cock jerked and, with a groan of completion, he erupted, his seed shooting from him as he pumped his hips in time to his pistoning fist.

Sidestepping the pool of semen gleaming whitely on the dark hardwood floor, he returned to the settee and her, his mouth twisted in a self-derisive grimace. "You've unmanned me, Chassy. Before now, I've never feared failing my partner to the point I had to bring myself off before mounting her."

If possible, her eyes widened even more. "But doesn't that mean you can't do anything now?" She pointed to the cooling pool of come.

His lips parted in an amused smile. Her question showed her true innocence. He gestured at his lower body. "Take a good look at me."

He waited until she obeyed him, until her mouth fell open at the sight of his still rampant cock. "Now I can take you as slowly as you need, baby."

She reached up and circled his cock, surprising him, her fingers warm and smooth on his aroused flesh. "I need you, want you, any way you will take me."

He eased her hand off him, his balls gone shockingly tight again. *So soon.* "Damn, Chassy, you're a dangerous woman! That kind of action will get you fucked instead of courted."

"I don't need courting." She pouted, coming up on her knees to wrap her arms around his waist. "I need you deep inside of me, filling my emptiness. Only you can do that."

"I can hardly contain myself as it is. When you talk like that..." He shook his head. "Lie down and lift your legs up."

She quickly obeyed, and he circled her ankles with both hands, lifted her legs higher and stepping up between her wide-splayed thighs. Rubbing his cock up and down her shallow groove, he pressed hard enough to part her labia, hard enough to slide the tip of his bulbous head through her drenched folds.

Her flesh was hot and wet, and he could see her clit pulsating, her intimate sex lips fluttering. Imagining her closing around his swollen penis was enough to push his vaunted control to the limit.

He gathered his courage and met her eyes, knowing she could see mingled hope and fear in his. "You're so wet and ready. That kind of reaction can't be faked. You really want me?"

She nodded, looking confused at his question. "I really want you, not your wicked reputation or your notorious past. Just you, Dare—and your cock in my pussy, fucking me like you mean it."

My heart in your hands, loving *you like no one else ever will.* But he hadn't gathered enough courage to say that out loud. "So be it." He rubbed against her again, cock sliding and slipping in her wetness. She was as ready as he could make her.

Using his thumb and middle finger, he parted her and fit his dripping head to her opening. Taking a deep breath, he began pressing, slowly easing his way in.

Her flesh parted and gave way before him, reforming around his thickness like a tailored glove, firm and tight. Nothing had ever felt better than her pussy opening and clenching around him, welcoming him, taking him as deep as he could go.

Not quite, he thought, coming up against her maiden's barrier. He slowed his forward momentum.

"We've encountered a road block." His voice gruff with holding back, he commanded, "Take a deep breath and lift your hips to me."

When he felt her inner muscles relax, he surged into her, breaking past the thin membrane guarding her innocence.

"Yes! Oh, yes, Dare, take me! Make me yours!" She cried out, but not with pain. And he pulled out—her nether lips clinging to his thick width—just enough to slam back into her.

Her body quaked, breasts and belly shaking with the impact. He rolled his hips and fed her another inch of his cock, gasping at the sensation, his blood racing, fire running from the back of his legs, up his buttocks, and into his balls.

Sinking down over her, he took her lips, devoured her mouth, thrusting his tongue into her honeyed depths to the same cadence he thrust into her pussy. He drove in, drove deep, *deeper,* trying to find his home, his soul. "Damn it, Chassy, you feel so good, so tight, so hot…"

Her legs dropped from his shoulders and clasped about his waist, her body working with his, straining to take him in and hold him. "More, Dare…harder and deeper…*deeper,* damn you!"

"Oh, hell, yeah!" Dare shouted, increasing the depth and angle of his strokes. Drawing his hand back, he slapped her flank, a sharp pat that was more sound than fury.

She erupted under him, screeching and arching and twisting. Her legs tightened about him, clung as she tried to climb up his body.

"Again! Do that again!" She panted, eyes wide, gazing up at him in wonder, the brown depths revealing a lust that rivaled what poured through him.

The growl he released was part wild animal and all male. "You like that, baby?" he asked, bringing his hand down again, a little harder. He could feel her intimate muscles grab hold of him, squeezing his cock with desperate strength. "I can feel you do. Okay then," he said, returning to devouring her mouth as he rained a flurry of hard spanks to her flanks and the lower curve of her luscious ass.

Throwing her head back, she screamed, convulsing and shuddering. Heat poured over his cock head, a liquid stream, filling her pussy and spilling over as she climaxed in his arms.

Her explosion triggered the beginning of his, and he bared his teeth, groaning as his spine stiffened. Semen boiled in his balls, the weighty sacs drew up close to the base of his penis. His cock swelled and lengthened, preparing to spew, and her pussy seemed to shrink around him, becoming a tighter fit.

A firestorm of heat slammed into the back of his head, bowing his neck as flames licked up his spine. Mouth open in a soundless wail, he locked his fingers in the cheeks of her ass and lifted her into his thrusts, driving his cock to the depths again and again. Knees shaking, he leaned against the settee and folded her legs over his arms, rolling her bottom up for better purchase. One hand curled around her thigh and attacked her clit, rolling and tweaking it, tugging and stretching it, flicking it hard.

"Come, damn you. Come now!" Voice hoarse, he shouted orders at her, desperate for her to finish climaxing before he came like the original landing shuttle, crashing through the atmosphere and burning to cinders.

She dug her nails into his back, clinging to him like a leech as her orgasm slammed into her. Thankful for mercies shown, he dropped his head to her shoulder and nuzzled her fragrant skin as he drilled into her a few more times before pressing in as far as he could go. Pressing in and letting go.

Come blasted through his cock, pulsed deep and hot in her core. His hips bucked and rolled as waves of semen poured out of him like a jet stream. He continued working her clit as he emptied himself inside her and collapsed at her side.

With a groan, she pushed up on her elbows and dropped a kiss on his open lips before flopping back down beside him in a boneless sprawl. "Thank you...thank you..."

He'd never felt more complete.

Chapter Ten

A week later, she woke to a broad finger running tight circles around her puckered opening. She reared in fright. "What are you doing? Stop that!"

"I want to fuck you here."

"No way!"

"You'll love it. I promise to make it beyond good for you." He pushed against the tiny orifice, fingertip sinking in and stretching the untried opening. It burned.

She slapped at his hand, twisting to lie on her back. Staring up at him in hurt accusation, she shook her head no. "I may have been a virgin, but I know enough to figure out you're too big to get inside of there. Your finger doesn't even fit. You'd rip me open."

"I won't." Dare's hands gripped her thighs and lifted, bowing her up until her anus was again exposed to him. His eyes gleamed with a shocking heat. She'd never seen such lust or such fevered, intense wanting. Her lips went dry. Down below, her vaginal lips were drenched with the flow of her arousal.

He took quick advantage of her involuntary reaction. Lowering his chest over her thighs, he held her in place, freeing his hands to roam at will over the round curve of her hips and between her legs. He gathered her juices and spread them over her cheeks, rubbed them over and in the puckered door. Her muscles clenched, pushed his finger out. He slapped her butt.

"Stop squirming. You're no longer a virgin...except for here...and not for long."

His insistence irritated her. He'd pinned her so securely she could do no more than wiggle beneath him. Staring up at him, using words as a whip, she lashed at him. "I said no, Dare! And since I pay the shot, I call the play."

The glow in his eyes snapped off like a light turned out by an impatient hand. He released her and backed away, his eyes hooded and shielded from her gaze. His jaw clenched so tight she could see the muscle ticking beneath the skin, while his lips folded in until their sexy curve disappeared. Without a word, he stood and walked away.

"Dare, where are you going? Come back. I didn't mean to say that."

Pausing in the bedroom doorway, he looked back, chiseled face stern and closed—the face of a crusader confronting a dragon. "It sounded like just what you meant to say."

She couldn't believe how easily he'd taken offense. Why did men always do that?

"I also said I was sorry, and I meant that, too. Please, come back."

Head tilted to the side, he weighed her words, his options, and then approached her, steps dragging. The loss of his eagerness was a bitter taste on her tongue.

"Why be sorry? After all, you spoke only the truth. Look around." He unclenched his hands, fanned them to indicate their surroundings. "Everything you see is yours: this flat, the furniture...me. Like my apartment, my servants, and clothes, you've bought me, soul and body."

Tears started, stinging her eyes. "No!" She sat up, held out her hands. "Oh, Dare, I never...I don't want you thinking I just want to own you. I'd rather die than hurt your feelings. I..."

He caught her hands and subdued them, his face still and blank. When he spoke, his voice was harsh enough to grind stone into gravel. "Hush, babe, don't fret so."

Once she was calmer, he carefully placed her hands in her lap and withdrew until he faced her from a space of two or so feet.

"We all make choices, Chassy, and I don't regret making this one. While I fully intended to continue rejecting your offer out of hand, I hadn't steeled myself to finding you on my doorstep. Your beauty knocked me off kilter. I couldn't resist you."

He wiped the tears from her face. Bending, he pressed his mouth against hers, licked the seam of her lips, wordlessly demanding she open to him. "I don't regret my choices...often."

She hiccupped. "I don't want you to ever regret choosing me. I knew your father had disinherited you, knew you were short of money. I have an obscene amount so why should you be in need? I didn't figure you for the sort of man who accepts charity, so I racked my brains and came up with the idea of offering you carte blanche."

He flinched, and she was quick to notice the betraying movement. "Why are you so bothered by the term?"

"To be the kept man of a woman is degrading. No man worth his salt would be comfortable in such a situation."

Chastity bristled. "So if I had accepted the same offer from you, I would be a degraded woman in your sight?"

His eyebrows creased in a quick frown. "Of course not."

"What would be the difference?" She leaned on one arm and cocked her head, eyes narrowing as she perused his stiff posture. "Haven't you ever offered carte blanche to anyone?"

"No." He looked relieved to be able to answer in the negative.

"But you have had mistresses...?"

His answer came slower this time. "Of course, yes. I'm a man. I've been mature for a long time, Chassy. You can't possibly have expected me to come to you a virgin."

She crooked an eyebrow. "Why not? Why must women be the ones to remain pure while you men flit from pussy to pussy like damned tom cats? Why haven't you ever offered any woman carte blanche?"

Exasperation sounded in his heavy sigh. "I have never cared for a woman enough to honor her with that level of trust."

"Ahh!" Chassy sagely nodded her head. "I have never offered a man carte blanche before. Until now, I have never cared enough for a man to honor him with this level of trust. But to you, my offering is an insult. Perhaps you would have preferred to be the one offering the blank letter...to uphold your manhood!"

"Damn it, Chassy, I would have preferred to be the one offering marriage."

Dare closed the short distance between them. Easing down on the mattress beside her, he cradled the back of her head and drew her into a soft, warm kiss, his lips gently moving on hers. An eon later, he pulled back and met her eyes. "From the first time I saw you, marriage was the only thought in my mind. I knew immediately we belonged together. Before you walked into view, I'd been searching for a likely fuck-partner. Then I saw you. Not a woman there could hold a candle to you. They all faded to shadow. Every man in the Avondales' ballroom became my enemy. I didn't want their eyes on you, didn't like seeing the lust they felt for you. I didn't fall in love with you, Chassy—I stepped into it with both eyes open."

She could drown in his gaze, lose herself in the wide, fathomless black pupils. The naked truth shone out of them, and her heart lurched somewhere in her chest. She recognized love when she saw it. Crying, she flung herself into his embrace.

"I'm so sorry." She gulped on tears, moved beyond the capacity to hold them in. "I'd dreamed of you all my life, measured all other men against your standard. I was used to wanting you, but there was no reason to expect you to feel the same connectedness. I've never wanted marriage before meeting you, and because of what father terms my 'hoydenish behavior,' I never dreamed you would want to marry me. I thought I could settle for an affair. Your rejection almost ripped my heart out of my chest. I'd never felt such pain."

"I refused the carte blanche because I wanted more. I still want more—more even than marriage with you. Chassy, I don't want a society bargain like my parents endured. I'd like a true partnership, a blending of our hearts and bodies. I want to have children with you...not just an heir and a spare. I want so much..."

Smiling through her tears, she lifted her hand to his beloved face, tracing the mobile lips and firm jaw. He dipped his head and rubbed his cheek against her palm, the gesture oddly submissive and manly at the same time. "I want to give you everything you desire. Everything."

His face snapped up, eyes glittered with newly awakened lust. "You mean…?"

Though still wary of all it might entail, she wouldn't deny him anything. Nibbling on her bottom lip, eyes shyly dropping from his dark gaze, she nodded. He didn't allow her to escape so easily. A finger beneath her chin lifted her head until she found herself mirrored in his pupils. "Say it."

"I want you to take my anal virginity." Her voice trembled.

He chuckled. "Now say it like you mean it."

She couldn't fool him. He knew her too well, understood her fears better than she did. But she could do this because she loved him and trusted him not to willingly hurt her. Laughter welled up at the thought of how he would react to her next actions.

With a last puckish kiss, she backed up on her knees, turned, and stretched her upper body out in a lazy curve. Widening her legs, she lifted her bottom, presenting her cheeks to him in a saucy pose that had her juices running forward to dampen the tight curls covering her mons. She gave her ass a flirty little wiggle and couldn't hold back a sharp sigh when the flat of his hand landed against the rounded curve of her buttocks.

"Oh, you're a nasty little thing, aren't you?"

He rubbed the stinging spot, bent and strung a line of sucking kisses along the crease between her full cheeks. She shivered and moaned at the intense and frightening feelings his touch awakened. She'd never felt such heat from simple mouth-to-flesh contact.

Another slap fell, sharper than before. Her nipples tightened.

"Get that ass higher in the air...and get those legs further apart. I want to see your sweet little pussy winking at me."

She obeyed, shaking with the arousal his words caused. The muscles low in her belly clenched and quivered. "Flying angel-serpents, Dare. I love when you talk to me like this!"

"I promise you, you're going to love everything I do to you." His hands coasted up and down her back, soothing her jangled nerves before he stung her bottom with another random swat.

Her knees gave way, but his forearm was under her, around her waist. He lifted her back into position and barked an order for her to remain still. She felt his hand between her legs, two fingers tunneling into her dripping vagina, a little rough and urgent. Just the way she liked.

"You are such a little slut puppy, aren't you? I've never felt you so wet." He clicked his tongue at her. "Naughty Chassy. Why are you pretending to be reluctant when you obviously want this ass fucking?"

He didn't give her time to answer. Good thing, because she couldn't have spoken to save her life. He was right. With lightning quickness, she'd gone from leery to lusty. Butterflies still beat frantically in her belly, not from dread of what was ahead, but from fear he might think she still protested and cease his thrilling actions.

His fingers dug in her liquid channel again, gathered the creamy moisture, and slathered it into the crease of her ass and all over the puckered entry to her most secret place. One well-lubricated finger pressed into the tight orifice, and she jumped, shocked at the pleasure pouring over her at the intrusion.

The finger retreated, surged back in. It hurt. And it didn't. His finger's movement became her focus. In…hurting; out…wondrous delight. In…pushing against resisting tissue, and out…gliding along nerve-rich membranes.

Her entire body registered what happened in that one place, became malleable, pliant. Soon the inward movement blended with the outward until the pleasure grew and swelled.

And stopped.

Dare's lips nuzzling her lobe, his tongue swirling in her ear, his voice gruff and hoarse, whispering dark secrets as his hands soothed and petted, brought her down where she could think again.

She didn't want to think—she wanted to feel.

"That was just my finger. Think about having me fuck your tight, sweet ass with my long, thick cock." He rubbed said cock against her, slid it up and down her crease and circled the broad head over her anus again and again.

She pushed back toward him, showing her willingness, her desire for him to take her last virginity.

A heavy groan sounded in her ear. A moment later, his hands were gripping her cheeks, prying them apart. He sank down, fit his cock to her pussy, and took her from behind, burying himself to the hilt with one thrust.

His fingers plucked her nipples, tugging and pinching and rolling the aching tips until they throbbed and burned. He buried his mouth in her neck, sucking her flesh between his teeth, leaving his mark on her, in her. He pounded into her, his hips slamming against the cushion of her ass, his wiry pubic curls scraping the sensitive skin of her bottom.

Seated deep within her, he helped her sit up, her back to his chest. He showed her the rhythm he wanted her to maintain, then set to work tormenting her clit. One hand worked lazy patterns on the heaving surface of her belly, while the other tweaked and thumbed the stiff bit of flesh at the zenith of her thighs. Not content to pinch and pull on her clit, he stuffed two fingers in her pussy, alongside his pistoning cock.

The resultant pressure was too much. She screamed, bucking against his thighs, the pleasure so intense she thought her body would disintegrate under the onslaught.

He tipped her head back and took her mouth, his tongue forceful and insistent. She opened to him, his woman to command, demanding more from him even as she surrendered.

He gave her more than she sought, working his fingers in tandem with his cock, his thumb riding her clit, supplying a counterpoint to his thrusts…and his other hand rooting at her ass, a finger forging past her sphincter.

Bliss.

Ecstasy.

And at the climax…his words in her ear, his promise of things to come. "One finger is nothing, love. When I fuck your ass, you are going to melt. You are going to go nova from the explosions, I promise you. But I'm not going to take your sweet ass until our wedding night. I want you to be able to wear white at our ceremony, so we'll keep at least one virginity intact."

"Dare, please!"

Chapter Eleven

Darian had an appointment in the city. Forced to emerge from their weeklong sex-fest, Chastity decided she might as well utilize the empty hours until his return to fulfill her promise to visit the duchess of Pettibone.

"This won't take long, I promise. Two hours, tops." Dare kissed her, his lips and tongue knowing just where and how to touch her to make her go weak with longing. "By then, I'll be ready for some more of your sweet, rich pussy."

"Keep it up and you'll miss that appointment." She wasn't kidding. They'd spent the entire night fucking, barely taking a break between torrid sessions, and he had but to kiss her to have her primed for more hot action. "You've made me need you again."

"I need you, too," Dare groaned. "Right now."

Glancing left and right, finding the street empty, he snatched her up in his arms and entered the hovering flitter. Hurrying to the long couch in the back, he deposited her on the firm cushion.

Her skirts went up about her waist in a quick move that screamed of plenty of practice. His buttons flew from their loops, and his cock sprang out, thick and high. He entered her so fast she barely had time to spread her legs.

"Damn, Chassy, you've got me hard as a glazed brick." He groaned. "I'm afraid this won't last long. Come soon, or forever hold your peace."

Chassy shuddered as heat and laughter ran through her. She clutched at him, arms about his shoulders, legs clinging tight to his flexing buttocks. "How can you make me laugh when you're fucking me so hard I want to scream?"

He gritted his teeth. "I don't know...I don't care. I have to come now, baby. Oh, god, tell me you're there!"

She flung her head back as lightning struck, sizzled down her nerve endings. "I'm there! I'm there!"

* * *

Slumped on the couch, Chastity barely had the strength to push her skirts down. Thank goodness Dare had programmed the flitter with the coordinates for the hours-long journey to the Pettibones' main residence and set the controls to auto-flight before he left.

Wriggling to get more comfortable, she settled back against the leather squabs and closed her eyes. Immediately, a vivid memory of Dare, naked and aroused, formed in her mind.

Chassy's lips widened, parting in astonishment as she shivered with rising need, sexual heat blossoming between her thighs. There was no controlling her body's reaction to its new conditioning.

Chilling fire raced up her spine, spilled across her shoulders, and flowed down to her breasts. Static electricity snapped and sparked in the tips of her engorging nipples. Her clit throbbed in time to the increased beating of her heart.

Glorious flying angel-serpents, but the man was gorgeous...and he can fuck! Through the roaring of her pulse, she seemed to hear Dare's voice urging her to grip him tighter, ride him harder. Her muscles closed on nothing, and she pressed her legs together, rubbed her thighs against each other, desperate to ease the flames licking at her from within.

She shifted on the seat, twisting in need. She couldn't believe how quickly her lust had risen. Though abashed over missing Dare so soon, she couldn't help but wish he was with her now, *in* her, once more filling the empty chasm of her welling vagina with his thick, hard cock.

He'd done this to her. Made her perpetually horny, addicted her to the frequent thrusting of his body in hers. She was a junky for the climaxes he wrung from her with such ease.

Chastity sighed, thinking about how she'd begged him to take her anally, to use her any way he wanted. Liana had been right to warn her of the folly of passing up life's greatest adventure, but she'd neglected to warn her about the stubbornness of men.

He'd fucked her numerous times last night, but he'd never satisfied her curiosity or satiated her longing for the salacious act of sodomy. Oh, he teased and flirted, ran his fingers and mouth over and around what he called her "tiny rosebud," but now that she longed for him to do so, he wouldn't fuck her there.

Her body made hot and itchy by the memories of their lovemaking, she ached with the urge to turn the flitter around, hunt him down, and force him to satisfy her needs.

Driven half-wild, she gathered the slim skirts of her morning gown in one hand and hoisted a leg up on the seat. She slipped her hand between her thighs and let her fingers coast over warm, damp flesh.

Muscles twitched and jumped beneath the surface as her body tensed, anticipating the pleasure ahead. Her breath caught, stalled in her throat as her hand reached its destination. Twirling a finger in the tight curls covering her mons, she circled her clit, fingertips slipping in moisture as her copious flow coated her hand.

A frown puckered her brow. The sensations weren't as strong or sweet as when Dare touched her, stroked her. She pinched her clit, hoping to ignite something more than frustration, but the feelings eluded her.

With a tortured groan, Chastity withdrew her hand and let her head drop back on the plush leather. Reaching for a handful of tissues, she cleansed herself as well as she could. Finished, she tossed the sodden mass into the trash and smoothed her skirts down over legs still weak and shaky.

Darian Acer was going to pay for making her immune to anyone but himself. When she returned home, she was going to fuck that man bowlegged.

Chapter Twelve

"I am here to see the duchess." Chastity handed her card to the cardboard-cutout figure pretending to be the Pettibones' butler.

The thin, haughty man took the small rectangle between thumb and forefinger, holding it from his body as if he feared infection. "Please be seated, Lady Chastity." His nostrils flared and chin lifted as he indicated a backless retiring bench situated a few feet away. "I shall ascertain whether Her Grace is at home."

"...*to you,*" he might as well have added. His supercilious tone said he doubted the duchess would deign to meet with the likes of her.

Chassy settled on the thin cushion with ill grace. *Damn pretentious man.* "You'd think *he* was the duke and not the servant with all the airs he put on," she muttered half under her breath.

I'll show him airs! He'd best remember I am the daughter of a duke, myself.

The butler returned quickly, his mouth drawn in a disapproving moue. Reluctantly polite, he intoned, "If milady will follow me...?"

Giving her his back—instead of inviting her to go before him as he ought—he led the way down a long, wide hall.

Chastity made an unladylike moue of her own as she trailed behind the butler. The loveliness of the duchess's décor caught her attention, and she quickly found herself drinking in the magnificent artwork and furnishings.

Covered in pale ecru cream wallpaper that intersected with a furniture rail bisecting the upper and lower halves of the walls, the wide corridor stretched for what seemed acres before her. Blond wainscoting covered the bottom half.

When she recognized the pale paneling as stykewood, found only on the winter continent at the top of the world, her eyebrows shot up. She whistled soundlessly, impressed against her will. Stykewood wasn't easy to come by. This corridor represented wealth on a scale unknown to most of Paradyse's inhabitants. Until today, she'd been aware of only one person rich enough to afford to panel a hallway with the stuff: her father.

Why would the duchess summon me? What could possibly be behind her furtive comments? Why did she insist time was of the essence?

Chassy sighed. She'd asked herself these questions over and over and had yet to come up with any reasonable answer. She hoped the duchess had good information, or at least a lead on her father's would-be killer, because she resented having to be away from Dare for even the short time this morning visit would take.

The butler halted before tall double doors and gestured for her to wait. Flinging the panels open, he stepped into the room and announced, "The Lady Chastity Tilson to see you, Your Grace."

Chastity sank into a graceful curtsey. "Your Grace…"

"Well, it's about time, young lady!"

Chastity's head snapped up. Her eyes widened in shock. Glad tears blurred her vision. *"Father!"*

"Yes, *Father.* Your poor old father who has cooled his heels for over a week, waiting for his wayward daughter." He held his arms out, a teasing smile wreathing his face.

Completely forgetting the presence of the duchess, she flew into her father's embrace, reduced to the little girl who had often sought comfort in his lap. In his arms, the constant fear and dread she'd lived with since his injury fell away. Only now did she realize how heavy the burden of wariness had weighed on her. Feeling light enough to fly, she laughed aloud, hugged her father, and burrowed closer as reaction finally set in.

He patted her back, his tentative, awkward caresses so much a part of their relationship. Poor Dad—he never knew what to do with her when she became emotional. She'd used his confusion to her advantage many a time.

With a last hiccup, Chassy leaned back and scanned her father's face, searching for signs of lingering illness. His face glowed with health, his ruddy complexion offset by his dear, familiar bushy eyebrows. He caught her watching and waggled them at her.

She squeezed her eyes shut and whispered a heartfelt prayer of thanks. Her brows lowered and she stepped back, hands shooting to her waist. "You want to tell me why Liana stopped sending me reports? And why you never wrote to tell me you were okay...and why you hid *here,* instead of coming to Uncle David's house?" She gasped, remembering something Liana had said. "Is he involved? Is that why you didn't...?"

Her father laid a finger across her lips, shushing her. "No, David may be a scoundrel, but he would never sully his hands by becoming involved in a murder. It wouldn't be proper."

He fished out his handkerchief and mopped up her tears. "There. Are you better now?"

She nodded, blowing her nose vigorously. She held out her hand, playfully offering to return the sodden cloth. She knew his fastidiousness. With a wry chuckle, the duke shook his head and backed away from the limp rag. "I think not, young lady!" He pointed at the used napkin. "That's yours...at least until you have it laundered."

They both laughed, recalling numerous such times in their shared past. Cedric sobered. "It is good to be reunited with you. I wouldn't have believed how much and how soon I missed you, child."

"I missed you, too, Daddy."

His face softened at the beloved term. "You haven't called me that in a long time."

She smiled, tears near the surface again. "I know."

"I need your help, Chastity."

"Anything, of course."

"You're not going to like your part, I'm afraid."

"What do you mean? What part?"

Cedric exchanged a cryptic glance with Lucynda before addressing Chassy. "I understand you've begun an affai—uh...an *association* with young Darian Acer." A scowl twisted his face.

"Not the sort of information a father wants to hear about his only daughter, by the way."

Chassy's face flamed, the heat sudden and intense. She hated blushing. It made her look guilty when she felt no such emotion. "To be precise, I offered him carte blanche. We have since decided to marry."

Cedric grimaced. "You'll be marrying, but the groom won't be Dare-the-devil Acer." He said the name with a sneer in his voice.

Cold speared through her chest. Dread's chilled fingers twisted her gut in knots. "Don't blame Dare for this situation, Father. I love him and he loves me. I hurt him dreadfully by offering him carte blanche when he planned to offer marriage. He refused me, but I wouldn't take no for an answer. I seduced him into making love to me. I can't marry another, not even for you."

"Utter nonsense, m'dear. Most of Society doesn't hold such antiquated ideas anymore. You're the daughter of a duke, and the man I have in mind will gladly overlook your absent virginity. Talk to your uncle. Have him arrange the match."

"No. Besides, I still have a virginity…of sorts."

Her father's entire face twitched as her meaning sank in. His mouth twisted. "Too much information, Chassy," he wheezed, thumping his chest with a closed fist. "Have a care for my heart, young lady, and remember you're talking to your father." He sobered. "Have you forgotten I am trying to flush out a killer?"

She frowned in confusion. "How will my marrying some man advance your program?" She thought a moment. "You know who it is. You've always known."

"Yes. However, I am not at liberty to disclose the person's identity…" He glanced over at the rotund duchess. "A prior promise constrains me."

She followed his gaze and another piece of the puzzle fell into place. "The duchess has something to do with this. That's why you came here."

Cedric nodded. "Her husband is an old friend. He is remaining silent about my visit while I clear up the misunderstanding with the crown. He knows nothing of Lucynda's involvement."

She quirked an eyebrow. "Neither do I, but that doesn't matter. I've promised to marry Darian Acer, and I intend to honor that promise."

"And so you shall. Your groom is none other than the earl of Chesley."

The ringing in her ears drowned out her father's voice. She heard nothing after the words, *earl of Chesley.* Vertigo swept over her and she fumbled her way to a settee. Plopping down, she closed her eyes and concentrated on staying conscious.

"His *father.*" Angry tears flooded her eyes. Hatred for the man who'd abandoned his own son blazed within, the flames so hot their residue charred her vision, turned everything gray. "I loathe him," she spat. "You have no idea the pain he's put Dare through. He wouldn't even allow Dare to attend his own mother's funeral! And this is the man you want to marry me off to…?"

"'Chesley' is a Landing title. Under the circumstances, he's a fitting choice. You might not be able to do better."

She countered, a sneer curling her lip. "I can do a *lot* better! His title does not erase his past. The earl of Chesley—your contemporary—is an old man, a mean, womanizing despot. He drove his son away and drove his wife insane with his infidelities."

"You know, Cedric, Chastity's right. I certainly wouldn't want any daughter of mine tied to that monster." Lucynda joined the conversation for the first time.

Chassy smiled at her, thankful for the support. Her father raised his hands in surrender. "All right, you two, I know when I'm beaten. You needn't marry the man, but I need the ceremony to take place." The two women opened their mouths to protest, and he hurried on before they could get their angry words out. "To *almost* take place." He noticed their skeptical expressions. He placed his right hand over his heart. "I give my solemn promise I'll stop the wedding before vows are exchanged if our culprit doesn't show up."

"You'd better...or I will." Chassy stood up, righted her dress, and made sure she had her reticule. "I need to get back and tell Dare about—"

"No, you can tell him nothing."

Chassy's hands tightened on the strings of her small purse. "Of course I must. He's sure to hear the rumors about town, and I don't want him upset or thinking I'd actually marry his father, for star's sake."

Her father came to her, placed his hands on her shoulders, and drew her into his embrace. "Does your Dare love you enough to forgive you?"

"What are you saying, Dad?" she whispered, tears clogging her throat. She didn't want to hear whatever it was. The thought of making Dare believe she would dump him for another...seeing the hurt betrayal in his eyes... She closed hers. "I can't bear to hurt him."

"If Dare learns the truth, his reaction will not be authentic. Our prey has eyes and ears among society. They will know if something, any little thing, is amiss. We'll lose this opportunity. I'm not the only target. My would-be killer has to think you are in my confidence. You have now become an equal or greater threat."

He patted her shoulder, offering the only comfort he knew how. "People who know Dare will look for him to react a certain way. We need your ex-lover's anger, his hurt bellowing, to make this appear legitimate. When this is all over, I will explain everything to him. I promise to make all right again."

"What if he can't forgive me, Dad? What if I lose him forever?"

"If he truly loves you..." Her father paused at the fierce look she shot him.

"What do you know of true love?"

He paled.

"If I lose Dare over this, I'll never forgive you. Your killer might as well shoot me, too, for I'll be dead inside." Sinking back down onto the settee, Chastity folded her arms on the raised rolled arm, tucked her face in the crook of her elbow, and burst into jagged tears.

Chapter Thirteen

It had been two weeks since Chastity gave Dare his *conge,* and Chezann was becoming worried. Dare hadn't gotten over being dumped. It didn't look as if he ever would. "Dare, please stop. If you drink any more, *I'll* throw up."

"Shut up, C.C.," Darian snarled, snatching the brimming tumbler from the reluctant waiter before his brother could intercept. His hand shook as he brought the glass to his lips. "I can still *smell* her—*taste* her, so I can't have drunk enough, yet."

Chezann propped his elbow on the bar, his chin on his palm, and gazed in pity at his older brother. He'd never seen Dare like this. Even in the days directly following the death of his brother and mother, his sibling had radiated an air of aloofness, maintained the impression he was impervious to pain.

Today, the man looked a mess. Clothes wrinkled and unkempt, he slouched at the card table, idly rifling a worn deck of *fago* cards. Hair uncombed and beard unshaven, his bloodshot eyes glared out at the world, counting every inhabitant his mortal enemy.

C.C.'s eyes narrowed. Jaw tight, he thought about Chastity and her fickle heartlessness, glad beyond words she'd seen fit to pass him up. The woman played hardball with people's emotions, and he wished she'd one day experience even a small portion of the pain she so blithely dished out.

Dare didn't deserve what she'd done to him. It wasn't right for her to use him then discard him for... *How had she put it?*... "The catch of the season."

"If she'd chosen any one other than my *father,* I could have understood it." Darian had lifted his head and mumbled the words through dry, cracked lips. One glimpse of his eyes had C.C. lowering his, unwilling to see that level of gut-deep pain.

"I mean, let's face it—I'm *not* the best catch. Disowned by my family, looked down upon by society—she could easily find a better man than—"

"Oh, hell, Dare. Spare me the self-pitying spiel." C.C. slapped his hands on the table and leaned into his brother's surprised face. "I've had it up to here with your sad rendition of a woman scorned."

Dare straightened up, his back stiffening against the chair. His lips thinned as he narrowed his eyes and tried to focus on his brother. "I thought you, of all men, would understand."

"The thing is, I do understand, Dare. I understand that you are going to sit here drinking yourself to death while the woman you love marries our father." The thought made him sick to his stomach. Maybe he could make his brother sick enough to put a halt to the monumental disaster taking place as they spoke.

"Just think about it…in a little while they'll leave the church. Knowing our randy parent, he won't wait long before he lifts her skirts—probably stop along the way and fuck her in the carriage. Yeah, and while he has her heels in the air, she can grip his thick cock with her pussy—hey, did I ever tell you how my mother went on and on about him being built like a horse? —and scream his name. Can't you hear it?" Speaking in falsetto, he chimed, "Oh, Darian, yes…fuck me with your big cock, ram that pole up my tiny little ass!"

"Mother *fucker*, C.C., shut the fuck *up!*"

Outside, a cloud of angel-serpents spun and dipped in frenzied flight, their shrill cries disturbing and nerve-jangling.

C.C. watched them, stunned at how they mirrored Dare's emotions, had always done so. They and his brother shared a connection that had baffled the naturalists for years. No one else, before or since, had bonded with so many of the finicky avians.

Moved by Dare's pain, irritated by the high-pitched screams of the serpents, he still couldn't allow himself to stop prodding. The wedding was scheduled for twelve o'clock, and it was past eleven. He had to shake Dare's aplomb, force him into action before it was too late.

"Ah, but you've already heard those words, haven't you?" His hand gripped his brother's arm. "Can you bear thinking about her calling *your* name while she lies under our grunting father, getting your next little brother or sister plowed into her? Can you *bear* it? Because I don't think I can. I don't want that lecher putting his filthy hands on her. If you don't want her, I'll take her. I'm going to try to stop the wedding."

A thud sounded against the window, and then another and another until the glass shook under the impact. The angel-serpents were attacking the window, trying to get in, trying to get to Dare.

A waiter, frightened at the cacophony, ran from the room, a salver held over his head as a protective shield. On desperate impulse, C.C. went to the window and flung it open.

A cloud of small bodies rushed past him, arrowing toward his brother. At the last minute, most veered off, content to circle his head and coo at him. Four of the largest mantled Darian's shoulders and arms, rubbed their sinuous heads against him, their tiny forefeet petting and rubbing him. The fifth creature settled in his lap, reared up to place her small feet on his chest, and stared into his eyes, crooning a little trilling song.

Dare broke.

C.C. reacted quickly, knowing his brother would rather die than expose his feelings to the public. "Everybody out!" he shouted, waving his arms and herding the patrons and serving staff from the establishment. As he pushed the complaining owner toward the door, he thrust a thick wad of bills into the man's hand. "I'm renting your place for the rest of the afternoon. Keep everyone out of here." The owner shut up and closed the door behind him, his face wreathed in smiles.

C.C. returned to his brother to find him literally covered in angel-serpents. Their mournful accompaniment was the perfect foil for a strong man's tears, but the low, ululating cries raised the hair on his arms.

Dare's shoulders heaved as sobs poured from him, a rain of tears flooding his face. His body shook uncontrollably. "I love her. I love her until my heart hurts with it. I'd walk barefoot across glass shards to her, and she threw me away like yesterday's trash."

"If you'd walk across glass, how hard can it be to walk across town? Or are you going to sit here and wallow in sorrow when you have one more chance to change her mind?"

"You didn't hear what she said to me when she gave me that obscene amount of money and told me we were finished. That she had a position to maintain and, as a society lady, she was expected to wed a particular type of man."

"Wait, Dare, hold it!" C.C.'s heart thumped with excitement. "She said all that, in those exact words? Are you sure?"

"It's burned in my memory. Her words will smolder in my mind 'til the day I die."

A grin spread his mouth wide. "Oh, brother, you need to get home and clean up. Better yet, clean up later. We have a wedding to halt."

"What are you talking about? Haven't you heard a word I said?"

He couldn't help smiling. "I heard you, Dare. After all my work on getting you two back together, I want the first boy named after me. 'Crofton,' not 'Chezann.' No one deserves to be stuck with a name like 'Chezann.'"

The angel-serpents' lilting song registered the renewal of Dare's hope before his face revealed what he was feeling. "You know something I don't?"

"I know she must have been trying to give you a message, but she sent it through the wrong brother. Chassy is totally against society marriages and never planned to make one. Her father and she fought about it on a regular basis. If you don't believe me, ask her."

"I believe I will." Dare surged to his feet and jammed his arms into his jacket, his abrupt movements startling his bevy of angel-serpents. They flew up and circled him, crying and—C.C. could swear—giggling, their iridescent wings a beautiful kaleidoscope of ever-changing, shifting colors.

C.C. opened the door and out they flew, staying in tight formation around Dare's rushing figure. He brushed past C.C. with a muttered apology, long legs carrying him after the serpents, which were all heading toward the Landing cathedral in the midst of town.

"Hurry up, little brother. We have a wedding to crash!"

Chapter Fourteen

Chastity sighed deeply. Listening to her young cousins chattering about her wedding did nothing to raise her spirits.

"Be still. I only have a little more to do." Alicia spoke around a mouthful of pins. Stoically holding her pose while Alicia fidgeted and twitched and pinned her gown into place for what felt like the tenth time, Chassy sighed again.

"All done. Now, step out of the dress. The seamstress needs to take it up one last time." Getting up off her knees, Alicia dusted the non-existent dust from her shins. "Thank goodness the wedding is today. You've lost so much weight we've had to take your dress in five times."

I haven't lost enough weight to suit me. I want to fade right away and become nothingness.

"I wish my father were here." *So I can strangle him for making me do this.*

"Oh, honey, I know!" Ali threw her arms around her, gave her a loving squeeze. "But soon you'll have someone of your very own. Someone to keep you company and—"

Chassy stared at Ali as if she had two heads. "Are you totally insane, Ali? The earl of Chesley is the biggest womanizer since Landing. The man's a sleaze, a dog—my apologies to dogs everywhere—and a total reprobate. How could you possibly imagine I'd be happy with him?"

Ali swallowed. "B-because you asked Father to arrange a contract of marriage with him...?"

"*Arrgh!*" Chassy reached toward her hair, seriously contemplating yanking the unruly mass out by the roots.

"Don't do that!" Ali screeched, running forward and grabbing her cousin's hands. "The hairdresser took two hours creating this masterpiece. Don't you *dare* make a mess... Oh!" She slapped palm over her mouth. "I said the 'D' word. I'm so sorry."

Chastity tapped her cousin's forehead. "I know you have a brain in there, Ali; I've heard it rotating."

"How can you be so mean on your wedding day?"

"Oh, this is the day to be mean, trust me."

One of the cousins stuck their head around the door. "The bridegroom has arrived. Everyone get ready."

The seamstress returned with her modified dress and helped her slip it carefully over the hairdresser's masterpiece.

Shrieking and laughing, the girls scrambled to get ready. Grabbing up their bouquets and slipping on their shoes, they lined up in order.

Chassy couldn't help smiling. In their gowns colored all rainbow shades, her little cousins looked like a bunch of willowy flowers. The one good thing this mock marriage had done was bring all her family together. It had been eons since she'd seen most of the people that had gathered under one roof to wish her happy.

The duchess of Pettibone sailed through the door, cutting a swath through the spectators and participants with equal disdain. "Everybody out, please; I need to speak to the bride."

Alicia bristled. "I'm the matron of honor. Why do I have to leave?"

"Because you *are* the matron, dear, while she is an unmarried woman without a mother. I am here to deliver the requisite prenuptial speech. Now shoo!"

Once the room emptied, she turned to Chassy with her usual calm smile. Lowering her voice, she whispered, "Your father is secreted off the main sanctuary. We've wired the small office so he can monitor everything. I have to get back out to my husband now." She started for the door.

"Hey!"

She looked back. "Yes, dear?"

"What about my talk?"

The grandmotherly duchess chuckled. "My dear Chastity, you have been Darian Acer's lover. I should be asking *you* for advice. You could probably teach me a thing or three." She winked as she stepped through the door and closed it gently behind her.

Chassy took a deep breath. Time to get this show on the road...

* * *

"Dearly beloved, we are gathered here today in the presence of friends and loved ones to unite these two people in holy matrimony..."

Chastity glanced through the hazy gauze of her veil at the tall man standing beside her—Dare's father, and C.C.'s. *He looks like them...or should I say, they look like him? Dammit, why can't everyone see how much he resembles C.C.?*

The width of shoulder and length of leg, all three men shared between them. The differences were in their coloring. C.C. had to take after his mother, his blond, blue-eyed handsomeness a far cry from his half-brother. While Dare probably hated that he looked so much like the father who'd thrown him away.

She snuck another sideways glance at the man towering over her and saw the strong line of jaw was the same as his son's. So were the liquid black eyes, shadowed with long, thick lashes. Shoulders and chest and thighs, all found their echoes in the beloved flesh she'd recently stroked and measured. A fleeting question regarding similarity in length elsewhere crossed her mind, and she grimaced and shooed it away. She didn't care beans about the earl's hidden assets. She was a one-man woman.

She wished the murderer would hurry and show up. This ceremony was getting frighteningly close to becoming real.

"If there be anyone here who knows just cause why this marriage should not go forward, let them speak now or forever hold their peace!"

"I know!"

"I know!"

The crowd gasped in one voice as the words rang out from opposite sides of the church in synchronization.

Chastity whipped about, searching for a glimpse of those who'd shouted their opposition. That had not been her father's voice, but she could have sworn one of the voices had been female.

The priest's stentorian tones rang out. "Come forward and state your objection before God and this assembly."

Darian stepped from behind a pillar and made his way toward the front of the church. C.C. followed close behind. "I claim the woman by dual right of possession and declaration. She belongs to me."

Chassy stopped breathing.

He looked magnificent. His hair wasn't combed, and his clothes were wrinkled and...not up to his usual sartorial elegance, but the expression in his eyes as he approached lit her heart until it flamed like a miniature sun.

"No! I'll not lose another son to an unworthy female. I'll see her dead, first!"

A shot rang out, the sound deafening and echoing in the vaulted chamber. A hard push from the side sent Chastity hurling down the stairs, out of the path of the projectile.

Screams.

Shouts.

Pandemonium.

Strong hands lifted her off the floor. "Chastity, darling, are you okay?" Those beloved hands ran over her shoulders and arms, traced her torso, checking for injuries.

Dare.

Laughing and crying, she went into his arms, everything and everyone around her fading into insignificance measured against the joy of having the only man she'd ever loved at her side. "Oh, Dare, oh, darling, I'm fine now that you're here." She looked around. "What's happening?"

Darian's lips tightened. He drew her tighter against his shoulder. "Apparently, my mother is still alive, but perhaps not for long. She just tried to kill you."

Chassy stiffened. "What? Where's my father?"

It was his turn to stiffen. "Chassy, don't you remember? Your father is dead."

She avoided his concerned eyes. "Yeah, well...he's about as dead as your mom is." She cringed at his stony expression. "I can explain..."

He nodded, lips folded in a disapproving line. "Later. Right now, I need to check on my father. He took the shot meant for you when he pushed you out of the way."

"Oh, my goodness," she gasped. "Is he all right? Does this mean I can't hate him any longer?"

That surprised a smile out of him. "I think he'll be fine. He's still worthy of hate. It didn't look too serious. Probably just a flesh wound. Come on." He took her hand and pulled her after him.

She held back. "Wait. I want to ask the priest something."

She walked over to the prelate and tugged his sleeve. He bent to her, listening with a growing expression of shock and doubt. When she finished, he laughed aloud and nodded. "Well, why not, milady? Stranger things have happened in this church."

Epilogue

"I am glad your father reinstated you to your title and inheritance, but so sorry about your mother." Chassy snuggled up beside her new husband and slipped her hand into his. He squeezed her fingers, feeling a mix of emotions hard to put a name to.

"Thank you, darling. She was truly insane. I never dreamed she'd try to kill you again. When she came at us, the serpents thought she was attacking me. At least it was quick, if painful. Being struck by so many angel-serpents—the venom acted blindingly fast."

"She wasn't really to blame for her actions. Our father drove her out of her mind with all his infidelities." C.C. lounged on the couch opposite them, sipping brandy and recovering from the wild events of the day.

"At least he wasn't to blame for our brother's fiancée's death. According to what Mom confessed, he was blind drunk when Eschell crawled into his bed, and he never knew he'd slept with her. Her mistake was bragging to Mom about the pregnancy. When Daniel discovered Mom after she'd drowned Eschell, she begged him not to turn her over to the authorities. You remember how he was?" he asked C.C., sorrow threatening to crush him as he recalled the brother he'd worshiped while growing up under his shadow.

"I remember. Straight as an arrow, but lamentably narrow in thought."

That gave Dare pause. "That's a pretty dead-on evaluation. Anyway, the only alternative for him was to end his own life. And she killed her maid in order to fake her death in that chamber fire. She disappeared and started a new life away from father and her guilt over Daniel's suicide. Strange," he mused almost to himself, "she killed several people and suffered no remorse. Daniel kills himself and she can't live with that. I wonder if she ever loved me."

Chassy leaned up and kissed him, peppering soft kisses all over his face. "I love you. That's all that matters."

Everyone was quiet for a while. After a few more sips, Chezann broke the silence. "I didn't catch how your father came into this, Chassy."

She turned her face toward him but didn't lift her head from Dare's shoulder. "Simple. Father caught sight of Dare's mother in New India and recognized her. He and the earl had been drinking buddies. He told me she hated him almost as much as she did her husband. She blamed Dad for some of your father's excesses. Thinking he would contact your father and tell him her whereabouts, she came to our plantation and tried to kill him." She shrugged. "We decided I'd come to New Britain and pretend she'd succeeded, to give Father a chance to recuperate. The day I visited the duchess of Pettibone was the day he revealed this plot to flush out your mother. She was such a stickler for upholding appearances he figured she wouldn't, couldn't, allow your father to remarry as long as she lived.

"I didn't find out until you did that the duchess was her half-sister and your aunt. Your mother refused to recognize her. Their relationship was nothing like you two have. Father had made her a promise long ago never to reveal her relationship. The duke of Pettibone never knew she was not her father's true daughter."

Chastity looked up, and Dare saw her beautiful brown eyes swimming with tears. "It almost killed me to hurt you like I did. I told Father if I lost you, the murderer might as well have shot me, too, for I would be dead inside."

"You can't lose me."

"Unless he's buried in angel-serpents." C.C. chortled. He pointed over to the mantle where two serpents reclined, their wings furled along their backs, drowsing in the heat of the fireplace.

"I think you taught them about windows, C.C." Dare's accusation made Chassy smile. "When we came home, we found all the windows ajar and over twenty serpents checking out the house. I'm worried over what you've started."

"Then my work here is done!" With a laugh, C.C. jumped to his feet and placed his empty glass on the tea table. He touched Dare's shoulder in a fleeting brotherly caress and leaned over him to kiss Chassy on the mouth.

"Hey, none of that, young buck!"

He chuckled at Dare's not-so-fake grimace. "Relax, bro. I'm just kissing the bride...and my new sister." He opened the door. "I imagine I won't see you again until you two lovebirds decide to emerge from your nest."

Before he could close the door, a serpent zipped out the narrow opening and fluttered above his head, chittering madly. Eyes widening, C.C. tentatively raised his arm, offering the angel-serpent a perch. Moisture added a luster to the blueness of his eyes when the dainty creature settled carefully on her new friend.

"Did you see that?" he asked, his voice hushed with awe.

The serpents on the mantle giggled and trilled, their amusement so obvious, Dare wondered how he had missed seeing their high level of intelligence for so long.

"C.C."

"Yeah?"

"Congratulations. Now get out. I have to relieve my wife of her virginity, and you are cramping my style."

"But..."

His little lady serpent grabbed his earlobe between her two tiny forefeet and tugged just as Chastity reared up and threw a couch pillow at him. It missed him by an inch.

With a resigned sigh, Darian untangled his limbs and climbed to his feet. Stalking over to the still open door, he pushed his brother through, whispering, "C.C., I can't name what I can't make."

"Huh? Oh...*oh!* Okay." Dare shook his head as his sibling finally caught on. For a rakehell, C.C. was awfully slow sometimes. "'Crofton,' remember, not 'Chezann'!"

Latching the door, Dare leaned back, placed his hands behind him, and smiled at his wife. "You know, it occurs to me that C.C. needs to settle down."

"You men are all alike. Once you get married, you can't stand for your friends or brothers to remain single." Chassy sat up and tossed off her gown, baring her lush breasts to his interested gaze. "Enough about C.C. Come fuck me!"

Dare sauntered over to the love of his life, hiding a grin. "Oh, I don't think he's ready for marriage. I was thinking along the lines of him finding a good woman willing to offer him carte blanche!"

Camille Anthony

Camille Anthony is a pseudonym for the author who lives in the beautifully wild Low Country of South Carolina. She is a transplant from Sunny California. A fertile imagination and a love of romance fuels her writing, which she has been doing since grade school. Her favorite stories are those of strong, honorable people—whatever the race, or planet of origin—who are driven by love and lust to find and hold that one special someone. She likes her heroines feisty, her heroes dominant and her passion red hot!

She loves to hear from her readers. Your comments and suggestions are appreciated. Visit Camille on the Web at www.camilleanthony.com   or   e-mail   her   at camilleanthony@camilleanthony.com.

* * *

Read on for a tantalizing glimpse of
Queen's Rules 1: Every Good Boy Deserves Favor
by
Treva Harte
Available now in e-book format from Loose Id

Jewel heard the roar of male voices and the loud trumpeting beyond the Castle M'Cee walls. She pushed her purple-black hair back from her eyes, pausing for a moment. "Who is it this time?"

The deep-throated yells reached a crescendo, echoing through the outer walls of the castle. Jewel swore the keep trembled just slightly from the noise.

"Karenna, I think," Tess answered. "She always makes a good display for them. They love looking at her when she is as naked as possible. I wish I could manage to look good with just nipple chains."

"Better her than me." Jewel went back to weeding the tiny herb garden, tuning out the cries. "Being thrown once to those jackals was more than enough."

"The display starts the time of favor. That makes babies," Tess said. "And it keeps the men from trying to tear the place down, stone by stone, to get at us."

Jewel shrugged, dismissing the argument. Other women might accept or even enjoy the time of favor. She didn't. Never would. Fortunately, she had other gifts to bring to the keep's sisterhood. The Castle M'Cee might not depend on her healing gifts yet, but everyone knew she was one of the keep's more promising apprentices. She would never have to go through the whole ritual of giving favor again.

At least that was one of the endless, dreary tasks of the castle she could skip. She'd been living all her twenty-four years in the keep and knew this was where she'd be for the rest of her days, following the same routine. There was no other life for a female. No other tolerable life, anyhow. She'd heard rumors of what happened to unprotected females captured by males.

"Don't you ever get tired of this?" Jewel asked Tess, suddenly.

Tess blinked. "Tired of what?"

"Everything. You know what day it is because it is washday or sewing day or whatever task it was the week before. There's never anything new here." Jewel gestured to the tidy little garden. "We even plant the same herbs every year in the same spot."

Tess stared at her as if she'd grown wings and fangs.

"What do you mean, Jewel?"

"Never mind." Jewel dug hard into the earth and pulled.

"Jewel, that's coneflower, not a weed!" Tess snatched the plant from her hand, distressed. "Maybe you should go downstairs. There should be tea soon."

"Of course there will be tea soon. It's almost four o'clock isn't it?" Jewel muttered. She glanced at Tess and her worried face. She'd just confused the poor woman. "Tea would probably be a good idea."

Tess' frown lines smoothed out as she relaxed, clearly relieved. "It's very soothing, especially if it's—well, you know. Your time."

Jewel took a long, deep breath before she stood up. She wasn't going to snap at her companion. She wasn't. Tess was only saying what any woman in M'Cee would say, of course. Jewel could predict the conversations by now.

What would Tess say if Jewel told her only one more predictable word would set Jewel screaming and she wasn't sure she could stop? "She'd probably just be convinced it was my time," Jewel muttered.

"Any problem, dear?" Tess smiled up at her.

"No. None at all."

"Jewel!" KarLa, their Eldress, stepped into the tiny garden. "Come with me, please. I must speak to you immediately."

"Before tea?" Jewel asked. This must be an emergency. It certainly was a break with the routine.

"Before anything." The Eldress impatiently beckoned to her.

* * *

Ara stood, hands at her hips, breasts jutting forward, once again in the same stance she'd held far too often over the past year or two at Castle Bloomingdell. Maryam stooped before her, carefully painting and enhancing the redness of her nipples.

"Done!" she announced. "No, hold still. Now for the nipple ornaments."

Ara sighed as the first one was fastened into place. Someone behind her began to brush her white hair while another painted glitter into the strands. Every part of her body was to be put on show during the display. Was it really her fault she'd been subjected to this so often? The initial excitement was gone. The terror left next. Now she was more bored than anything else. Bored and faintly repulsed. She was just plain tired of giving her favor.

"Girdle or not? What do you think?" Maryam asked over her shoulder of the other two women.

"The girdle makes it hard to breathe when you cinch it so tightly," Ara said. No one responded.

She didn't even have a say anymore in what she should use to entice the waiting men. Not that she cared.

"I wonder how the bigger castles make a display with their females," the Eldress wondered aloud thoughtfully, pinching at Ara's nipple so that Maryam could push the jeweled bar in easily. Ara's smaller, everyday ornaments were carelessly pushed aside. "Perhaps we are too old-fashioned. I could contact Castle M'Cee with an e to find out what they do."

Ara shifted uncomfortably. Having these nipple ornaments in, both pleased and tormented her. The slight pleasure/pain made her restless in ways she couldn't quite describe. Goddess knew that fulfilling her obligations during the time of favor didn't satisfy that restlessness. Once in awhile being alone with a special dildo came close—not that there would be any private time anytime soon. Ara tried to focus her mind on something else.

"I haven't seen any of the men losing interest," Maryam answered with a sniff. "I think I create a damn fine display with the talent I've been given."

"No offense meant. However, with but three women to display—" The Eldress began.

"—and with us being put on display every month—" Reina agreed.

"—the last thing we need is for the men to get restless or bored," the Eldress finished.

The last thing we need is for the men to get restless or bored? A pox on the men. What about *her?* Ara scowled.

"Don't ruin the makeup, girl," Maryam warned, absently. "It took near an hour to do properly."

"What difference does any of this make?" Ara said. "Ulrich will win me. He always wins all of us. I won't breed. No one will breed. Then we'll do this all over again next month. We have to change something. It's time to realize we have some big problems."

No one said anything.

"I hate to agree with such a peevish wench, but she has a point," Maryam said at last.

"Change what?" Reina asked, fearfully. "This is what we've always done."

"We need advice." The Eldress pulled at her chin. "Somewhere some of our sisters will know what is wrong and how to remedy our problems. I've already begun to e the larger keeps."

"But we have the problem right now," Ara pointed out. "How long can we wait?"

No one answered.

* * *

"The men will be at the gate, waiting for the champion to enter the keep." KarLa drummed her fingers against the computer. "If we want to get anyone out, that would be the time."

"Very well." Jewel swallowed the nervous excitement rising in her throat and tried to sound matter-of-fact. "That's as good a time as any."

"None of us have been outside Castle M'Cee for a generation, at least. We can't tell you what to expect. I'm only doing this because Bloomingdell has such an emergency. It's a terrible pity their only healer died." KarLa frowned. "Their Eldress is a good woman but—ah well, she does her best. It's our duty to help."

"Of course." Sisterhood was one of the only defenses against the rest of the world. Jewel had had that drummed into her since childhood. When there were but a handful of women in the world you had to help your fellow females.

"You may pass for a boy with your looks, but we can't count on that. Put a dagger in each boot. Don't forget to use them if you have to." The Eldress gripped Jewel's hands. "Be alert. Be careful."

"Eldress."

"Yes?" KarLa asked.

"You're telling me very old news. Don't worry. I'll get to the Castle Bloomingdell. I don't know yet why their women haven't been able to get pregnant, but I've been trained to diagnose and heal such disorders. I'll e you from there in no time at all."

"See that you do, Jewel."

* * *

"Mama Zee?" Jewel looked into the tiny library.

"What is it, child?" Zee looked up from her book. "I was right in the middle of my studies. In fact, I was just reading the most fascinating—well, never mind that. Why aren't you at tea?"

Jewel bit her lip. Zee was a wonderful healer but her "studies" tended to include far more of the ancient romance novels than medical books. It didn't matter. No one in the keep dared point such a thing out to the woman who had ushered almost all of them into the world.

Why did Mama Zee bother, anyhow? That old romance world, one where men and women chose a mate for themselves, without needing to worry about pregnancy or kidnapping, was long past. Romance had blown up, along with history, generations back. It might as well be a fairy tale for all the good such stories did now.

Jewel sighed. She didn't have the luxury of pausing to wonder why Mama Zee did such things.

"I haven't much time." Jewel put her hands on the small woman's shoulders. "I have to fix an emergency. I can't explain much, but I thought if anyone could give me some advice, it would be you."

"I love to give advice." Zee smiled at her and put down her book. "What do you need to know?"

"Causes of female infertility."

Zee snorted. "That is something I never had to worry about. Eeee. I have eight boys and two girls and you ask me about infertility? If not for my medical work, I'd probably have had ten more, Goddess pity me."

"Zee, seriously. I need to know."

"Well, I'm not a writer, but I do have a little list of instructions on the subject. That was from back when darling P'Trice was having her troubles...or was that Karenna? Ay, there are so many of you girls I sometimes can't remember who had what ailment." Zee began to fumble through the books scattered on the shelves. "Hmmm. Here. It's also on the puters, of course. You don't need my old-fashioned lists."

"I may not have access to a puter where I'm going," Jewel snatched the tiny book from Zee's hands. She knew Zee had done a fine job with her list. Otherwise the Eldress would never have allowed her to use any of their precious paper.

"Darling! Where are you going if there is no—"

"I can't explain now. When I get back!" Jewel blew her a kiss and hoped Mama Zee was as clever about infertility as she was about midwifery. Clutching her book, she began to make her way down to the kitchens and from there to the outside world. Was she truly prepared?

It didn't matter. She was as prepared as she could be, given that she had but a few more minutes to safely leave while the men were distracted.

* * *

"Ladies, may we announce the champion of our latest tournament and winner of your lady's favor at Castle Bloomingdell." Ara looked at the unctuous little man and wondered how many times she'd have to hear those words in that same oily tone. "Lady Ara, our champion is Ulrich."

Ara refrained from rolling her eyes. A giant of a man loomed behind the herald. His cheek held scars from an old swordfight. He scowled menacingly, as if he were facing down another horde of males set to win favor rather than the lady whose favor he had gained.

Ulrich.

He was bigger and faster and meaner than any of the other handful of males who camped outside the castle. He'd won every championship for the last seven months or more.

"Lady Ara." His voice came out as a low growl.

"My champion." She tried very, very hard to sound gracious and not bored. Ara wasn't sure if she pulled it off.

"Let us hope for a successful outcome to our mating." Ulrich spoke the traditional words, his growl making the flowery words sound even more ridiculous than they were.

"Nonsense!" The word burst out of Ara instead of the ones she was supposed to say.

Everyone gasped.

"Lady?" Ulrich asked.

"I said nonsense. We haven't had any pregnancies in the castle for the past year."

"You women are failing to do your duty! We grow tired of the wait," one of the men in the crowd blurted out. "Once Ulrich gets you pregnant then he must step aside and give the rest of us a chance."

"You dolts! We women aren't failing. It's your precious champion who can't make us pregnant!" Ara snapped.

The whole crowd fell silent.

Oh my Goddess. Had she actually said that? Out loud? In front of a sea of huge males, all sweaty and edgy after their stupid championship battles? Ara would have clapped her hands to her mouth but it was too late.

"What do you mean by *that?*" Ulrich's voice raised to a roar.

"Exactly what I said. Or are you stupid along with your other fa…" A hand was clapped over her mouth. Maryam's.

"Ara is a little over-excited by giving favor today." The Eldress stepped forward, her hand on Ara's shoulder. She squeezed it, hard.

"She hasn't given anyone favor. All she's done so far is give me sass!" Ulrich scowled so hard Ara wondered if he could be displayed as a gargoyle on the castle turret. "Maybe I don't need this one's favor. And maybe you don't need my tribute."

The women looked down at the pile of venison, raspberries, and other delights the men always brought in tribute at the start of giving favor. None of those things could be obtained within the castle walls unless someone brought it to them.

"If you don't want Ara's favor, I'm sure we can come to a reasonable compromise," the Eldress said. "Just let me confer with my Council."

The two other women of the castle's council scuttled to her side and began to whisper. Ulrich's glare trained itself on Ara. She held her chin up, but she could feel her palms begin to sweat a bit. Ara was very aware that the only thing she had to hide her perspiration was body paint. Good Goddess. She had just insulted the most powerful male in their region. A male who was supposed to have intercourse with her for the next week.

Would the Council ever stop those endless deliberations? Ulrich's glare didn't cease the whole while. Everything, from his coppery, braided hair down to his tree-trunk-sized legs, bristled with annoyance. Maybe with something even more frightening than annoyance. He wouldn't hurt her, would he? Males were supposed to confine their hostilities to other males. But Ulrich was so particularly large and so particularly hostile. Ara forced herself not to shift her feet nervously, but time began to feel as if it was carried by a very slow turtle.

The Eldress broke free of her Council. At last! Ara could have sobbed with relief. The older woman walked to Ulrich, a tentative smile on her face.

"Champion," the Eldress began.

"I won't have her." Ulrich crossed his arms. "Lady Ara is no lady and not worth my efforts."

Maryam clamped her hand over Ara's mouth again.

"Very well." The Eldress bowed her head in respect. "We would not force her on you. We offer an alternative."

"What?"

"We have another available female. She is a bit older than the others but she was the last female in our castle to bear children. Three children. One of them was female, a blessed and rare event among us." Maryam made a noise in the back of her throat before she dropped her hand. "We offer you Lady Maryam in the Lady Ara's stead."

"Wha—" Maryam clapped a hand to her own mouth.

Ara fought her laughter. Maryam had been retired from giving favor after the birth of little Stefani almost six years ago—a suitable reward for such a wonderful event.

But who could argue with the Eldress' public announcement? Especially now that Ulrich was turning his angry gaze from Ara to Maryam, beginning to smile.

"I accept your compromise."

* * *

Turn the page for an exciting excerpt from

Ice Man

by

Samantha Winston

Available now in e-book format from Loose Id

The trip had been easier than she'd dared dream. The pills had worked their magic, and she'd slept through the whole trip, only waking up when the plane landed. The miracles of modern medicine; she could fly!

She got her luggage and followed Mr. Smith through the busy air terminal. *Wait a minute. The exit was that way.* She tapped his arm. "Excuse me. Why are we going towards gates one through ten?"

"We're taking a private jet to the air force base. You didn't think we'd be in the middle of a city, did you? We're going to a secret station in the Arctic."

Her steps faltered. Panic froze her limbs and she stumbled. Oh God. If she died of a heart attack, would they be able to revive *her* at that secret station?

The plane looked too small to fly. It perched on the icy tarmac like a child's toy. Her teeth chattered and her hands felt like blocks of ice. She could hardly fasten her seatbelt. When the plane took off she jumbled all her prayers together and squeezed her eyes shut. Then the plane hit a cloud and started to bounce, and she passed out.

"Miss O'Shea, you can open your eyes now. We've arrived." Mr. Smith sounded exasperated. *Tough.* She opened one eye, then another.

"It's getting dark." She unclenched her fingers from the arm of the seat and looked at her watch. They'd only been in the air for two hours. It shouldn't be dark yet.

"We're above the Arctic Circle. It's still dark most of the time. Get up and get your things. I hope you brought a warmer coat than that," he added, looking at her down jacket.

"I never get cold," she said, shrugging into her plum-colored jacket and making sure she had her purse and her luggage. She stepped out of the plane and a gust of wind knocked her sideways. She skidded on ice and would have fallen, but a soldier dressed in a white snowsuit grabbed her and pushed her towards a door, seemingly set into a snow bank.

Before entering, she turned and looked at the airfield. Airfield? She saw nothing but ice and snow. No buildings anywhere, only a line of blue lights showing the runway. Then the plane left with a roar, and soldiers turned off the blue lights. Nothing was left but murky darkness and whispering snow. A shiver tightened her belly and she turned and entered the station.

Warmth and light greeted her at the end of a narrow tunnel. She stopped and stared. As huge as an airplane hangar, the underground station looked like a set from a sci-fi movie. She stood at the top of a metal platform and looked down at a beehive of activity.

Harsh neon lights dazzled her eyes. A steady electrical hum formed a background to the sound of echoing footsteps, the murmur of voices, and the rustle of papers. Everyone, it seemed, carried a clipboard.

Hesitantly, she walked towards a pod elevator where Mr. Smith motioned impatiently. "You can sight-see later. I have to introduce you to the group leader, Captain Bide. The man is waking up faster than we expected. Hurry!"

His words jolted her out of her stupor and she rushed to the pod. Her luggage didn't fit, so she left it on the platform. Someone would bring it to her room, Mr. Smith informed her tersely. The pod slid down a cable like a ski lift and deposited them next to a low building in the middle of the hangar. A crowd stood at the doorway, and as she got out of the pod, a tall, thin man in a white lab coat ran to her and grabbed her hand.

"No time for chit-chat. Let's get you dressed now. The subject is nearly awake and we can't wait any longer."

The next few minutes flew by in a blur as she took off her clothes in a cubicle and pulled on a leather dress, leather boots, and a bear claw necklace. A bear claw necklace? She made a face as she touched one of the long sharp claws.

"That will impress him; you'll be a shaman, all right?" A gray-haired woman with a clipboard poked her head in the cubicle and beamed at her. "Let's hurry now. No time to talk. Come on!"

Before she could protest that she didn't think the necklace was a good idea, Allie found her arm in the grip of an athletic looking man who jogged her to a small door set in the wall. "Don't be alarmed. He seems groggy, but he's rapidly gaining consciousness. We'll be following everything with a camera and we'll be able to hear everything you say. Good luck." He opened the door and shoved her inside.

She found herself in what looked like a Viking longhouse. A nude man lay on a furry pallet near the fire. Firelight ran over his body, gilding it and showing flowing muscles beneath his smooth skin. He had dark brown hair, cut short and lifting in curls off his temples. Not very tall, but exceedingly well made and strong, the man's physique took her breath away. Her nipples tingled and her belly tightened at the sight of him in a purely animal response to his nudity. He moaned and stirred, but his eyes remained closed.

Her heart somewhere in her throat, she crept towards him, stopping long enough to take off the stupid bear claw necklace.

If he were a Celt or a Viking, the necklace would frighten and confuse him. A young woman would not wear such a symbol of power; only a very old woman could aspire to such trappings.

She knelt by the pallet and shook her head. He would not like waking up on the floor either. He should be on a bed. She looked upwards, trying to spot the camera. They hadn't tried to hide it, probably figuring the man wouldn't be looking for them. A small camera peered out of a chink in the wall. She looked at it and said, "Can someone come inside and help me get him into a decent bed?"

The door opened in the wall, and a man poked his head in and whispered agitatedly, "Do not, I repeat, do not try to contact us. Pretend you are in a primitive land and just do what you have to do. We will not come in unless your life is in danger. And Dr. Paula says to put the necklace back on." He glared at her and shut the door.

She sighed and looked down at the man.

Dark brown eyes stared back at her. He looked puzzled, but not frightened. He studied her for a long moment, his eyes going from her hair to her feet. Then they settled on her breasts. His eyebrows lifted a fraction.

Allie felt hot blood burn her cheeks, and then she remembered. She'd forgotten to take off the silver crescent moon necklace she always wore. It lay between her breasts, probably a glaring anachronism that would send the man into hysterics.

He cleared his throat and a few guttural sounds came out. Nothing she recognized as speech. Great, she wouldn't be of any help at all.

Then he lifted himself on one elbow and said, in a halting, broken voice, "I have great thirst."

She understood! Granted, the accent didn't sound like anything she'd ever heard, but she'd understood what he'd meant. He spoke Latin, but hesitantly, in a strange dialect. Who was he and where did he come from? So many questions jumbled in her head!

He coughed and pointed to his throat. "Do you have anything to drink?"

"A thousand pardons," she said. A pitcher of water stood nearby, and she poured him a cup. Everything was made of glazed pottery. She wondered if it looked odd to him.

He sat up and drank, the water moving in knots down his throat. He wiped his arm across his mouth and nodded. "Thank ye."

"You speak Latin. Are you Roman?" She read he'd been found in northern Scandinavia. Could he be a Roman soldier?

He rubbed his hands over his face. "Nay. I am Celt from the kingdom of Gaul."

"You speak Latin well." She couldn't take her eyes off him. Never had she seen such a handsome man. He seemed as unaware of his nudity as a wild animal, and like a wild animal he stretched and flexed his muscles, testing his arms and legs as he spoke.

"I also speak Greek, Goth, Pict and Celt." He broke off and looked at her thoughtfully. "I know not who you are, nor where I am. 'Tis strange. I can recall the tongues of man, but not my own name." He looked around the room. "This place calls not to my memory. Where am I?"

Perhaps he would be more comfortable speaking his own language, although his Latin was passable. In Celtic she said, "You have been ill for a long time. We brought you here to heal your wounds. My name is Allie."

His eyes widened. "You speak Celt?"

She hadn't considered what to tell him about herself. "My father was Celt." Well, close enough. He was Irish. "Can you remember your name?"

He closed his eyes, then opened them. "I seem to hear the name 'Kell', but whether it is mine or not, I cannot be sure."

"I'll call you Kell, then; perhaps it will help you remember."

"You wear the pendant of the crescent moon. Are you an adept of the moon goddess?" His fingertip nearly touched her skin, stopping a hairsbreadth from the pendant. She could have sworn she felt the heat emanating from his body, and a shiver ran through her.

"No. This belonged to my mother."

"Ah." The man drew back slightly and looked around the room, his eyes taking in every detail. "You said 'we' brought me to this place. Where are the others?"

"They have gone…er…hunting." That sounded right. She smiled. "Can you remember your name now?"

He shook his head, his eyes still scanning the room. "In my bones, I feel a strangeness. Is this the land of the dead? I have died, haven't I, and you are the goddess come to carry me to paradise." He chuckled and before she could react, reached out and touched her breast. "Such a beauty you are. My life on earth must have been exemplary if the gods sent you to me."

The touch of his hand on her breast sent a delicious tingle through her body, but Allie drew back, her heart pounding. "You are mistaken. You are very much alive. Here, let me get you something to eat."

"I feel no hunger." He shook his head as if to clear it and rubbed a hand over his face. His hand lingered, and he frowned. "Who shaved me?"

"Uh, the healer." Allie gulped. Had he worn a beard when he'd fallen into the icy water? Would he go crazy on her now and attack her, ripping her from limb to limb? She peered at him. No, he looked perfectly civilized, despite the aura of raw energy that surrounded him.

"A healer?" He cocked an eyebrow at her and she saw a spark of humor in the depths of his dark brown eyes. "Are you a healer too? Is that why you watch over me like a mother hawk with her young?"

Had she been staring at him? She lowered her eyes. Would he take offense if she stared at him? She had no idea. "Excuse me. I'm just a foolish woman."

"Why do you beg my pardon?" He reached out and touched her chin, lifting it so that her eyes met his again. "Don't tell me you're a Greek. The women there are downtrodden, but in my land they are equals."

His gentle touch reassured her. Whatever apprehension she'd had about him vanished. He was no savage. "No, I'm not Greek."

"I didn't think so. Your accent is strange but definitely not Greek. I have traveled far, but I've yet to hear someone with your accent." He let go of her chin and sat back, examining her from head to toe. "There is something very strange going on. I cannot recall my own name, and I have no idea where I am or who you are, but I can recall certain things like the sight of white swans on a small pond and the smell of fresh lavender. Can you tell me who and where I am?" For the first time his voice wavered slightly, as if from fear.

"Do you trust me?" she asked.

He hesitated a long time before he spoke, and when he did, his voice was soft. "Yes, for some reason, I do. I think I must be in the land between the living and the dead. My memories have fled, but my body is still intact. Perhaps I have to accomplish some feat before I can go join my ancestors." He looked at her, his gaze smoldering. "You must be the goddess who will lead me to the land of the dead. I am glad it is you, for you please me, Allie."

Her cheeks burned. "I am not a goddess and you are not dead, I promise. Let me get you some more to drink. You must be thirsty."

"No." He knelt and took her wrist, pressing it to his lips. "You please me, Allie, handmaiden to the gods. Come warm my body with your caresses."

She pulled back, but his grip tightened like a steel trap. "Let go!"

"Are you married?" The question surprised her.

"No."

"Then I will be gentle." He flashed a grin, surprising her. Still kneeling, he pulled her close and, without letting go of her arm, he stroked her hair. "I think I will claim you for my own, maiden Allie." He chuckled. "Your heart races like a hare in flight. I feel your desire like a firebrand; do you deny it? Come, refuse me no longer." He reached down and stroked his cock, which swelled and hardened.

Allie's mouth went dry. A flood of hot wetness dampened her inner thighs, and she realized she hadn't any panties. Underpants didn't exist until the twentieth century.

She glanced beseechingly at the camera in the wall. *Please, someone come in here quickly.* But she knew no one would unless he started to hurt her, and he wasn't hurting her at all. Perversely, she wanted him to continue stroking her breast. Her mind grew curiously numb even while her body seemed to come almost painfully alive.

"Kell, please let go of me." She managed to get the words past her lips, all the while wondering what it would be like to feel those strong arms wrapped around her... *No! That is enough!* 'Easy Allie' — that's what the boys in school called her. She'd sworn to stop saying 'yes' on the first date. As that thought flitted through her mind she almost laughed.

"Why do you smile?" Kell let go of her wrist and stood, stretching languorously. "I have let go of you, but I will have you, Allie, don't doubt it for a minute."

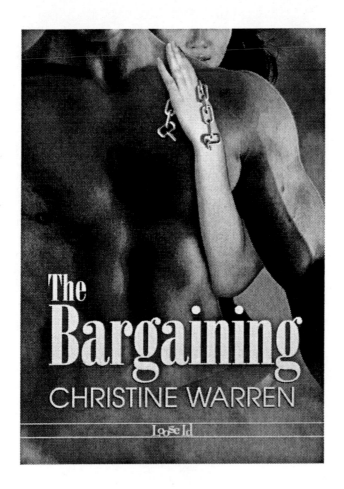

Kili's a sex slave. Deacon's a rebel prisoner. She knows the planet. He's got the skills. He's in no position to reject her offer, and after one taste of her passion, he's pretty sure he doesn't want to.

Let the bargaining begin...

Christine Warren's *The Bargaining*

Now Available in E-book Format

www.loose-id.com

Printed in the United States
36265LVS00004B/100